# The Dark Queen

D1736337

1

# The Dark Queen

*"Mirror, mirror on the wall. Who's the fairest one of all?"*
We all know the legend, or so we think. But what do you really know of the woman behind the myth? Fable of Seren—daughter of the Sea King, and granddaughter of both Calypso and Hades. The blood of gods runs through her veins, but the young girl destined to one day wear the title of The Evil Queen is now seventeen and wants nothing more than to see the land above the waves, to be part of the human realm. One fine day she does just that, but the heaven she imagined turns into a terrible nightmare of pain, suffering, and lies that twists the heart of this starry-eyed girl into one of darkness and hate.
*Villains aren't born; they're made.*
But sometimes even villains get a second chance. Calypso, seeing the suffering of her granddaughter has concocted a brilliantly, clever plan—The Love Games. In Kingdom, there is one magic more powerful than even the darkest of spells...true love, and with the help of her BFF—Aphrodite, *the* Goddess of Love—Calypso knows exactly who Fable's truest love is. A Native American god called, Owiot. Can this gentle, star-eyed god help Fable see there is another path she can take before it's too late and the evil that beats within her heart consumes her soul for good?

# The Dark Queen: Part I

*Inside each of us, there is the seed of both good and evil. It's a constant struggle as to which one will win. And one cannot exist without the other ~Eric Burdon*

*In this life, we have to make many choices. Some are very important choices. Some are not. Many of our choices are between good and evil. The choices we make, however, determine to a large extent our happiness or our unhappiness, because we have to live with the consequences of our actions~ James E. Faust*

# Forward

*Many names has she been called. Evil. Vain. Tempestuous. Jealous...*
  *~Writ by The Brothers*

No doubt you all think you know the true story of the woman they call the evil queen. Cruel. Unmerciful. Prideful. The queen is called the fairest in all the lands until the day her magick mirror tells her there is one more fair, a child by the name of Snow White. The queen, in a fit of rage, demands her huntsman take care of the problem once and for all. Take Snow out into the Enchanted Forest, kill her and bring back her heart. He does. Or so it seems because little Snow with her guileless beauty and beatific smile weakens his resolve, and instead he sticks and kills a swine, bringing it and not Snow's heart back to his Queen. The Queen eventually discovers his deception and henceforth is on a mission to end the beautiful and innocent daughter of the King. Turning into a crone and offering the pretty lady a poisoned apple. One bite is all it takes to send Snow into a catatonic trance, never to be broken...save for true love's kiss. In the end, the terrible and dark queen receives her just reward as she is violently punished, forced to dance in heated iron boots to her death.

Well, that's how the story goes anyway. But as we all know, in Kingdom stories are rarely what they seem. What if the tales were all wrong? What if what you think you know is nothing more than smoke and mirrors? What if the Dark Queen isn't who you think she is at all?

This then is the true tale of Fable, the most beautiful woman in all of Kingdom with skin dark as night, eyes more golden than the sun, and hair the shade of deepest ebony.

I will tell this story differently than I tell the others. I've given her permission to pen you a short introduction letter.

Now let us begin this story as all good stories do.

Once.

Upon.

A.

Time...
  *~Anonymous, one of the 13 keepers of the* **Tales.**

# An open letter to you, dear readers...

*Fable*

It all started the day I was born.

I knew I was different when I opened my eyes and saw a world full of sea monsters, smiles, and gods.

Calypso, my grandmother, and Hades, my grandfather, told me I would be destined for greatness. But I never believed it. Born a twin, I felt very lacking when compared to my brother.

Where I was human form, he was merfolk. The first male since my father born with a tail—the revelry and wine flowed for nearly two weeks after his announcement. I was dark; he was light. My hair was black as night, his as electrifyingly blue as the sky above our waters.

The folk beneath the waves loved me and kept a watchful eye on me, but always I felt less than. Lacking in ways, I couldn't quite understand.

Don't mistake me; I loved my life. A girl couldn't have asked for better parents. My father was the King of the Sea. You should have seen the magick he created for me on a whim. Chariots of water, steeds built from the icy waves beneath the Northern shores, gardens that glowed green and blue and twinkled like stars, anything, and everything to keep me happy.

But always I knew I could not be as happy as my mother had been in the below. She, the daughter of the infamous Captain Hook, willingly choose to live her life beneath the sea, choosing love above all else.

Uriah, my brother, could never understand my sullenness; he loved the waters and its people. And I did too, but I envied the life my mother had given up. It was the little things that drove my curiosity.

How would it feel to breathe, not through gills, but through my nose? Would it tickle, or feel wet as it did now? Walking, I'd heard, was much more cumbersome above because of this crazy thing called gravity. Walking in the below felt weightless, effortless, dreamlike.

Much like my life sometimes did.

Like it wasn't real, just a waking dream I partook in until the day I could finally wake up and see the world above. I'd seen glimpses of it, of course. Like when my Aunt Aphrodite would come over for a quick spot of tea and she'd painted images of Mt. Olympus on the sea bubbles.

It was full of gods. Of more people who weren't quite like me. I had power, but I was no god.

I knew I was different than most.

And usually it didn't bother me, but sometimes it did. Like, when growing up, I'd join in on the mermaid games of catch and chase. Even in the below, without a tail, I was slow and cumbersome compared to the folk. After getting caught for the tenth time, I'd become frustrated and cranky and without thought, I'd shifted to shadow.

I have magick. Strong magick. Magick that I cannot always control, though I try. I try so hard, but sometimes my emotions...they get the better of me. They make me do things, terrible things, things I'm ashamed of.

My parents understand, and my grandmother and grandfather, I think, actually love me more because of my seed of power. Uriah for all his beauty will never know what it is like to taste near a tenth of my magick—as my grandmother says with a touch of pride in her voice.

And sometimes, yes, I see him look upon my art with longing, but truthfully it is he I envy. Knowing that you were born in exactly the right place and amongst the right people, what a wonderful feeling that must be.

I yearned for my freedom, yearned for more, and then one day...it happened.

The Queen of the Enchanted Forest had died, and the king was in search of his new bride, the ripples of her death had spread far and wide and even into the below.

I did not know who the King was or what he might look like, nor did I care. I knew I could make him happy, I would make him happy, and I knew that he could make me happy too. Even if all I was to him was queen in name only. But for a chance to be above land, for a chance to be amongst my kind, not to be gawked and stared at because I lacked a tail or godhood, gods above I would have given anything.

Mother and father did not want me to go. Eventually, it was grandmother who helped them see that, just like Uriah, I too needed to spread my wings and fly.

There were many tears, and much heartache—even from me—but eventually we agreed it was time for me to be "human."

With a final hug to them both, I turned and proudly marched into my future, holding fast to my grandfather's gift before leaving—an enchanted mirror. A true friend, he told me, and someone on whom I could always depend on.

I just knew I was stepping into a wonderful and glorious new life, the kind of life I'd always imagined. One full of laughter, happiness, and possibly even love.

Looking back on it now...if I had to do it over again, I think I would have told my younger self to run and never to look back. Of course, I wouldn't have met "him." So maybe in the end happiness can only truly be found after the torments of the fire take you down to your very lowest self.

Now I'll let the keeper tell you my tale, only please, do not judge me too harshly, for had you been in my shoes I'm not sure you wouldn't have done exactly as I did...

# Chapter 1

*Fable*

*Many, many, many years ago...*

Stepping through the watery portal, Fable took a look around and almost forgot how to breathe.

There were trees everywhere. Beautiful, towering trees that seemed to reach gnarled fingers in prayerful worship toward the cerulean sky; their chartreuse leaves almost gleaming like twinkling, polished gems in the wash of golden sunlight. Trails of fairy light were easy enough to make out, strands of glimmering red, blue, purple, and silver.

Apple trees in abundance filled the enchanted forest with their fruity, ripe scent. Fable had been surrounded by all that was most beautiful in the below, but nothing, nothing, compared to what she now saw.

She smiled as a gentle breeze feathered across her forehead, smelling scents she'd never smelled before in her life. Pines. Berries. And so many others she had no name for them.

The gills she'd used in Seren hadn't followed her into the above. Closing her eyes, she tipped her face toward the sun and inhaled deeply. Letting her senses soak it all in.

Damp leaves.

Fresh earth.

And flowers. So many flowers. This was heaven on earth, and for the first time in her life, she felt her soul smile.

"Oh gods," she moaned, inhaling even harder with the next breath. She didn't know what kind of flower it was as she'd so rarely smelled the ones in the above before, but whatever it was, she loved it.

Fragrant with a heady nip of roses to it, but not quite a rose...a little more citrusy maybe? Also, breathing didn't tickle.

She'd almost hoped it would. A grin she couldn't contain stretched wide on her face.

"So this is the above," she whispered in an awed hush. "Happy birthday to me."

Today she'd turned seventeen. A woman grown now, she had plans. So many plans. She'd find and marry her King; she'd be the people's benevolent queen and a good wife. Those were things she desired above all else. And she knew she'd do it too.

"Watch out!" A man's sharp cry startled her from her contemplative reverie.

With a startled yip, she backpedaled, hugging the awkwardly shaped mirror tight to her breast and staring at him in wide-eyed shock.

The man—who sat upon the rickety seat of a Hackney led by two tired looking old mules—was dirty. His face smudged with dirt, grime, and sweat. His dark hair matted to his head and held tight with a dingy green ribbon. He wore a patchwork vest over a threadbare, yellowish—which must have surely once been cream—colored shirt.

He sneered, showing off several missing teeth. "Ye almost broke my wheels, you wench!"

She looked, and sure enough, there was a wide swerve in the muddy trail. Blinking, confused by his anger and his manner she shook her head. "I'm...I'm sor—"

"Save yer sorry, female." He said, and immediately his harsh tone shifted into something more lecherous. His lips turned from a hard, nasty line to a lascivious leer. His gaze turned from hard to slow and measuring, she shivered under his intense and gimleted stare.

Fable had been studying the above all her life, she knew women's fashion and knew she'd dressed the part of a noblewoman. Because that's exactly what she was. Her father was king of Seren, in the above or the below that meant something.

7

Her cloak was frost-white colored and threaded through with swirls of silver that winked like fairy light as she moved. Her dark hair had been caught up in a loose and feminine bun, highlighting the sharply sculpted planes of her cheekbones.

She'd worn no face paint, but then she needed none. Fable wasn't prideful, but she knew her beauty was exotic and unique. The flare of interest in his dull brown eyes was immediately evident.

Wetting his thin lips, he curled them into a lewd twist. "Well, now aren't ye a fine bit of feminine flesh."

Biting down on her back teeth she notched her chin high. Fable knew that if she called out to Calypso, her grandmother would come in a heartbeat and smite the rat with a mere flick of her dainty finger.

But Fable had learned one thing growing up, the blood of her father and mother flowed through her veins, she was not powerless. Notching her chin, she gathered her courage and looked him straight in the eye.

"Apologize," she said in a clear, but not near as strong a voice as she would have liked.

His nostrils flared, and his Adam's apple rolled as his slight belly shook with laughter. "Excuse me?"

"Were...were you never taught not to speak to a lady that way?" Her heart fluttered and her fingers tingled with a case of fear and nerves.

Again he wet his lips, but this time, he released the loose reins in his grip and moved as though he meant to step down from the Hackney.

As a princess, Fable had never known a day of impoliteness in her life. And if the male had only been cruel, she'd have overlooked it, but the intent to do her harm burned through his mean, little eyes.

Planting his hands on his hips, he spread his thin legs wide, perhaps to show off the bulge in his trousers.

Her pulse beat loudly in her ears; she tried to swallow the thick knot of her fear in her throat. She could not lose control of her powers. Breathing steadily through her nose and pushing it out between her lips, she counted slowly to ten in her head, trying to calm the adrenaline pumping through her veins.

Hand reaching down to his bulge, he gently stroked himself as he asked, "Have you ever sucked, woman?"

Fingers digging into the mirror with such strength that she snapped two of her nails, she opened her mouth, ready to say...only goddess knew what when the sharp neighs of more horses cut through her tension.

"Get away from her!" Another male thundered.

Fable, now more than upset, was ready to crack and let loose her magic on both men. It was only her first day on the above; she couldn't fail already. She couldn't go back home with her tail between her legs; she had to prove to her parents that she was capable and as able as they, but one look at the still nameless male and the words died on her tongue.

The male sat upon a white and noble steed. Golden haired with deep blue eyes, a sharp nose that was just shy of being too beakish—but fit his square-jawed face perfectly—and with a ready smile shining with bright white teeth, he could be none other than the king of the Enchanted Forest.

"Sire!" The rat-faced beast whimpered, dropping so sharply to his knees that even Fable couldn't help but wince at what would surely be bruised knees in the morning.

Only once rat face had bowed did she realize that she stood still gawking at the king like a simpleton.

"My lord," she said softly, and gracefully bowed. Or as gracefully as she could manage, refusing for even a moment to release her grip on the mirror.

"Go." Was all the King said.

But Fable knew he'd not said it to her, when rat face, with a silent nod, whipped up his reins, flicked his poor animals, and raced away as fast as his crooked wheels allowed.

"Look at me, woman," the king said, and Fable did, heart beating like a wild thing in her chest as she fell a little more in love with him.

Never could she have imagined that the king of the enchanted forest would be so handsome. There was a little silver beginning to show at his temples, but his shoulders were wide and powerful looking, and his grip on his horse's reins sure.

She'd come with the expectation of finding an older male, well beyond his prime. King George had been ruling the enchanted forest for many decades now; his wife had been in her early fifties when she'd passed, which was very young by Kingdom standards.

There had also been rumors surrounding her death. How could such a young woman in the prime of her vigor have died so suddenly? Death did not come easily to Kingdomers, though it happened, it rarely occurred due to natural means.

"Are you hurt?" George asked softly, cutting through her musing.

Just then more horses carrying riders—no doubt the royal guard since they were all dressed in white armor and carrying golden scabbards—came galloping over the grassy knoll.

"Sire!" the lead rider cried, "you should not race so fast, it is not safe."

Holding up his hand for silence, the king shook his head. Immediately the lead guard snapped his mouth shut, looking stunned to see her standing there. He had a neatly trimmed, black goatee and sharply raised dark brows, which made her think him akin to the devil in looks.

Not at all unpleasing to the eye, though King George was more her type.

"Lady?" George said again, gently.

Shaking off her own stunned stupor, she nodded. "Yes. Yes, thank you, King George, I am well."

His smile grew radiant, and she knew she was halfway to being in love with him already.

"And what, pray tell, are you doing out here in my woods all alone? You look like a woman of stature and means."

Implied, but unspoken was that noblewomen should never walk about on their own. Which Fable found to be rather archaic thinking, but he was so handsome, and she was quite smitten, so she shrugged it off. He was a king after all, and they tended to be a tad old-fashioned, she should know; she'd lived with one all her life.

Smiling gently, she nodded. "I am a woman of stature. You are correct. Though I am not of the above."

His eyes widened for a moment, and then his entire face broke out into a smile. "You must be she. The princess of shadow and night."

It was her turn to be shocked. "You...you know of me?"

Though knights surrounded them, it felt as though the world had slowly faded away to only him and her. Fable was aware of nothing other than the sound of his voice and the beat of her heart.

"I believe all of Kingdom has heard of you, Fable, daughter of King Sircco and granddaughter to both Hook and Hades. Though I must say, your beauty far surpasses even your legend."

"Good gods," she couldn't help but mumble, planting a hand on her burning cheek.

He threw his head back and chuckled, causing his own Adam's apple to roll. But unlike the revulsion she'd felt for rat face, the sight of his enchanted her. If Auntie Aphrodite had been here, she was sure there'd be little hearts floating around her and George.

Was this true love?

Mother said that when she'd first seen father she'd felt the powerful magic of true love beat through her soul. That was how love worked in Kingdom, immediately and powerfully when two destined souls met.

Her smile grew bright, sure that she'd just met her perfect, other half.

"And may I ask, if I might be so presumptuous—"

As if a king ever needed to ask for permission, she chuckled softly to herself but said nothing except to nod for him to continue.

"—if you had any plans for tonight?"

She'd come to the above with one intention only, to find the king and make him fall in love with her. So far her plan was coming to fruition. Little did she know that she too would feel the pleasant sting of it.

"No, my liege, no plans at all."

With a gentle roll of his hips, George caused his horse to canter slowly toward her.

9

"Charles! Come and take this ladies mirror from her and carry it safely to my home," George cried.

The lead guardsman came up to her then, and his look was serious and intent. He really was handsome, up close she could also tell that he had unnaturally long lashes for a male, her heart fluttered a tiny bit. Though that emotion was nothing to what she currently felt for George.

Happily she lifted the mirror to him.

"My lady," Charles said slowly when he got near enough to take it.

And when he grabbed hold, his fingers gently brushed hers. Not in an obvious manner, but in a way to catch her attention. She looked up at him with a question only to note that his eyes had taken on an emotion she couldn't quite place.

Steady.

Studious.

Fearful?

She blinked, sure it had only been an illusion of light and shadow, because as soon as he'd taken the mirror, he bowed his head and turned, his features looking as distant and implacable as before.

But she quickly forgot her unease when the king gave her his hand.

"Please do me the great honor of being my guest this evening," he said, and she was more than happy to oblige.

"Yes, I will."

One night soon turned to two. Then three. A week. A month. And in next to no time the banners had been raised.

King George had found his new bride, and her name was Fable of the Seren Seas—the fairest of them all.

Sadly, the night of the wedding was the last night of joy she'd know for a very, very long time.

# Chapter 2

*Fable*

"Let me out of here!" She screamed passionately, kicking at the door with her slippered foot in her fearful desire to leave the tower.

"Ye heard the King!" The rickety voice of George's mother cackled through the thick walnut doors. "Ye've been a bad, bad girl, Fable, and needs be punished."

She sobbed, shaking the handle impudently, knowing her meager strength could do nothing against the magick holding it fast.

The only crime she'd committed this morning had been to remain in her robes, laid up in bed rather than greet him as the rest of the castle did at the start of each day. Fable had felt pain in her head, and had taken too much of the witch's "healing brew" she'd felt weak and helpless and unable to rise and had known much too late that Brunhilda had put something into the potion to make her sick as she was.

"You know he wouldn't like this!" Fable screamed louder as she heard his mother's footsteps retreating. "If he finds out what you've done to me! He'll—"

Immediately Brunhilda returned, moving fleet of foot—much faster than an aged crone of a millennia should. Or at least that's how old Fable judged her to be the one time she'd caught Brunhilda transform from a woman of moderate years to something ancient, powerful, and full of the very darkest kind of magick.

Fable had almost not believed what she'd seen, except for the fact that as the months in this wretched castle passed she'd witnessed the witch do other, even more, amazing feats.

"He'd do what, huh?" she taunted, voice sounding as dry and dusty as brittle bones, "we both know who's the true power here, wench, and it ain't him and it ain't you. I own him, always have. Always will. Besides..."

Nails dragged down the door, the squeal sounding like the death throes of a dying swine, and Fable clapped hands over her ears, biting down on her back teeth as she trembled and shook, hating the witch with a fury that rocked her to her very core.

"...we both know there's nothing you can do about it. *Dark Queen.*" Cackling laughter trailed in her wake.

It took several moments before Fable could even move. Only in the deep silence of knowing she was truly alone, did she finally take a tentative step back. Then another. And another.

Until finally she sat on the edge of the massively large bed covered in the skins of a giant deer and looked around the lonely tower she'd no doubt call home for the next fortnight until George's return.

Luxury dripped from every corner of the tower. There were fairy globes glittering with green and blue light above her. Artist's renderings of the previous kings and queens through several dynasties past. Paintings of the Enchanted Forest directly surrounding the castle's walls.

Stitched together furs from hundreds of sacrificed snow foxes on the black marble floor. A massive table with a silver bowl in its center that would magically fill with whatever food and drink she so desired.

She had a trunk full of the most lush and provocative fashions meant to make any queen appear the grandest of them all at any ball or gathering.

Surrounded by everything, and yet she had nothing.

Blinking back tears, she stared at the thin iron shackle on her wrist. "A gift," Brunhilda had said, after Fable's marriage to her son.

She'd never suspected George's mother of subterfuge. Not the comely woman with a crown of lovely snow-white hair that fell in graceful waves down her back. Not the woman with a face as smooth and unlined as a female in her youth. Not a woman with clear blue eyes whose smile was as open and honest as her sons.

No, Fable had taken that *gift*, smiled her thanks and of her own volition had sealed her doom when she'd locked it around her wrist.

The moment the iron had clapped down, she'd felt it—the burn and sizzle of the loss of her magic. The violence of losing it had driven her straight to her knees in horror and distress, only to hear the witch's dulcet voice proclaim that none would ever rule this kingdom beside her son, but she.

Fable had made the mistake of telling George. And the warm, caring, kindhearted man she'd fallen in love with back in the Glen had merely looked at her, patted her head and shambled off as though he'd not heard her. It was then that Fable finally understood why her husband never removed the thin, delicate iron chain around his neck.

By the time it had finally dawned on Fable that the witch had full possession of George as well, it had been far too late for her to do anything about it.

Fable was as helpless as a human and too far away from Seren to alert her parents to her newfound horrors. The witch, clever as she was, and knowing exactly who Fable was, had even made it impossible for her to call on her own grandmother and grandfather, who could have surely come to her aid had they only known.

But the moment Fable had opened her mouth to scream out their names, her molars had clicked shut, and her tongue had swollen to twice its size, making her fear she'd suffocate on her own tongue.

That was when she fully understand the power Brunhilda wielded; the witch had thought of everything.

Feeling hopeless and lost, she stood and walked slowly toward the only window in the tower staring out at the beautiful blue sky, watching the fanciful flight of a sparrow sail past and wishing with all her heart and mind that she'd never left Seren.

That she could roll time back and never come here.

Planting her hand on the stone, Fable rested her forehead against the cold, and unyielding gray stone, pretending for a moment that she rested her head on the chest of her lover and that he held her back, reassuring her that all would be well again.

But there was no lover. Not even George. Not after the night of the wedding. He'd never touched her again. Never kissed her again. And rarely spoke more than two words to her.

Her solace in this whole miserable place was two. Her mirror. And George's little girl by his first wife—Snow White.

"Mirror," she said softly.

Immediately she felt the prickle of the mirror's power roll to life as it washed against her back. Brunhilda had been thorough in her torture of Fable; the witch had allowed Fable to keep her mirror. Which should have been a great act of kindness, but was, in fact, the very worst sort of torture there was. When she grew really heartsick and desperate, she'd ask Mirror to show her Seren, her family. It was a blade to the heart to see them all so happy, smiling and laughing and having the time of their lives, no doubt resting securely in the knowledge that Fable was too. To see them, but not to hear them, not to talk with them, or beg them to come and snatch her away from this misery, it was a form of torment far worse than almost anything else the witch could have devised.

"Yes, my queen," he said in that deeply pitched voice that somehow always reminded Fable of the deep waters of home.

Twirling on her heel, she stared at her final gift from her grandfather.

No doubt as a joke, grandfather had crafted the image within to resemble that of Uriah. Fable hadn't been too fond of that aspect at first, but now she found that even a false connection to her brother had become a lifeline to her sanity.

Bottomless blue eyes stared at her quizzically. "My queen?" he asked again.

And her heart clenched all over again at the image of her brother. So strong and virile and handsome with his electrifying blue hair framing his face and his masculine jaw, in coloration he looked nothing like her parents, but in features he took after father completely.

It was her Uriah in many ways; only Mirror lacked the rascally twinkle in his eyes that showed her brother was perpetually up to no good.

"It seems we are trapped in the tower again," she said softly.

He looked around. At times, it still amazed her how sentient the mirror was. How aware and thoughtful.

"True," he finally said, "though considering I am always trapped, I do not find my new surroundings to be much different."

His grin was commiserating.

She sighed, then chuckled softly and hugged the robe tight around her. The tower was always damp and far too cold for her. Seren's waters were deep and warm. Ironic, she'd never given much thought to the beauty of her world until she'd come to the place she'd always known would make her "happy."

Fable was not happy now. And she feared she might never be happy again.

"No, I guess it wouldn't. What am I to do? Each time we are locked away, the days grow longer and more taxing. I cannot sit up here for hours upon a day eating nothing but bonbons and watching birds fly by; I would go mad. I know I would."

Mirror cocked his head, staring at her a long moment before asking, "What would you like to do?"

She blinked, not exactly sure herself. Fable had come here with very little thought in mind other than making the king fall deliriously in love with her and living happily ever after.

Wasn't that how the stories went?

The lovers met. The lovers loved. The lovers stayed gloriously, forever, and eternally happy? What a stupid fool she'd been to think any man could ever become the sole source of her happiness.

Mother had often warned Fable not to keep her head in the clouds, but she'd just known that someday too her own prince would come. That they'd rule their kingdom justly and with a sound and fair hand. That they'd be beloved by their people and children.

In the eight months since her marriage Fable had been alone with George only once, and even then things had been rushed and hurried, after that, she'd been nothing more than a title to him. Dolled up and paraded out before the masses to be gawked and stared at by all other noblemen and women.

The only time Fable was truly happy were the rare and stolen moments she got to share with Snow. But even the little princess was kept under tight supervision by the witch.

It was like the entire castle was under Brunhilda's spell, but none of them knew it. And then in one of those rare flashbacks, where her mind suddenly recalled a memory it hadn't in ages, the image of the guardsman who'd taken her mirror came sharply to mind.

"Where is Charles!" she asked, voice rising with the thought of salvation.

Uriah Mirror, far more unflappable than Uriah her brother, said without missing a beat, "King George's guardsman was unable to follow his liege this morning, he recently broke his arm and—"

She held up her hand. "I do not care what's happened to him, only that he is here on the premises."

"Yes, my queen, he is."

Wetting her lips, an idea suddenly came to her. She'd never tried this before, but her grandfather's magick was powerful. Powerful enough that when Brunhilda tried to strip the man from the mirror she could not.

For so long having Mirror in her room was a constant reminder of all that she'd lost. But through the weeks and months that had followed she'd begun to learn that Mirror was so much more than merely a two-way device that allowed her to talk with her family. Mirror was smart, and above all, loyal. All she knew was that she was grateful now more than ever for him.

"Mirror," she said softly, "I wonder, can you travel between looking glasses?"

He blinked, as though startled. Then looked at her with wide, rounded eyes. "Why yes, it seems that I can, my queen."

13

She grinned, feeling more positive and excited about this than she had about anything since arriving in the above.

"Go to him then and deliver a message—"

"My queen, if I may."

She lifted a brow.

"There is a secret tunnel into here."

"What! Where?" She turned; ready to run far from here. She could leave the castle grounds, find a lake and call for her father. She could be hom—

Mirror shook his head, a look of distress pinching his features. "I am sorry, my queen, to have caused you such excitement only to have to be the bearer of bad news now."

Immediately her heart plummeted to her knees and a scream wedged tight in her throat, to have been given a glimpse of freedom only to have it dashed, it was all she could do to remain standing and not crumble to the floor.

Squaring her shoulders, remembering the words of her mother, she shook off the disappointment as best she could.

"What is it, Mirror?"

"You cannot leave, my queen. The witch has spelled the tunnel, should you pass through it, you would surely die."

"What?" She shook her head, knowing she'd heard wrong. It was near to impossible to die in Kingdom, only by weapon or magick...

"You would die, Fable," he repeated.

Her jaw dropped, and her ears thundered with the beat of her racing pulse. Grasping hold of the edge of her robe, she shuffled back toward the edge of the bed, landing with a soft thud onto the mattress and staring at the walls in dawning horror.

"Are you sure? How do you know this?"

He remained perfectly still as he said, "She carted me up here hours before she had you locked away. I saw her weave the spell. I can only assume she allowed me to witness what she'd done to torment you with an avenue of escape you could never possibly use."

Fable's jaw dropped. That the witch should do such a thing spoke volumes as to just how evil, and wicked she was. The witch had sent her off on a fool's errand yesterday morning, begging Fable to run into town and fetch her a basket of golden apples from the vendor at the marketplace because only those golden apples were the very best with which to make the King's favorite pie.

She'd thought the request an odd one, considering there were servants to handle such chores, but she'd been happy enough to get away from the depressive castle for a few hours. Like a fool she'd happily agreed to the task, all the while Brunhilda had been weaving an enchantment meant to keep Fable locked away.

"But...but...when George returns surely, he will—"

"I do not think she means you to ever leave."

Pain lanced through her heart like a thorn ripping through her flesh.

"But...but..." Were the only words she could seem to stutter. "He wouldn't allow it, surely."

Why did her tongue feel so numb of a sudden and her head so dizzy?

There was too much noise, too many questions bombarding her consciousness to get any one of them out. The room was suddenly spinning out of focus. George was under Brunhilda's spell, surely if there were someway to rip the necklace off him Fable could reach him, the real him and alert him to what the witch was doing. There was still hope.

Right?

She must have spoken her words aloud, because Mirror said, "The chance is slim, but yes, my queen, there is always hope. If only you had a fairy godmother."

14

Being a natural born denizen of the under meant Fable was never given a godmother. But she'd never needed one. Her magic was strong and powerful, and if she should fail, then there was always her father's, grandmother's, or grandfather's to back her up.

She'd always been protected, cherished.

Loved.

A wretched sound suddenly filtered through the room. The sound like that of a dying animal, only there was no animal dying, the sound came from deep inside of her as the hopelessness and emptiness of her future rolled out before her.

To never leave this tower.

To never know her magic again.

To never know love.

To always remain alone.

Alone.

Unwanted.

And unloved.

"Oh, my gods..." She rested her cold fingertips against her blazing hot cheeks.

"Look at me," Mirror spoke to her in a tone he'd never taken with her before.

She wiped at her tears, looking up at him.

"Remember who you are."

Frowning, she shook her head. "I know who I am."

"No!" He said with authority. "Remember who you are. Whose you are. You are the daughter of The King. You are the Queen of Shadows and Night, shackled or not; you are powerful and mighty. Mightier than that evil witch down there. It is why she's chained you, Fable. It is why she's locked you away. To control what she could not otherwise. Do not forget yourself."

Fable hadn't realized she'd been walking toward the mirror until suddenly her hands were pressed against her *brother's* face. "Why do you care? You're just a mirror, you're—"

His eyes flashed with thunder and lightning, and ephemeral blue smoke coiled around his striking features. "I am so much more than that. I am a sliver of your grandfather's soul. Meaning, I care for you deeply, my queen. I love you as he does. You are not alone, thought it might feel so."

"What?" She could hardly swallow her throat felt so tight. "He...he, did what?"

Grandfather had spelled a sliver of his soul into the mirror? It made sense now why Brunhilda had not known the depths of Mirror's powers. No witch—no matter how powerful—was stronger than the will of a god.

"I know what that witch has done, my queen. And someday, it will not matter. For you will be mightier than she, even with your shackle on," Mirror said gently.

A different kind of emotion pounded through her veins then, fear, but also apprehension. Mirror had never spoken to her this way before. With such force and authority behind it.

And she believed him.

"You can free me from here? If you're part of my grandfather, surely you're powerful enough to break this enchantment." She lifted her wrist.

"No, not I, Fable." He shook his head sadly. "But you. You are young, but someday you won't be. Someday you'll know who you really are."

"And who am I?"

His grin was so heartachingly similar to her brother's that she forgot he wasn't. Fingers twitching against the cool glass surface, she could almost feel his soft skin and imagine his arms wrapping around her for a much-needed embrace.

"You are the Queen of Darkness. Now, let me go find the guardsman, for he bears a tale worth hearing."

15

Mirror was gone for so long that day shifted into night, and the emotional high she'd experienced after his pep talk began to wan with the setting sun. By the time he finally returned she was sure she'd remain forever alone. Forgotten and doomed to live out her near eternity in isolation.

But as promised, "Uriah" returned to his mirror and mere seconds later there was a quiet knock in the stone wall behind her. A banging echo that caused her to jump and twirl. So there was the infamous hidden doorway, oh the temptation to run to it was great. Immediately her hand rushed to the column of her throat in a nervous reflex.

Mirror nodded for her to answer it.

"Come. Come in," she breathed, then cleared her throat.

He looked a little different than he had that day in the woods. But Charles still cut a striking figure.

Tall, broad of shoulders and narrow of hips, Fable felt something squeeze through her heart she hadn't in ages.

Curiosity.

"Charles," she said slowly.

His look was cursory, but thorough, before he nodded, dropped to a chain-mailed knee and bowed his head.

"My queen. Why have you summoned me?"

# Chapter 3

*Fable*

Clutching at her soft pink colored robe, she curled her fingers tight into the fabric and tried to swallow her nerves, though she knew her voice sounded strained by the emotion.

"Thank you for coming," she said softly, cutting a quick glance toward the doorway that had vanished the moment he'd stepped through. The tunnel, or staircase—whatever it had been—vanished the moment he stepped through into her room. Freedom was so close and yet so far from her.

Maybe Mirror was wrong. Maybe it wasn't enchanted to kill her; maybe it would sting a little? But no sooner had she thought it then she knew she was grasping at straws.

Mirror would never lie to her. If he said it was enchanted to kill her, that's exactly what it would do.

He rose back to his feet, and again Fable suffered a strange roll of emotion. Her heart stuttered powerfully in her chest, and her stomach kneaded with tight knots. She'd not been alone in a room with a man for so long that to do so now felt foreign and almost uncomfortable for her.

Unlike the day in the woods, his look now was open and curious. And she drank in the sight of his handsome face. She'd forgotten just how good looking the male was, when she'd seen him last her heart had been captured by George, but it had been some time since she'd felt anything for George other than quiet detachment.

Now here was a strong, virile male looking at her with a spark in his eye she'd not seen for some time.

"You shaved," she said, then twitched uncomfortably, realizing she'd spoken her thoughts aloud.

He moved deeper into the room, rubbing his jaw idly, as though unaware of the action.

"Some time ago, yes."

"Why?" she asked, talking of nonsense until she could gather enough nerve to get to the real reason for why she'd asked him to come see her.

He paused in his walk, cocking his head and looking at her far more heatedly than before.

Nothing inappropriate, but with an obvious flare of curiosity burning in his pretty brown eyes, and suddenly she wished she'd taken greater care with her appearance.

Whenever she was viewed out in public, she would never be caught dead in anything other than a princess gown with her hair done up in a fashionable queue and her face painted with bright, bold colors to highlight the natural dark hue of her skin.

Now she wore only a thin, transparent white slip beneath her thick robe. Her hair hung long down her shoulders, covering both breasts with the very tips reaching to her waistline. And no shoes. She had however painted her toenails a pretty shade of lavender. Wiggling her toes and feeling altogether self-conscious she blew out a heavy breath, ready to turn her gaze to the side so that she would no longer need to look at him.

"I suppose," he finally said, "that I felt the need for a change."

She swallowed hard, wishing she weren't quite so aware of just how big and imposing Charles was. Even with one arm in a sling, he was clearly a powerful man. His skin was firm and unmarred by either wrinkles or marks. He had a very strong, masculine face that was offset by those pretty eyelashes of his.

A wide—though not overly so—mouth with a full bottom lip. She swallowed hard, palming her chest nervously.

As though sensing how fidgety and nervous she was, he thankfully came no closer.

"My queen—"

"Call me, Fable," she automatically corrected, knowing she broke protocol by doing so, but for the first time in months, she didn't feel weighed down by the responsibilities of being a queen and all that the title entailed.

She expected him to shake his head and tell her he could not do that. He was George's captain of the guard and punctilious about the title and position. Yes, she'd watched him now and again. Had seen him roam the halls of the massive castle and grounds, once she'd even spotted him training with his men, shirtless and drenched in sweat in the setting evening sun. It was with some shock that she realized she'd been on the look out for him almost constantly.

Sucking her bottom lip between her teeth, she worried the flesh, suddenly more nervous and anxious than before.

He paused for so long; she thought for sure he'd let out a cry to the castle, telling everyone of what she was about. What she was doing?

Though it wasn't wrong, suddenly it felt like she was wicked for bringing him into her room. Alone and unchaperoned, Brunhilda would certainly not take kindly to this.

"Fable," he said then, with a much deeper, scratchy sounding voice than she'd heard him use before. Then tucking his good arm against his waist, he bowed deeply before her.

Feeling the heat of a blush wash through her cheeks, she stuttered, "A...arise, knight."

When he finally did, she knew the moment of truth had arrived, and she could delay no more.

"The day we met in the—"

"Enchanted Forest," he finished for her, shaking his head, "I could never forget."

She sucked in a sharp breath, stomach twisting powerfully inside of her and making her feel strangely ill.

"Oh," was all she could manage to say for a moment, needing a second—or ten—to gather her wits. When she finally did, she could hear the strain beating through her words. "I...I saw something in your eyes that day. Something I have come to consider often and now wonder if...if..."

She flicked her wrist, feeling suddenly foolish for calling him up to her. What if that really had been nothing more than the flicker of light dancing through his eyes? Why had she called him to her based on a memory nearly ten months old? She was a foolish, stupid woman grasping at straws—

"I tried to warn you as best I could, my queen."

Her eyes widened, knowing she'd not imagined the truth of it. "Wh—what?"

For a brief second, he closed his eyes, and it was such an odd emotion to feel, but she almost cried out in fear, desperate to keep any form of human contact she could and when he did open them again, she nearly sobbed with relief.

Shaking and trembling all over like a sapling caught in a strong breeze, she shook her head.

Charles glanced over his shoulder, no doubt as nervous as she, before taking another step toward her. Now nothing but ten feet separated them, but it felt so much closer.

Her body trembled with the prickles of his heat rubbing up against her. Fable hadn't realized how starved for company she'd been until just now.

"My first queen, her death was not..."

His words trailed off, and Fable stuck her thumbnail between her lips, ready to chew it down to the quick from the razor tipped butterfly wings wreaking havoc on her nerves.

"What, Charles? Her death was not what?"

He sucked in a trembly breath, and it was a relief to know she wasn't the only one feeling nervous.

Again he closed his eyes, this time keeping them shut longer. "I should not speak this. *She* has eyes and ears everywhere."

Refusing to let him scare himself into not talking, she switched tactics.

"Who is Brunhilda? Really?"

Something had always felt off about the Dowager Queen, and not just because she was clearly a witch of some form. Deep down, Fable had sensed that all wasn't well within this realm. There was something very wrong, very twisted in it, and all of it centered around George's mother.

18

Charles jerked, and the muscle in his jaw twitched rapid-fire, as though he nervously clenched and unclenched his molars.

Eyes flicking toward her, something hard passed over his face. A sentiment or emotion that let her know he'd come to a decision and she was suddenly terrified that he meant to leave.

Taking an involuntary step forward, she held out her arm causing the grip on her robes to loosen and reveal just a sliver of her body beneath.

Heat rolled through his eyes briefly before he turned his gaze down to his feet.

"You have no right to trust me, Fable," he said slowly, "but I vow to you I am not your enemy here."

"Then who is? The witch?"

He looked back at her and again a wealth of emotions whispered through his astute gaze.

"I will probably regret this," he muttered more to himself than for her benefit, and then he was marching toward her with purposeful steps.

Letting out a startled yip, when his warm hand wrapped around her elbow, she couldn't move. Frozen by fear, doubt, and something far deeper.

Touch.

Though his grip was firm, almost to the point of pain, she shivered into it, desperate for more. Instead of moving back—as she probably should have done—she moved infinitesimally closer. When he breathed, his chest grazed hers.

They locked eyes at the same moment, and something within Fable's soul shifted. When he leaned forward, so that his mouth rested against her ear, she shivered.

His deep voice filled her heart like angel song.

"Brunhilda is not his mother."

She sucked in a sharp breath. "Wh—"

He shook his head, cupping the corner of her jaw with his callused palm so that she could not move.

"I only learned of this myself last year," he whispered quickly. "What I tell you now, none but us will know. Should any other learn of it, we would surely die."

She frowned, heart beating like horses' hooves in her chest.

"Brunhilda is a witch," he said.

"I know—"

"No, you don't." He shook his head, and idly she realized that his fingers had begun to feather delicately along her jawline, breaking her out in a wash of heated goose bumps.

"Brunhilda, the real Brunhilda was also a witch. But I know it was not real mother who won George his seat at power."

She frowned, having a hard time understanding that. "Seat of power? Real mother? But he's the male heir; the seat should have passed to—"

"No, there was another. The real George, his twin brother. This George wasn't born George at all, but William."

She gasped. "Are you saying that—"

He nodded quickly. "Yes. *William*," he finger quoted, "had a terrible accident the day before he turned eighteen. The day before his brother was to inherit the title and throne. The castle and everyone in it were told to cover up the true details of *William's* death. That he'd broken his neck falling off his favored Stallion—Devil. The fact was William had eaten of the foxglove berries."

She shuddered knowing exactly what those were. Berries the color of deepest magenta that could stop a heart cold in less than a minute. Even she, born in Seren, knew to stay well clear of those poisonous little berries.

Fable frowned. "But that makes no sense."

19

"We all thought so too. But we were ordered by the then queen mother to silence. For many years, I believed William truly had died, that he'd committed suicide because he'd been envious that George and not he would get to become king."

A cold chill worked down her spine. She knew there had to be more to this story. "So how did you learn that George and William were—"

"I began to see slight differences at first. George and William were so similar that only those truly closest to them would have ever noticed anything amiss. But where George excelled in math, William excelled in the arts. Most notably the art of seduction. He was a well-known cad and Casanova. George always had his nose stuck in the books."

She clenched her jaw. "George, *my George*, never reads."

His look was sad but honest. "I began to suspect that it had been George and not William who'd met his untimely demise. And when I thought that, it wasn't a far stretch to imagine that William had also been the one to poison his own brother. At first, I thought myself mad. Thought I had to be seeing shadows and ghosts where there were none. It had been so long, and people change. But the more I noticed, the more I began to notice too. Like the dowager—how she too changed in the months following William's death. I was George's oldest and truest friend. The differences with her were so slight as to be subtle. Her favorite color, which had once been rose red shifted to black. Her food preferences changed." He shrugged. "Like I said, small things."

Though she loved the way he still stroked her skin, she had to look him eye to eye. Pulling back just enough to do it, she searched his gaze for any sign of deception but found none.

"What happened?" Her whisper sounded like cannon fire in her ears and she was sure they'd be caught. But though her knees trembled, Fable would hear him out.

Wetting his lips, he blinked rapidly several times before saying. "One day I spotted Brunhilda working magic."

"But I thought you said she was a witch."

He shook his head slightly. "Not magic, Fable. But *magick*. The dark kind."

She swallowed hard, wondering if he knew that she too worked magick. Though she'd not sold her soul to do it, her powers were more akin to her grandfather's Hades than a fairy godmother's.

"Brunhilda did not know magick like that."

"Like what?"

"Like death curses." He nodded slowly, as though reinforcing that he did not lie. "The first queen's death was no accident of fate. It was deliberate and caused by the dowager."

Her nostrils flared, deep down Fable had already suspected this, but hearing him say it now made her feel scared and terrified. "Are...are you sure?"

Nodding once, he again drew her chin back, curving his large palm against her neck and odd as it was, Fable felt safe for the first time since being tossed in the tower.

"Many months back I visited a witch, and not just any witch, but *the* witch. Baba Yaga. I thought I was going mad. I had to make sure. I had to know the truth, one way or the other."

Immediately Fable shivered, everyone in Kingdom knew of the child eater. Her powers were terrifying, mythical, and nearly godlike by comparison. Anyone would be a fool to seek out that woman. A fool or desperate.

"She told you?"

He clipped his head once. "Aye. She did."

Baba did not lie. The witch had many flaws, but one thing was known to be constant with her, if you paid in enough gold, the truth you'd know.

"She verified everything I'd already suspected. Brunhilda, George's real mother, died the night before George took the throne. This witch, whoever she really is, did it and took on her form. I knew then that to betray those truths to anyone would become my eventual demise. So I never told a soul. Until now. Until you."

20

Trembling with the enormity of this reveal, only one thought pierced Fable's heart. "Is it possible that perhaps the witch had her hook's in William before he—"

When Charles wrapped his arm around her waist, she didn't complain, and she didn't pull back. His touch upon her spine soothed her raging nerves.

"He knows, Fable. For he is the one who set the whole thing up."

# Chapter 4

*Fable*

Fable hadn't been able to sleep that night, or the next, or even the next week as Charles' words continued to echo through her head.

*George did it...*

Gripping the golden lion's head bedpost, she stared at nothing as growing dread continued to consume her soul.

*George did it...*

George...

George knew.

He knew.

He wasn't bespelled. And he wasn't really George; he was an imposter. An evil twin with a heart full of hate and lust.

Squeezing her eyes shut, a lone tear rolled down her cheek. For days, she'd attempted to reconcile Charles's revelation with what few memories she had with her king, and though it pained Fable to admit it, she had to concede that it all made horrible sense.

His easy disregard for her.

The way he'd so easily batted away her words when she'd spoken to him of her misgivings concerning his mother. It was a fact within Seren that nothing happened there that her father wasn't always aware of; any good king knew what happened within his own walls.

Fable had tried to brush off her unease in the beginning, how he'd so easily disregard her thoughts or feelings. How little he seemed to care whether she was in his presence or not. The long leash he continually gave to Brunhilda.

And once she'd been tricked into putting on the wrist cuff, cutting off her powers, Fable had latched onto that, choosing desperately to believe that George was under the same sort of enchantment as she.

What if Charles was wrong? What if he lied? Could she even trust him? She didn't know him, he could be trying to manipulate her mind, could be trying to...

But no more had she thought it then she knew it wasn't so because Charles hadn't sought her out in the first place. Fable had brought him to her.

"My queen," Mirror spoke gravely, "your thoughts are so heavy as to smother me."

Shoulders drooping, she turned bleary-eyed toward her only friend and gave him a small, pitiful smile. "I am sorry, Mirror. And you are right; my thoughts are grave today."

His handsome face scanned the corners of the tower. "May I help?"

She sighed. "I wouldn't know how. Unless you know magick and can release me of this chain."

Fable held up her wrist, showing off the iron shackle.

He shook his head, but said, "It's been some days since last you've seen Snow. I could try and fetch her for you."

Immediately the thought of company livened Fable's sour mood. And a real smile spread upon her lips. "I'd like that."

Mirror's smile was as large as hers. "Only give me a moment, my queen. I shall return soon."

And just like before when he'd gone to fetch Charles, Uriah vanished from within the looking glass.

Knowing she'd be in for a long wait, Fable rose and decided that she was done torturing herself with unanswerable questions. Taking care of her morning ablution, she took time with her appearance. Getting out of her sleep things for the first time in a week and slipping into one of her prettier, yet more sedate gowns.

A confectioner's delight of spun frothy fabric dyed a beguiling shade of silvery-lavender. It cinched tight at the waist, but the strings were in the front and not the back, so she could take care of dressing herself.

Her hair, however, was another matter. A few quick brushes to get out the worst of the tangles was all she could manage before there was a soft, hesitant knock at the door.

Gasping from a powerful case of nerves and happiness, Fable ran to the front door, idly wondering why Snow hadn't come in the back way as Charles had.

"Come in, come in, my little—" She gasped. Her happy greeting for Snow died on her tongue as George tossed the doors wide and stepped through.

Handsome as ever, and dressed in a burgundy wine colored smock that highlighted the gold strands of his hair and captivatingly attractive features, he looked around the room slowly.

Pausing briefly when his gaze landed on her discarded clothing on the floor.

"Are you well?" he asked slowly, and she frowned, hearing a note in his voice that she'd so often heard before but had refused to speculate on.

That note was the sound of utter boredom.

George was uninterested in her. To have a king grow bored with his queen was a never a good thing, far too many queens had lost their heads for less.

Her soul trembled, and it was all she could do to remain standing. So often she'd heard this and every time she'd made excuses for his behavior, cold hard reality was like a smack of ice water to her face.

Not wanting him to know or suspect at all that she was starting to see the truth, she wrung her fingers together and clasped them tightly in front of her, forcing her lips to rise into a facsimile of a smile.

"Yes, George, I am." Her words had sounded unsure and hesitant.

But then, that's how it had sounded lately when around him.

"You're back soon," she said, for lack of anything better to say. Brunhilda had mentioned him being gone a fortnight; he'd barely been gone a week.

"I've been made aware of important matters to attend to back home."

She swallowed hard, not liking the sound of that one bit. Without asking, she knew he spoke of her. But she needed the confirmation.

"Me? Matters pertaining to me?"

Why did her heart flutter so strangely in her chest?

He grunted with a nod, then he looked her up and down, and for the first time, she spotted something other than quiet detachment in his gaze.

"You look...nice." He wet his lips, taking a step further into her room.

So far they'd been talking with the door open, and when she glanced out, she realized with a start that Charles stood outside and was looking at her with anguish in his brown eyes. They'd not spoken since that day in her tower. She wet her lips, hating that it bothered her so much.

He'd been out there the entire time and she'd not known it. But he'd never returned, never even looked up at her tower when out in the fields practicing with the other knights.

Grabbing hold of her stomach, she nodded. "Thank...thank you."

But George wasn't done. He invaded her space so that he and she shared breath. His hands wrapped hotly around her waist, and his smooth cheek rested proprietarily against her own.

He smelled of pine and sandalwood, two scents she'd once loved. But now her flesh prickled with revulsion at his touch. She wanted to shake him off her, but she knew to do so might well be the last act she ever committed.

His lips feathered along her skin. "Mmm, my dark beauty. Tonight I shall return to you. Dress in white. You look pure in white."

As opposed to not pure in white? The bastard. She'd been pure when she'd come to him; he'd been the only man to lay claim to her body, and she hated him for it. If only she could have her magick back, she'd leave. Leave and never return again.

Anger burned through her belly. And with it came a hot rush of tears jammed tight in her throat.

Fable swallowed hard determined not to show him just how upset she now was. "Yes, my king."

Lowering his hand, until his palm cupped her bottom, he squeezed to the point of pain, making her lift up on her toes. But she'd be damned if she made a noise of protest, burying the pain, she swallowed the sound and held her head high.

"Tonight you will make me a child," he said.

She sucked in a sharp breath.

Taking her face in his hands, he jerked her forward, slamming his lips to hers, and without a word of warning crammed his tongue inside of her mouth like a javelin.

She tasted spearmint on it.

The only way to not shove him off her as she wished to do was to transport her mind someplace else. To a safe place, a happy place. Home. In the below. With her family. Why had she ever thought herself unhappy there?

He bit so hard on her bottom lip at one point that she felt the burn of tearing and tasted the copper of her own blood. Pulling back with a satisfied grin, George patted her on the head like she was nothing more than a good, little pet and smirked.

"Until tonight. Kitten."

And there could be no more denying the cold, hard, brutal facts that George was exactly who Charles claimed he'd been because the cruel petting session had exposed his neck.

His very naked neck.

The iron necklace she'd sworn had to have been enchanted by Brunhilda wasn't on him today.

Fable didn't cry until he'd turned away from her, marching back down the stairs without looking back once. Charles lingered only a moment longer, shaking his head softly before reluctantly locking her in the tower once more. She'd hoped Charles might be the one to help save her. That perhaps she'd found a kindred spirit in him, but she'd been wrong.

Though he knew the truth, he would not do a thing to help. And that was a terrible feeling, to know that she truly was all alone.

She stood exactly where she was until she heard the last echo of his footsteps melt away.

In fact, she didn't move at all until suddenly tiny arms had wound themselves around her waist.

With a start, Fable twirled, and couldn't help but choke up with relief at the sight of the little girl who had begun to feel more like a daughter of blood than of marriage to her.

"Snow!" she cried with joy, dropping to her knees and hugging the sweet girl tight to her breast.

Snow began to sob, and the sound tore Fable in two.

"What is wrong, my love? Why do you cry?"

Snow was nearing eleven years of age now, and it was obvious to one and all that when she grew fully, she'd be a beauty beyond compare. Prettier even than Fable, and she wasn't afraid to own up to that fact.

With her milky ivory complexion, ebony colored hair as dark as Fable's own, and enchanting blue eyes, she was exactly what a fairy tale princess should look like. Mixed in with her sweet disposition, and Fable knew that to know Snow was to love Snow White.

It was impossible to hate anyone so pure and beautiful.

"Why has grandmum hidden you from me?" She hiccupped, wiping at her nose with the back of her hand. "I asked for you for days and was told to shut up or I'd be thrashed but good."

24

Her tiny shoulders trembled as she continued to sob silent tears.

"Oh, my sweet, beautiful girl. I'm okay, see. They haven't harmed me." Fable tried not to choke on the lie, but for the benefit of the girl, she plastered on a tight smile and twirled for her.

No sense in adding to the girl's unease by admitting that her grandmother was a vile witch and her father a horrible, wicked man. Somehow, someway when Fable left this place, and she would, she was going to figure out a way to take the girl with her.

Wiggling as tight into Fable's side as she possibly could, Snow sighed deeply as though releasing all the cares of the world and a real smile tugged at Fable's lips because there wasn't anything she loved in this castle the way she did this little girl.

After clinging tightly for another few minutes, Fable reluctantly pulled back, wiping up the girls tears.

"There now, my dear, smile, for we are together again."

Long lashes matted with tears, Snow sniffed an unladylike little sniff and shook. "Fable?" she said slowly.

Hearing the question in her name, Fable cocked her head. "Love, what is it?"

"Mirror spoke to me today. Is it true what he said?"

Mouth suddenly going dry as she tried to imagine just what her mirror could have possibly said to the little girl, she was hesitant to ask. "Wh...what did Mirror say to you?"

"That my grandma is a very bad witch."

Gasping, she shot a heated look toward Mirror, which still lacked Uriah's face, no doubt the miserable cur was hiding from her wrath. The cheeky bastard.

"It's not tr—"

Snow's face set into a hard line. "Don't lie to me too, Fable. Everyone else in this place lies to me. Please, don't be like everyone else. Is it true?"

Her words were so strong, so evident of the little princess she was. Young as she was, there was no mistaking the budding nobility standing before her.

Heart sinking, because she did not want to admit to this, but knowing she now had no choice, Fable softly said, "Yes. It's true."

"She has locked you away, hasn't she?"

Again, it felt like she spoke not to an immature eleven-year-old, but a mature and reasonable adult.

Closing her eyes, she shamefully admitted the truth. "Yes, Snow, she has locked me away."

"She's not my real grandmother, is she?"

Fable couldn't help the gasp of shock that fell from her. "Where...where did you hear such a thing?"

If Mirror had told the little girl all this, Fable was half-tempted to break him herself.

Where once it had seemed like she'd been talking to an adult, now Snow looked her age as her small shoulders slumped, and she released another silent sob. "My fairy godmother, the Blue, told me."

Clenching tight to her upper arms fear beat a terrible rhythm in Fable's heart; she shook her head. "Now you listen to me, little one. You tell no one of this. No one. Do you understand?"

Her brows lowered. "But father would—"

So she didn't know just what kind of man her father actually was. Good. Because at least Fable wouldn't be forced to shatter the poor girl's entire world tonight. "Leave him out of this, do you hear me?"

"But we can't just stand back and let this happen, Fable; we must do something—"

"Yes." She nodded brusquely. "And we will. *I* will. Not you. Do you hear me? You stay out of this, Snow White. Promise me."

A stubborn look pinched her pretty features. "I can't—"

Fear twisted her heart in its vice grip, and Fable shook her hard. "You will!" she snapped. "Promise me!"

Startled at the vehemence and violence of Fable, Snow went absolutely still. Enough so that Fable, ashamed of what she'd done, snatched her hands back and curled them impotently upon her knees.

25

"I'm...I'm sorry, little Snow. Please forgive me. Only, I worry for you; you must know this. Promise me, child, promise me you will not go after your grandmother."

Blue eyes flashed with fury. "She is not my grandmother."

Her chin notched high, and for just a moment Fable saw George in her. Fable had seen the paintings of Violet, Snow's birth mother. In every way, she looked a mirror image of her, but the hardness and implacability were all George, and it saddened Fable to see it in Snow.

The fury eased from Snow's eyes, and with the enthusiasm of a child, she rushed Fable, wrapping her arms tight around her neck. "I promise, Fable. I promise. Only please don't get hurt, she is a bad woman. I know it. I know she is."

Relieved beyond imagining, Fable kissed the girl's temple, inhaling the heady scent of rose and lavender in her hair deep into her lungs. The girl was the only thing that made living in this castle bearable; Fable didn't know what she'd do if she ever lost her.

Hugging her tight, and wishing she didn't need to let her go ever, she finally forced herself to back off.

"You need to return to your room now, child, before your absence is noted."

Snow White nodded, wiping her nose again. "Okay. But what, what will you do?"

Giving her an immediate grin, Fable shrugged, affecting a nonchalant attitude she most certainly didn't feel. "Oh, don't you worry about me, little Snow. I'm resilient." She winked, and then kissed the girl's temple one last time. "Now go, sweetheart."

Squeezing her hand one last time, Snow turned and walked back toward the hidden stairwell Charles had used before. Even knowing that the wall would part, and the stairwell would magically appear, the magic was seamless that it felt like a strange dream when Snow left.

Immediately she sensed the prickle of Uriah back in his mirror.

"You're a bastard, Mirror," she said without preamble, still staring at the stone wall.

"She asked, my queen, I could not lie to her."

Twirling on her heel, she notched her chin, staring at his face in silence for several long heartbeats. Seeing Snow had resolved one thing in Fable's heart. Determination.

For a week now she'd walked about in a daze, hoping idealistically perhaps, that someone might still come along and save her from this hell. She had no innate magick anymore, no power...at least that's what she'd been telling herself, allowing her thoughts to sink deeper and deeper into depression.

But it wasn't just her in this mess; there was Snow White to consider. For if she didn't no one else would. That little girl would be lost and alone and raised to become one of the worst villains in all of Kingdom.

"No," she said slowly, and this time, when she spoke her voice did not ring with sorrow, but with resolution instead.

Resolution that Mirror clearly noted because his own features changed. Where once he'd appeared morose and sad, now he looked curious and thoughtful.

"My queen?"

"You remember telling me to remember who I am?"

He nodded. The blue smoke behind his face was now threaded through with deep veins of glittering sapphire.

"Yes." His voice echoed.

"I remember." She nodded. "I remember, and my training begins now."

# Chapter 5

*Fable*

Turning toward the only window in the tower, Fable walked up to it, gripped the edge and took several deep breaths.

What she was about to do was foolish by any stretch of the imagination, but she had no choice. The only one who could free her from this hell was her. Staring at the damnable wrist cuff, she clenched her jaw, took several deep breaths and began to spout off names to the wind.

"Aphrodite, come to me."

Seconds past but her aunt did not come.

She'd expected it, of course, but she continued down the list.

"Great goddess Calypso, I call you."

*Tick. Tock. Tick. Tock.* Nothing but crickets.

Squaring her shoulders, she pressed on.

"Hades, please hear me."

Nothing.

"Apollo. Zeus. Themis..."

And on and on and on she went down the long list of names, Brunhilda was crafty, but there was no way she'd enchanted the cuff against every magick wielder in Kingdom, she only needed one to hear her.

Turning from the Greek gods to different legends, she pressed on.

"Baba Yaga." Fable cringed after saying it, heart thundering like horses hooves in her chest, not sure she actually wanted the child eater to hear her cry.

But just as before, the witch did not answer.

Pressing on, determined to not allow herself to feel an ounce of disappointment, Fable carried on.

"Wicked Witch. Rumpelstiltskin. Bloody Mary..."

Time pressed on. The sun revolved, the sky deepened into twilight, and several hours had passed. Fable's voice was hoarse, and tears rolled unchecked down her cheeks as her resolve of earlier faded away with each name called.

"Godmothers of Kingdom."

Her voice cracked, and she hung her head.

Brunhilda had been far more thorough than she could have ever suspected. But to stop now meant giving up, and though she was on the verge of helplessness, Fable brokenly whispered, "Galeta the Blue, if you're there...please—"

Instantly the room snapped with a pop of power, and a roll of brilliant blue light swayed across her flesh.

Eyes wide, and breathing heavy, Fable twirled on her heel sure that Brunhilda had come, had heard her, was here to hurt her.

Her legs ached. Her back hurt. Her head throbbed, and Fable knew that she must either be dreaming or delirious because there could be no way the Fairy Queen was actually flitting in her room.

A miniature woman with massive blue wings, cotton candy blue hair that coiled in tight spirals around her cherubic face and sharp, tiny fangs poking out as she smirked back at her. Galeta was famous—or rather infamous—within Kingdom.

Rumor had it she was somewhere between pure evil and methodically wicked. But she was Snow's fairy godmother so she couldn't be all bad. No doubt the stories had been greatly exaggerated as they were when it came to most of Kingdom.

Narrowing ice blue eyes, Galeta spoke. And her words instantly filled the room with the sharp nip of frost.

"I wondered if you'd ever get around to me."

Wetting her lips, pulse pounding so hard in her ears Fable knew this couldn't possibly be a dream, she shook her head because at the moment all the words were a jumbled, chaos of noise in her head.

Flitting forward on those massive butterfly wings, Galeta flew slowly around her body. When she finally circled back to where she'd started from, she snorted.

"So you're the renowned darkness of legend, eh? Oh, what would your family think to see you now? Broken. Weak. And so very pathetic." Her lip lifted into a disgusted snarl.

Bleary eyed, and exhausted from the hours spent calling out; Fable was in no mood to deal with this fairy's nastiness. Notching her chin, she schooled her features into a cold wall and snapped, "If I'm so pathetic, why did you come?"

Galeta shrugged a pale shoulder that glimmered like freshly fallen snow in the sunlight. Her fairy dress, woven of what looked to be spiderweb silk and stained a deep blue, glinted with thousands of teardrop shaped snowflakes that had been threaded through the gown.

One thing was certain; Galeta definitely lived up to her more colorful moniker—*The Cold One*.

"Maybe," she said in the small, childlike voice common to the fairies of the south, "I know things."

Fable's nostrils flared. "What sorts of things."

Reaching a small hand up toward her hair, Galeta tugged on something and Fable flinched imagining all sorts of horrible things. Like a big hairy spider, or a slug. Hard to say with fairies, they bonded to the strangest things.

But instead of some frightening familiar, all she pulled out was a golden colored egg the size of her fist. Galeta stroked the egg tenderly with three fingers, and unbelievably the thing began to actually quiver. Like something, or someone was inside of it and enjoying the touch.

"That maybe, just maybe you and I are destined to cross paths. That perhaps, you're calling me was no last recourse as you might imagine, but fate intersecting our paths at the right and perfect time."

"What?" Her brows gathered in a sharp vee of confusion. "But I only called you to—"

Galeta smirked. "Oh, I know why you called me. To save you."

Well, that wasn't how she saw it. She'd called Galeta with the hopes of making a trade, bartering her wealth or even part of her kingdom for hers and Snow's release. A fair and even exchange.

"No." Galeta shrugged. "Not I, but you will save yourself."

"Why are you doing this? Why do you seem so willing to help?"

Fable was no fool; she'd known that to call any of the names she had meant she'd be required to give up something great in return. It was simply the way of magick; nothing ever came without a deep cost attached.

But Galeta hadn't even asked for payment; she simply continued to grin and stroke her egg.

The rumors of the fairy queen were hardly flattering. She was petty, cruel, and vindictive.

Nimue—Fable's mother—had had her own run-ins with The Blue. Fairies weren't the sweet, docile "grandmotherly" types they were made out to be in the legends; legends they themselves penned.

Of all the names Fable had called for, she'd not really seen The Blue as a threat, but standing here now with the fairy queen flitting before her wearing a calculated look, she shivered.

"Oh, I'm not really, dear. Believe me." Her laughter sounded like shards of ice crashing off a cliff's face. "You see I've seen the future. And there will come a time where you will pay me back in blood. Not much. You'll hardly even miss it. I promise."

Fable's jaw clenched, not liking the sound of this, but knowing she was stuck between a rock and a hard place. With the cuff on her wrist, she was unable to tap into her powers to free herself.

28

And based upon the fact that she'd called out names for hours, and only The Blue had come, her options were few, if any.

Biting onto her lip with her sharp little fangs, Galeta eyed Fable so hard that the muscles in her thighs began to tremble with anxiety. Mother had always said the fairies were nothing more than little demons with wings, and seeing her now, Fable was inclined to believe it.

Something wicked rolled through The Blue's head, she just knew it.

"How? How will I pay you in blood?"

Galeta flicked her words away with a roll of her wrist. "Let's save that discussion for a later day. Right now, I'm to teach you magick. And magick you shall learn."

"I know magick." She lifted her wrist. "But I cannot use any; I'm locked—"

Galeta snorted. "Such, a stupid little fool you are, darkness. Magick comes in many forms. Sometimes you are born with it. But sometimes...you have to make it grow."

When she said the last, the egg she'd held onto floated high off her palm and it started to shake.

Gently at first, then harder, and harder still, until it's movements were violent and erratic.

For a second Fable feared the demon hadn't been holding onto an egg at all but a weapon meant to end her until the egg suddenly stilled and then...a loud noise erupted, like the tremblings of the earth.

The castle shook. Cries sounded from within. And the floor beneath Fable's feet actually began to dance.

Terrified, she clutched onto the edge of the bed, unable to tear her gaze off the egg that now glowed a deep and bloody red flame color.

And then with a burst, it ruptured, and out popped a miniature dragon bellowing tiny jets of flame.

Blinking, because the castle walls still echoed with the screams and shouts from below, Fable couldn't seem to gather her thoughts into any sort of coherence.

"That tiny dragon caused the earth to shake," she muttered in awe.

And Galeta grinned. "It is why his kind is called Earth Shaker. And he will not remain tiny for long, will you Button?" she crooned to her new tiny pet, reaching out a hand as she scratched behind his earflaps.

The dragon gave a coughing sound that sounded suspiciously happy and coated Galeta's hand in his flame. She seemed completely unaffected by it. Looking back at Fable she nodded, causing her curls to bob and dance like charmed snakes around her heart shaped face.

"I will train you in the arts, Fable, and when I am done, it will be you who decides which path you'll choose."

Blinking, and completely confused, but also secretly thrilled at the prospect of learning magick at the hands of a dark faerie; Fable could only nod and say, "When can we start?"

"Why now. Of course."

They practiced for hours. Simple things. Learning to crush the proper herbs together to create a spell. Incantations. They worked until the sun began to set, and though Fable had created no magick to speak of, she'd been a woman possessed to learn all she could.

She did not doubt the veracity of The Blue. The fairy would demand her due, and knew the only way to ensure she got whatever it was she wanted she'd need to be honest in her dealings with Fable.

Fable's tongue had twisted trying to repeat the strange words in the strange books filled full of drawings that made her flesh tingle just to run her fingers across them.

She'd thought she'd known what magick was, but holding this leather bound book with depictions of demons and pentagrams, angels, and objects of great and sacred power, she felt fear.

Knew she dabbled in the type of darkness she should never knowingly dabble in. How had a fairy godmother gotten her hands on such a tome? Why did a being sworn to bring about the happily ever afters for the heroes of this world know such evil?

And though a side of Fable hated what she did, she knew she had no other choice in the matter.

"Enough," Galeta finally said, her voice so deep and thunderous that Fable jumped, so lost in the translation and speaking of the words that she'd forgotten for just a moment that she wasn't alone.

Blinking suddenly tear-filled eyes, she rubbed the grit from them with her arm and glanced around, shocked to note the twilight pallor filling her room and the fact that her stomach was so empty and hungry that it felt like it ground viciously against her spine.

Groaning, she leaned heavily against the wooden table and shook her head. "How long have we been at this?"

"Hours."

"But I still could—"

"No," Galeta petted the head of her now slumbering Earth Shaker, "you cannot. The King comes even now to lay claim to his bride."

Her laughter was full of wicked humor, and Fable decided that help or not, she did not trust The Blue. Licking sharp fangs, Galeta eyed Fable hard and long.

"What?" she snapped a moment later, unable to bear the tension of such a heated stare.

"Oh, nothing." Galeta shook her head, causing her curls to bob almost prettily.

In Kingdom, often the most wicked hearts hid behind the loveliest facades.

Fable didn't buy it. Which clearly Galeta realized, because laughing, she held her hand's palm up. "You wish to know, fine. I've seen your future—"

"You read futures?" Fable asked dubiously. She knew fairy lore and knew that only The Grey generally had such power.

Though there were rumors that Galeta, from time immemorial, had envied the skill and magick of The Gray and had done something awful to the fairy so as to gain the power for her own. Rumors were hard to substantiate in a land full of them, but one thing was certain, The Blue had retained authority over the faes for as long as history had recorded their existence. Which was a very, very long time.

Again a one-shouldered shrug and only a secret smile were her answer. "George will impregnate you."

Fable gasped, forgetting all about secret assassination attempts and coups for power as her world rocked violently.

"No," she breathed, as her hands began to tremble.

Galeta nodded gleefully. "Oh yes, a gaggle of them. All beautiful. Some dark, some light. All wicked, and one...one of them will end you."

Her eyes widened. "It's not possible." She held onto the flat of her stomach, curling her fingers into her gown and bunching it tight, feeling both hot and cold, dizzy and weightless. "You can't know this. You can't."

Snorting so loud that The Blue woke her dragon—who shook his head and belched a fiery burp before settling back down—Galeta laughed. "I can, and I do. I learned all I could of you Fable of the Seren Seas once I discovered our paths entwined."

"Why are you telling me this?"

Flitting those demonic blue wings that sported a massive moth's eye on each, she drew closer to Fable's side, before drawing a sharp nail along the corner of her jaw. She hissed as her flesh split like a thin ribbon beneath that wicked touch.

"I have my reasons, and they are not yours to know."

Fable desperately wanted to know why but sensed the Fairy would give her nothing more.

Finally, the nasty smirk slipped off the fae's face, and she said in a hard growl, "You must take this."

Tipping her palm over, a bottle in the shape of an apple suddenly appeared there. The glass was a deep red so dark it almost looked black, and every so often would glow like the pulse of a heartbeat.

Wetting her lips, Fable took an involuntary step back. "What...what is that?"

30

Ruby red lips curled upward as Galeta stroked the bottle's stopper and said in a dark, deadly whisper, "Your salvation. And your ruin. Drink it."

She thrust it into her chest. But Fable wanted no part of it. Stumbling back another step, she shook her head hard. "I'm not going to take that. Are you insane? What will it do to me?"

Just then the echoes of someone climbing the stairwell pricked Fable's ears, and she knew without being told that George had made good on his threat and was coming for her.

Swallowing hard, angry, upset, and terrified, she stared wide-eyed at the fairy who now flew within a foot of her face and said softly, "No babies for you, Fable. Ever. That is the price you'll pay for drinking this."

She gasped, throat squeezing tight because the thought of never bearing a child, it was almost too painful to consider.

There were too many questions without answers. Like, how did Galeta know this? Was it even true?

Learning of George's true colors made her never want to bear one of his, and knowing what Galeta had told her, that one of her offspring would be the death of her—whether true or not—had infected her with fear.

But she had hope of escaping, hope of someday being her own woman again. "Never?" she asked, voice reed-thin and scratchy.

Galeta's only answer was a terrible laugh. She tossed the vial at Fable, and without thought, she snatched it from the air, terrified of it crashing to the floor.

The footsteps grew louder.

"Decide quickly, darkness, for soon the matter will be taken out of your hands entirely."

Soon George would be here. Soon he'd force her to mate, and like Galeta said, she'd no longer have a choice in the matter. The thought of bearing George's children, of knowing that they'd be as trapped here as she, as Snow...it wasn't her eventual murder that decided her, but the fate of the beloved children she'd never know that steeled her nerves.

This could all be a lie.

A scheme concocted by a cold, and unfeeling heart. But time was not on her side, because if this was true, she had only seconds left to decide.

With a sinking heart and trembling fingers, Fable uncorked the bottle, tipped it up and drank deeply.

The thick fluid tasted of burnt cherries and made her gasp as she swallowed, feeling as though she'd consumed living flame.

Galeta vanished in a puff of silvery-blue snow crystals, the echo of her laughter chilling Fable's soul.

Tears burned her eyes.

The door opened.

George stood on the other side, holding only a lit torch and dressed in his kingly robes.

"Now," he said deeply, "take off your clothes, female."


The nights were the worst.

George had come that first night and every night since. He was not a sweet and caring lover. He did not hit her, but he did not tend to her either.

He'd enter her, whether she was physically ready or not. Give several hard thrusts before grunting a release, collapsing upon her for a quick rest, and then resume his task over again.

He was like a man possessed, consumed with her bearing him a child. A male heir, he'd always say.

It didn't take long for Fable to understand that he came to her out of duty and nothing more. No doubt by Brunhilda's lead.

Sometimes Fable thought it would have been preferable to feel wrath or anger come from him, as opposed to the oppressive nothing she got.

He did not kiss her. Did not hold her. He simply shoved his cock into her with no regard to her comfort or pleasure.

There were never any sweet words whispered, nor even petting of any kind.

But those nights were not the worst.

No, the worst was when George came to her room so drunk and half-cocked that he'd require help to "finish." Charles, his ever-devoted knight, would guide George's sometimes semi-flaccid penis directly into her.

Tears of shame would run down her face, and all she could do to get through it was to look up at the ceiling and pretend that it was all just a horrible, terrible nightmare.

And when it was done, and George had spilled his seed and collapsed in a heap beside her snoring heavily, Charles would give her a look that would split Fable's heart in two.

Pity.

And she hated him for it.

The days were better and made all the tortures of the night somewhat bearable. Galeta, as promised, returned every day. Now, months in into her training, Fable felt stronger.

The other day she'd created fire with nothing more than a spell.

She'd laughed and then cried, sensing the end of this miserable time here. And as she grew stronger, it became harder and harder to hide just what she could do. Every night that her bastard of a husband came to her she wanted to hurt him, end him.

And the need for that revenge only grew stronger and stronger within her.

But Galeta cautioned her not to. That she was still nowhere near as strong as Brunhilda and should the witch learn what Fable was really up to trapped in this tower of stone, she'd end it all.

So Fable forced herself to lie still and take the abuse, repeating to herself over and over that when she was finally strong enough, she was going to make them all pay.

Now, six months into her training, Fable was so lost in the learning of the newest spell—a killing curse— that she did not at first hear Galeta's words.

"Snap out of it, darkness!" Galeta snarled, shoving Fable so hard that she practically stumbled over her feet.

Frowning, and furious, she glared at the miniature woman. "What?"

Galeta's eyes were wide and with a flick of her wand, she vanished the book, herbs, and poisons now littering her worktable.

"I said, the witch comes." And then, just as she'd vanished everything else, so too did The Blue leave.

Fable had just enough time to twirl in surprise when the doors were tossed wide and landed with a violent bang against the walls.

Brunhilda, dressed in a moss green gown that fit snugly to her body, eyed the room critically, and Fable trembled, terrified that somehow the witch would know what had actually transpired just beneath her nose.

Knowing that to act guilty would make her look guilty, Fable instantly transformed into a thing of regal and arrogant beauty.

With the power she learned came now a new and innate strength she'd never known she'd actually possessed.

"What do you want, witch?" she hissed.

Snapping frosty blue eyes toward Fable, she lifted her nose and glared. "I've come to have a long overdue chat with you, woman."

She crossed her arms beneath her flat chest, causing them to swell and look bigger than they actually were. Brunhilda had wildflowers threaded together to create a garland upon the crown of her head.

Fable recognized Snow's handiwork and had to gnash her teeth not to say anything. Little Snow hadn't come to visit Fable in near a month now, and it worried her that she'd not seen the girl. Not only that but why was Snow creating garland wreaths for a grandmother she loathed? A terrible, sinking feeling wormed its way through her gut.

But until she grew stronger, she knew there was nothing she could do for the child.

"About what?" she asked crisply.

Brunhilda, without requesting permission, entered the room and snapped her fingers. Causing the doors to slam behind her with a thunderous thud.

Fable didn't flinch.

To the witch's credit, she did not beat around the bush or mince words. "You're not pregnant. You should be pregnant."

The way she said it. *Should be*, Fable knew instantly the witch had indeed spelled George's seed.

The pain of not bearing children no longer bothered Fable, and she was suddenly grateful that Galeta had given her that potion. Snow's mother had died, it was easy now to see that Brunhilda had definitely had a hand in her demise. Laughing on the inside, she said softly, "Some women can't get pregnant quickly."

Brunhilda snorted. "Aye. Some can't."

It was obvious by the way she spoke that she didn't believe Fable.

Lifting her brows, she shook her head. "Is there something you want to say to me, Brunhilda? Something you know that I don't?"

The dowager's smile was vicious and cruel. "I know you've done something, little bitch."

Fable couldn't quite hide the smirk. She sniffed and shook her head. "What could I have possibly done?" she lifted her wrist, showing off the damnable cuff still locked tight. "I have no magick. No one comes to me."

Not entirely true, but again, the witch didn't need to know that.

"Are you saying I'm more clever than you are?" Fable's words were sugar dipped in venom.

Fire burned through Brunhilda's eyes, and a snarl transformed her pretty face into that of a monster's. "Once I figure this out, and I will, you will pay, darkness. Mark my words."

"Get out of my room," Fable said unflinchingly.

Brunhilda stood exactly where she was.

Curling her fingers tight to her side, knowing she was still no match for the witch, Fable screamed, "Get. Out. Of. My. Room!"

The dowager stood there only a second longer, before snorting, turning on her heel and with a snap of her fingers, opened the doors and walked out without saying another word.

Fable sank to her knees the moment she was alone again, trembling not from fear, but from such a fierceness of rage that she thought she'd be consumed by it.

"Good on you, darkness. You will be a fine queen someday," Galeta said, startling Fable with her return.

Clenching her jaw, and snapping her own fingers to slam the doors shut and locking them this time, Fable glared up at the fairy. "I learn this magick so that I can leave here, I am no queen and I will not—"

Galeta's laughter was terrible. "You just keep on telling yourself that, darkness. Now come, you've still yet to master the killing curse."

# Chapter 6

*Calypso*

Twirling, Calypso eyed her mate.

Hades—who sat on a burnished mahogany leather tufted sofa before his massive, flame-lit hearth—slowly set down his reading papers and gave her a raised eyebrow in question.

Caly's heart flipped. Even now, after so many lifetimes together she adored her male. With his dark hair, olive toned skin, and mysterious eyes full of brimstone and madness he was her perfect match in every way.

He also knew her inside and out.

"My jewel?" he asked, in that deep sonorous voice of his that never failed to make her skin tingle. She might have jumped his bones just now if she wasn't so sick to her stomach.

Clenching onto her middle, she worried her bottom lip.

Calypso was never one to find herself tongue-tied, a fact that he knew well. Shooting to his feet, he marched toward her, the echoes of his shoes on the slate-gray marble floor of his mansion in the Underworld reverberated like cannon fire in her ears.

Reaching her side just a second later, he gripped her biceps and squeezed gently. "My love, you're worrying me, what is the matter?"

His gaze was searching.

Wetting her lips, knowing she needed to set his mind at ease, she shook her head. "It is...nothing. I don't know."

He looked shocked. "You don't know? Since when don't you know something, my heart?"

His grin was crooked, and she couldn't help but respond. Calypso loved her bubble butt, but right now sex and mating and flogging the blowhole were the very last thoughts on her mind.

Releasing a heavy sigh, she sagged into his comforting hold, running her fingers lightly up and down his spine to help soothe her own ragged nerves. "The truth is, Hades, I'm worried about Fable. And I have been for some time now."

Hades might not be her grandfather by blood, but he was definitely her grandfather by soul. His entire frame bristled at the notion of anything amiss with his beloved granddaughter.

And suddenly even the underworld itself seemed to go cold with his displeasure. The wails of the trapped souls floating within the River Styx echoed down the great halls mournfully as all of hell grew aware of their master's discontent.

Patting his hair back down into place, Caly nibbled on her bottom lip. She hadn't told Hades of her feelings because she'd not wanted to distress him unnecessarily.

In fact, for several months after the girl's nuptials to the handsomely aloof King George, Caly had thought her granddaughter deliriously happy and in love and thus why she'd made such little effort at reaching out to her clan.

Why when Hades and Caly had finally sealed the deal they'd rarely left her chambers for several decades straight—and only when forced to.

"What is the matter with Fable?" he growled, and in his anger, his face took on the hue and appearance of his other face. His true visage.

That of death incarnate.

His gorgeous features became more harsh and razor sculpted and a glow of crimson curled through his dark eyes.

34

Planting her hand on his chest, she rubbed a soothing circle, to ease the now rapid beating of his heart.

Shaking her head, and causing her octopi tentacle hair to undulate like a wave, she took a deep breath.

"Probably nothing, my love. You know how I am prone to worry when my family is involved."

But there was no pacifying the beast now. As she'd said, Hades knew her dark soul as well as he knew his and Caly was beyond anxious right now.

The flames in the hearth raged like a wildfire, leaving black markings behind on the ten-foot-thick river stone that lined it.

"Calypso," he growled a warning, letting her know that he wouldn't allow her to try and lessen the significance of what was going on.

Knowing that if she didn't stop him now, he'd tear down the worlds to get at his granddaughter and make sure for himself that she was safe, Calypso forced a lighthearted laugh to spill off her tongue.

"The truth is, my darling, that I really don't know. It could be nothing." She rolled her wrist airly, keeping her tone light and carefree.

His eyes thinned, but the walls of the castle still stood, so her prime piece of man meat wasn't totally losing his head just yet.

Most of the world believed it to be Zeus and not Hades who wielded all the power in Olympus, but the truth of it was their powers were equal and should the brothers choose to war very little could survive them.

"Then tell me now what is going on?" he demanded.

And normally, Calypso would bristle to hear his high-handed manner, but she also knew her spouse well, and Hades' sharp tongue was more a sign of his fear rather than of anger.

Exhaling, she forced herself to finally speak her worries. "For some time now I've wondered why it was that Fable hasn't reached out to any of us. Not her parents, us, not even Hook—who we both know she's terribly fond of."

Hades' eyes narrowed, but he remained silent. This was his thinker's pose, he was ingesting everything she said and would mull it over before giving his final thoughts.

"Of course, she is a newlywed, obviously. So I was content to merely sit back and relax and think no more of this."

"Then what is the problem now?" he asked, and his voice now sounded much less animalistic and more thoughtful and contemplative.

Even the fire in the hearth had settled down, and the flames in his eyes were mostly extinguished. Though the sharp bones and lines of his face hadn't smoothed out yet.

Laying a loving hand upon a slashing cheekbone, she gave him a soft smile. "The problem is I worry, my dear."

Calypso wasn't sure whether she should tell him the next part because now that she thought about it, she felt silly and foolish for jumping to conclusions. The only problem was she'd always considered herself to be a good judge of character and situations, and though there seemed to be a rational explanation for all of this, her brain continued to nag at her that all wasn't quite right.

He tenderly kissed the meat of her palm, nibbling on it just slightly, enough to make her hiss and tremble with an immediate wash of need.

Calypso's emotions were as temperamental as her seas—flighty, would be one way of putting it, and yet she'd never once grown bored with her male and truthfully doubted that she ever would.

He grinned a wicked grin, and she couldn't help but mimic it.

"So this is simply a case of nerves then? Is that all, my love?" He stepped in close, so close the heat of his body washed against her own, making her primordial form of glass-like water tremble.

Her thighs shook, and her insides quaked with a tsunami of desire. Talking to Hades and being able to think matters through was doing a miraculous job of easing her worries.

In all likelihood, she probably really was suffering from a case of empty nest. To be gone so many months without a word or a letter was unusual for Fable, but her granddaughter was part god. She had powerful magick to her. Powerful enough that nothing and no one could harm her.

Hades curled her octopi tentacle around his wrist, bringing her face scant inches from his so that she felt the roll of his minty breath linger along her lips like a delicate kiss.

"My, dear, sweet Calypso, the primordial goddess of great passions and power, brought low by the thought of our beautiful little granddaughter."

He said the words with an echo of great fondness and love and she couldn't help but snicker, feeling suddenly silly and foolish for worrying so.

"I do love you, woman," he said in a thick, raspy burr full of heat and longing.

Caly had forgotten to mention to him that when she'd attempted to get in touch with Fable this afternoon by sea orb, the image inside of it had been nothing but blackness.

Someone—and no doubt it could only be Fable since you'd have to be a powerful magick wielder—had blocked the sea orb's access.

In all likelihood, her precious darkness was busy corrupting the mind of her gallant King and did not wish to be disturbed by her meddling family of gods.

Hades palm cupped her breast, hefting it in his palm and Caly could not help but gasp her pleasure as her fingers curled into his jacket.

The length of his cock suddenly poked her hard in the thigh, and Caly knew her devil of a husband had much pleasanter ideas on his mind.

"Mmm," she moaned incoherently, and he smirked.

"Give her a few more days, love, if we do not hear from her then, I shall send one of my spies to seek her out just to assure you that our little granddaughter is fine and is no doubt desperate to do with her male as I now wish to do to you."

The husky tenor of his voice nearly made Calypso come. Her gown spun of colorful beta fish swirled around her trim body as they too responded to the heat in the Lord of the Underworld's voice.

"Okay?" he asked her.

And she nodded with a gulp when he flicked his wrist, using his own power to rid her of her gown so that she stood gloriously nude beneath his sharp and predatory gaze.

He was like a ravenous wolf ready to pounce, and she couldn't wait.

"It's a deal, my love," she said in a husky voice herself, then wrapped her arms around his neck and pulled his face down to hers, "now about those carrots..."

*Fable*

It had been two days since Brunhilda had come to threaten Fable. And in those two days, George hadn't come to visit once.

Which she was beyond grateful for. Maybe it was to "teach" Fable a lesson or simply that George was sick of slacking his lust on his "bride," and not one of his whores.

Rumors reached her ears even here of another dark-haired beauty now laying claim to his time and smiles. Her skin was said to be dusky and her eyes green, but Snow said the woman was nowhere near as pretty as Fable.

Not that Fable cared.

George could spill his seed in a cow if he wished to, just so long as she no longer had to suffer it.

The sun was still several hours away from rising, and Galeta had left her only three or so hours ago, but she couldn't sleep.

For days, Fable had practiced that killing curse and finally could say that she'd mastered it. She had no intention of using such a curse, but there was another one she'd like to look at.

"*Ignis*," she intoned, flipping her palm over and immediately a hard curl took the corners of her lips as she gazed transfixed at the fireball glowing on her palm.

Blood tingling with a rush of raw power, she knew that she was so close to the end of this nightmare that she could practically taste it. The anticipation of the end, it lingered on her tongue like the sweetest aroma.

Only a few more weeks, enough time to make sure she was stronger than Brunhilda, to break the cuff on her wrist and then she *would* free herself. Herself and Snow. She'd return to Seren, to father, and she'd never leave again.

They'd be safe and sound and never again have to worry about the wolves that lived and breathed in this wretched, horrible world called the above.

She might even find a new love someday.

"My queen," Mirror hissed urgently, "someone comes!"

She frowned, as immediately his mirror went dark. So lost in her head and her future plans that she'd forgotten to quell the flame in her palm when her door was suddenly slammed open, and there stood the king, the dowager, Charles, and a handful of royal guards.

Too terrified to make a sound, she held as still as field mice scenting danger, staring at the lot of them wide-eyed and disbelievingly.

Brunhilda wore a cruel smirk. George stood beside her looking bored. It was Charles's look, which finally caused the numbness in her brain to scatter.

His look was one of tortured regret.

"Charles?" she whispered, but the lead knight turned his face to the side and refused to look at her.

Brunhilda pointed a finger at her. "There, a witch. I told you! Burn her at the stake."

"Wait! What?" Fable jumped to her feet, finally quenching the magick, and clutched onto the edges of her robe with nerveless fingers, shaking her head. "What are you going on about? George, what is this?"

His lip curled into a look of disgust. "I will not harbor a witch in my presence. Behead it and burn it at the stake."

Jaw dropping; Fable couldn't believe what she was hearing. Or seeing.

Suddenly everything was moving too fast to process. The guards came pouring through her door, surrounding her in a circle. Their faces sharp, angry, and cold.

Charles led the pack, and he looked anguished and terrified. For her.

Blinking, trying to piece the fragments of this mad puzzle together, she backed up, until her back pressed against the stone wall and she could go no further.

Nothing made any sense. Why were they in her room? Why was Brunhilda calling her a witch as though it were a bad thing when the dowager queen was one herself? None of this made any sense.

"What is this!" she cried again, tongue feeling swollen and thick, throat too tight with fear so that it was hard to breathe.

Brunhilda wore a lecherous grin as she said, "We do not harbor witches in the Enchanted Forest. Do you not know your own tales, Darkness?"

Blinking, unable to believe this could really be happening, she shook her head. Mouth flopping open and shut like a dying fish on land. "But...but..."

Tossing her head back, the witch cackled, the sounds of which seemed to echo like madness through the rafters.

Why was everyone standing around looking at Fable as though she were the villain? Couldn't they sense the madness, the evil in the dowager? Or did they simply not care?

"You were supposed to give him an heir. Instead, you turned yourself sterile, you think I don't know. You reek of dark magick, the little fairy told us everything, do not think to lie to me again," she said it with far too much pleasure in her voice.

The little fairy?

There could only be one.

Fable's heart sank like a rock to her knees.

The Blue had betrayed her.

But why?

"No." Fable gripped her robe tighter, shaking her head and knowing she was still in shock. Desperate to believe this was nothing more than a dream, a strange, awful, and terrible dream. "No. You're a witch. You, not me. You!"

Brunhilda's face was transforming, literally before her eyes. Turning from the smooth-faced matronly beauty into the twisted and macabre mask of an ancient crone with withered flesh and a beak's nose.

"Me, a witch!" She cackled in a voice that seemed forged in the fires of the Underworld itself. "She is the witch."

She pointed a gnarled finger at Fable. And Fable felt the tightening of dark, ancient, and terrible magick pulse through the confines of her tower.

Saw the way the guard's irises flared so darkly that the entire color of the eyes now bled through with black so deep it seemed bottomless.

"George, look at this. Look at her!" She cried, shrinking in on herself, desperate that Charles be proven wrong. That for once the man she detested with her whole heart and soul might do one act of kindness in his whole, miserable, pathetic life. "Look at her!" she screamed.

But her king merely shook his head. "I know who she is, and who are you, Fable. You thought to make a fool of me, but no more. I do not want you, and I do not need you."

He snapped his fingers and instantly the guards were on her. Even Charles.

Their hands latched cruelly onto her arms, her legs, her waist, her hair; anywhere they could grab hold of. Yanking, tearing, squeezing so hard that tears rolled in great large clumps from the corners of her eyes.

"Stop"—she kicked and screamed, flailing pitifully—"Let me go! Don't do this, don't do this, please. I would be a good wife to you, George. I would be—"

"Burn it," he said again, and then turned on his heel. Brunhilda notched her skeletal chin, sneering maliciously, and something inside of Fable snapped then.

She'd never wanted to hurt anyone.

She'd only wanted her freedom.

Freedom from their pain, their abuse, from their tortures. Snapping her fingers, she slammed the doors shut, locking them tight so that not even dark magick could reopen them. Outside the remainder of George's men pounded on the doors, their cries of desperation to reach their King echoed through her chamber.

"*Ignis!*" she cried, and this time, fire didn't simply erupt from her palm, but from every inch of her.

George ran to the door, trying to open it, but it was no use. He kicked and screamed, demanding his Knights open it. But not even Brunhilda could undo what she'd wrought. Instead, the witch had jumped in front of the King with her arms spread wide and glaring hate at Fable.

Flame so hot it melted flesh on contact spread out from her body like a creeping vine. The guards screamed, dropping her instantly.

"*Fin!*" Brunhilda roared back, and the fires that had been reaching for her and George like ravenous fiery claws immediately ceased.

But the men continued to burn on; the magick once lit wouldn't stop until it had consumed them. They dropped her, scattering to all corners as they writhed and wailed, begging her to cease their torment.

Brunhilda's eyes burned hate.

Body aching, Fable pushed her way up shakily to her feet. But she knew she was still far from safe.

"Stop this," she squeezed out, unable to believe that that pitiful whimpering voice had been her own. Breathing hurt, her ribs were bruised, and she felt blood—her blood—oozing down from the countless wounds the guards had already inflicted upon her. "We don't have to kill each other."

Brunhilda's shrunken lips curled in disgust. "Of course, we do. You will rot in Tartarus for what you've done today. The sins you committed. Take a look around you, Queen of Darkness, and see the evil you've wrought."

And suddenly the entire world moved as in slow motion. Fable saw the crone lift her palm, and her months of studying under Galeta's tutelage helped her to see what she might have missed before. The spark of dark magick that suddenly flared to life on the aged crone's palm, the malevolent whisper of terrible power that squeezed the oxygen out of the air.

Brunhilda was going to throw not just any killing curse on her, but "the" killing curse. The sphere of ebony power gathered and grew, and there was only one shot of making it out of here alive.

She had to be the one to throw it first.

There was no time to form it into a tight sphere, no time to make sure that she harmed none but her intended, Fable opened her mouth and said the words she could never take back.

*"Occidiere maledictio."*

The ground shook, the wind shrieked, and the bolt of raw, primal magick blasted straight toward them.

No sooner had Fable released it, she wailed, desperate to take it back. She was no killer, not even to a wicked witch such as Brunhilda.

"No!" she cried, but it was too late. It was far too late.

Once released, the curse had to strike. And it did but in the worst possible way.

The doors were suddenly rammed open, giant splinters of wood erupted all around like tiny wooden projectiles, one of them catching Fable in the cheek and tearing her open.

George, who'd been somewhat hidden behind Brunhilda, was tripped by the blast, knocking him forward, directly into the path of the ebony bolt.

The magick took his head clean off, dropping him like a sack of stone to the ground. Instantly dead.

And Brunhilda, she wasn't safe from the blast's path either, she'd not gotten a direct blow, but the javelin of darkness pierced clean through the left side of her chest, opening a giant, gaping sucking wound.

She too dropped, eyes wide and staring at Fable with an incredulous shock. "What?" Was all she managed to whimper.

With a cry of alarm as the truth of what she'd finally done had dawned on her, Fable ran to them, dropping to her knees. There was nothing she could do for George, but maybe she could still spare the witch.

She grabbed Brunhilda's ice-cold hand and shook her head. "I didn't mean this. I didn't."

There was no love lost for the witch, but Fable was not a killer. A monster. An evil queen.

She wasn't.

She wasn't a villain.

Her soul trembled as the smells, and scents of blood and charred flesh filled her nostrils. The horrors of what she'd done were now crashing down on her.

"No. No. No," she whispered, shoving her hands against Brunhilda's chest to try and stem the bleeding, but it was no use.

With each pump of her heart, the witch bled out bucketfuls.

Brunhilda's face was an ashen, colorless white when her eyes finally opened. Her gaze was cloudy and drugged looking, and using the last bit of her strength she panted out three words that Fable knew would haunt her all the rest of her days.

"You. Did. This."

39

Gasping, she dropped the witch's hand as though burned, bringing her hands to her mouth she covered it as a strange, wild sound climbed out of her throat.

"Leave her."

The overly cheerful and exuberant voice of Galeta the Blue suddenly echoed like sunshine in the room. The happy, sunshiny tone was so wrong that it finally pierced the veil of Fable's shock.

Gasping, and shaking with tears and pain, Fable couldn't gather her words or thoughts into any sort of coherence. The only thing she could whisper was, "Why, Galeta? Why? Why did you betray me?"

She was so cold. All over. And rather sensed she was deep in shock, and that when it finally wore off all she'd be capable of feeling was fury and hate for what The Blue had done.

A few more days and she'd have been free of this torment. Only a few more days.

"Why?" Her voice shook, and her body trembled.

Galeta patted her head with her tiny hand, her sharp, fang-like teeth poking out menacingly from her curved lips. "Because we had a deal, Darkness. Did you think I'd forgotten?"

The patronizing manner with which she treated, Fable, caused her to grit her teeth and jump to her feet. Wiping her stinging eyes with her forearms, she shook her head.

"You said my blood. You'd take my blood. This was not our deal."

"I said, no such thing," Galeta chuckled the words, looking heartily pleased with herself. "I said you'd pay me in blood. And you have, sweet girl. You have."

"No." She hugged her arms to her chest, feeling a soul-sucking void of numbness begin to sweep over her consciousness. This couldn't be real. None of this could be real. This hadn't really happened.

"Why did you teach me something so vile? Why?" she muttered.

Galeta, who still smiled, was now humming cheerfully to herself as she reached into a pocket tucked into her gown and pulled out a green glass vial. Tipping it toward Fable, she winked.

"I told you why. And now I do believe that payment can be rendered. I needed the blood of a powerful witch you see, and since they're so selfish about giving that type of thing up, well...the end justifies the means, does it not?"

Flitting toward the now deathly still and silent Brunhilda, Galeta reached forward and dragged the vial through the ocean of red covering the fallen witch's chest.

"You're evil," Fable whispered as she watched the little fairy practically gleam with joy as she played in the blood.

"What's that?" Galeta turned to her, her glacial blue eyes cold and frosty. "Evil you say. Yes, well. I might be a tad bad, Darkness, but I've never destroyed an entire kingdom, now have I? You were very thorough, my dear."

"No. I didn't—"

A tiny feminine gasp had Fable's skin instantly crawling, heart pounding, and chest aching. She knew without even looking up who it was, and the minute her eyes landed on Snow's face, she went absolutely still.

Blue, blue eyes rimmed in red and crying large tears looked back at her. "You did this."

It wasn't a question.

"Snow, I—"

She reached out a hand, but the child screamed, and instantly a guard snatched her up, shoving her behind him and glaring hotly at Fable as though he meant to snuff the life from her.

But not a one of them moved. All of them were terrified; the emotion was clear in their wide and petrified gazes.

"I didn't mean to do this, Snow. I didn't. I—"

Galeta snickered. "Yeah, well, tough titties, oh evil one, cuz ya did. By the by, I'll be seeing you around, Darkness, you can count on it."

The fairy vanished with her prize in a puff of glittering blue.

The guards lifted their spears and Fable knew she would be transformed into a true monster in Snow's eyes now.

Shaking her head, and with giant tears rolling down her cheeks she whispered, "Lay them down."

But she'd unlocked her powers again, and the words were full of magick.

Immediately the spears were flung from their hands, clacking loudly against the stonewall before dropping to the ground.

"Go away!" She screamed, flinging them all from her sight. Careful not to toss the girl around, but needing those censorious eyes away from her.

The moment she was alone, she looked at what she'd done. The charred, crisped bodies of the knights, curled in fantastical poses of writhing agony as they'd succumbed to their deaths.

At their center, and closest to her side was Charles. Fable clenched her eyes shut, forcing herself to breathe in and out as suddenly her stomach heaved with the violence she'd committed.

Numb, still in shock, she walked in a daze over to Mirror. And gasped when she viewed herself.

She'd felt the aches and pains earlier, but had had no idea the violence that had been done to her.

One eye was almost completely swelled shut. Blood had matted her hair to her forehead and neck. Her dark flesh was covered in oozing slits of deepest crimson and already she could see the mottled purple tones covering most of her skin.

Fingers trembling she covered her mouth with her hands, that was how Uriah found her.

His dear face filled the looking glass so that she no longer had to look upon herself.

Scanning the room quickly, he then looked at her. "You had no choice, my queen. They meant to end you."

"But Snow White," she gasped, starting to shake violently now and having to clutch onto the wall for support.

His look spoke volumes. The girl would hate her forever.

"The effects of this night, I fear," he said quietly, "has only just begun, Fable. You must rule this kingdom now."

"After what I've just—"

"Regardless," he said gravely, "you are their queen, at least until Snow comes of age."

Tears blurred her vision. Fable latched onto his words like a lifeline. "Maybe if I stay, I can prove to her that I'm not evil. That I was simply defending myself, that—"

"Perhaps, my queen. Although I should tell you, our little Snow has escaped."

Heart gripping with fear, she clutched at her breast. "Escaped where! Stop her! She'll be hurt, injured, or worse. Please, Mirror, don't—"

He shook his head sadly. "I fear, my queen, that my reach can only extend through these castle walls. I simply do not know where she goes to now."

"What have I done, Uriah?" she wailed, losing what little control she still had left to her sanity.

She'd wanted her freedom yes, but not at the cost of Snow White's happiness. Snow had never known how wicked her father truly was, and now Fable would never get the chance to explain, to make her see...but no more had she thought it; then she knew it wouldn't have mattered.

Because as much as Fable loved Snow, George had been the girl's father.

Dropping to her knees, she buried her face in her hands and wailed in agony.

# Another letter to the reader

*Anonymous*

I never said that the telling of Fable's life would be easy or palatable. And though I rarely intercede on the behalf of others when I pen their tale, I felt I had to do so here.

You see Fable was placed in a situation with no recourse other than death. Hers, or theirs. By the time her family discovered that Fable's life had sunk into one of tragedy and pain, it was far too late.

The poor girl had been forever altered by the circumstances of that night.

She was now the dark queen in truth.

Her kingdom feared her, and there was always one coup or another to contend with. Simply to survive she had to continue to wear the mantle of the "evil queen." Fable could have returned to Seren at any time, but it was the love of a daughter that kept her where she stayed.

Snow White's heart had, sadly, been turned to hate for the woman who'd given up everything for her. The beautiful princess was obsessed with ruining her stepmother. In many ways the girl was good, but her venom for the queen would take a miracle to be extinguished.

And yet still Fable remained, knowing all hated her and weathering the storm as best she could.

She always tried to do right by her people, but rumors were a horrible shackle to break. And sorrowfully, Fable never could.

Her legend had become one of the most vile, and wicked villains in all the lands. Days rolled into months, then years, until finally several lifetimes later it was the love of a grandmother for a prodigal granddaughter that finally brought the beloved Fable out of the darkness she'd lived in for so long.

The seed of redemption had been born.

# The Dark Queen: Part 2

*Without change, something sleeps inside us, and seldom awakens. The sleeper must awaken~ Frank Herbert*
*Power is of two kinds. One is obtained by the fear of punishment and the other by acts of love. Power based on*
*love is a thousand times more effective and permanent than the one derived from fear of punishment~ Mahatma Gandhi*

# Chapter 7

*Calypso*

*Many lifetimes later...*

"I have to do something." Calypso wrung her hands together, pleading silently with Aphrodite, not even sure what she was pleading for, but desperate her friend hear and understand the secret yearnings of her heart.

Aphrodite, dressed in a gown of glittering starlight, walked toward Calypso, grabbed her hands and squeezed them tight.

"I hear you, Caly. I hear you. I will help you fix Fable anyway I possibly can. Only tell me what to do."

For years, Calypso blamed herself for the tragedies that had gone down that night. Not the fact that humans had perished, she hoped they rotted in Tartarus an eternity for the pain and torment they'd put her granddaughter through, no, what hurt was the pain and torment that Fable now inflected upon herself for her actions of that night.

She blamed herself for the pain she'd put Snow through. Blamed herself for calling to The Blue in the first place and learning such dark magick, but mostly, Fable blamed herself for ever leaving Seren in the first place.

And the truth of it was, all that blame belonged squarely on Calypso's shoulders, because had she not gone to Nimue to plead on Fable's behalf, the sweet girl would never have left the safety of Seren in the first place.

"She's lost, Dite. Lost and terrified, and so broken I fear I can never fix her again."

She sniffed pitifully, feeling wretched and ill at ease.

For a time following the deaths, Calypso had protected Fable in the only way she'd known how. By drowning anyone who'd come against her granddaughter. By killing anything, that tried to harm her.

And though those deaths too had been justified, the damage to Fable's reputation was nearly beyond repair.

Caly knew her granddaughter, she was not a wicked, evil woman and yet to the rest of Kingdom; that's exactly who Fable had become.

An image that Fable herself embraced by dressing in dark gowns full of metal accouterments meant to make her look fierce and unapproachable.

The mask Fable had worn for so long had permanently etched itself onto her face, so that Calypso was sure her granddaughter no longer even knew how to smile or laugh with joy.

She was mired in so much pain and heartache that she drowned in it daily, and Calypso was desperate to fix this mess she'd wrought by simply telling her mother Fable needed to see the above.

"Gods, if I could go back in time. If I could slap some sense into me, I would have. I would never have done this to my poor darling if I'd only but known."

Dite shrugged delicately, sliding a strand of Caly's kelp green hair across her shoulder. "If I might ask, sweetheart. Why now? It has been years since the, um...*accident*," she stressed, though they both knew what Fable had done had been a deliberate and conscious action, it was just easier to pretend it wasn't sometimes, "Fable has learned to live with who she is."

"Yes, but not well!" Caly shrugged out of Aphrodite's grip, and in her anger the waters of her home began to froth and churn, the ships riding her waves started to toss and buckle, and she had to close her eyes and count to ten to get her emotions under control.

Hades had made her promise to learn how to control her mercurial temper, and she was trying, ye gods was she trying. But it was so hard, especially when the fate of a beloved grandchild rested in her hands.

Squeezing her temple, she took several long, deep breaths before gently saying, "I am sorry, Dite. You do not deserve my rage. And I am not mad at you, truly, you are my dearest friend, it is why I come to you and no one else. The reason why I need to do this now is because I just have to. Fable is strong, but she is also weak. She is dying inside. I see it each time I visit her. The fake smiles, the witty banal banter that she uses to keep anyone who loves her at a distance. She is hurting, and I simply cannot stand it anymore."

Dite nodded, and Calypso was ready to plead her case further when suddenly a tiny ghost of a smile crossed her pretty, ruby red lips.

Freezing, because Calypso recognized that look instantly, she pounced. "What! Tell me now, what is it?"

Clear blue eyes snared Caly's, and then Aphrodite's grin grew brighter than the sun. "Remember you telling me about Fiera? Her demand that you find her a mate?"

Caly frowned sharply. "Yes, what of it?"

Shrugging one pale, lovely shoulder, Aphrodite began to walk slowly around Calypso.

"Well, only that I've been thinking about how one could go about finding a mate for a primordial goddess of fire, which could be said to be impossible for anyone but me, and now to hear of Fable, it all seems so simple. Doesn't it?"

She was at Calypso's back when she said that last part, but everything inside of Caly froze because she knew instantly what Dite meant.

"A love match? For Fable?"

Coming to stand in front of her friend again, Aphrodite's grin hadn't wavered an inch. "Well, don't you see, Caly? For all the gods strengths in this world and the next, there is one strength that defies most of us—true love. True love, and I speak only of the truest and most purest form of it, can mend even the hardest of souls."

Calypso might be goddess of the waters, but even she couldn't deny that simple truth because the moment she'd locked eyes on Hades she'd known she'd move heaven and hell to make him hers forever.

She'd been born to be a virgin goddess but had willingly given it all up for the love of her bubble butt.

Grabbing hold of her chest, to try and stem the now rapid beating of her excited heart she nodded. "Yes. Yes, I do believe you are right, Dites. Love can fix my baby. But who, who would be good enough for her? She's been ruined by men. By love, it would take someone—"

Aphrodite's eyes turned soft and her smile with it. "—it would take the undying love and devotion of one just as broken as she. Caly, I know who your Fable belongs with. A god who's been waiting his whole life for her, he simply didn't know it yet."

Frowning, and cocking her head, because Calypso couldn't think of a single Greek deity worthy of her beautiful granddaughter's heart, she asked, "Who?"

"Owiot. But I've always just called him, Sadness."

Sadness? For Fable? Caly wasn't sure.

She shook her head, but Dite grabbed her hands in a shockingly strong grip and said heatedly, "Trust me, Caly. If you've never done it before. Do it now. And believe me."

Calypso would do anything to see her granddaughter smile again, but pairing her with a male that Dite called Sadness seemed beyond cruel. Still, this was Aphrodite—*The* Goddess of Love. If anyone knew anything about love and hearts or even broken ones, it would be her.

Sighing deeply, she squeezed her fingers back and said, "If you were anyone else, I think I'd murder you for the suggestion. But I know you love my Fable as much as I do. So yes, Dite, I'll trust you."

"Good, then I think we can kill many birds with one stone, don't you?"

"A love tournament?" Calypso said, knowing exactly where her friend's thoughts had led.

Aphrodite nodded. "Yes. Now let's get the pieces in place, shall we?"

*Fable*

*Present Day*

"There's an uprising taking place in the Southern reaches of the Enchanted Forest," Mirror said, breaking through Fable's concentration as she tried to master the spell of silence.

And not just any kind of silence either. But deep, and bottomless, and terrible silence. The type of silence that echoed through the soul and made one feel hollow, feel alone, feel completely and totally forlorn.

It was black magick, but most of what she did now was black magick to one extent or another.

Fable had been a fool when she'd first arrived in the above. A silly, naïve, stupid little princess with visions of knights, and goodly kings, and happily ever afters imprinted on her heart.

The truth was, this world was an ugly, foul, wicked place and though she'd once felt like she didn't belong to it, in the years since George's *sad*—she snorted—demise, she'd become very good at one thing. Embracing her inner darkness.

Maybe she'd started out on the side of good and righteousness and justice and blah, blah, blah...but she'd been an idiot to believe in any of that. If there was one thing this world had taught her was that nothing good ever came to you unless you *made it* happen. Period.

She exhaled. "There's always an uprising against me, Mirror. Or haven't you learned that by now?"

Many years had passed since Fable had been tossed into the tower, and though she was now Queen of the Enchanted Forest in truth, she found that she'd grown to prefer her cell over any other room in the castle. It was a good reminder to her of where she'd been and just how far she'd come.

"Now, hush so that I can finalize this last bit of—"

"Yes, but Snow leads the charge," he said softly.

Spine stiffening, Fable pushed her grimoire back a tad with the tip of her long, pointed black and red painted nail. "So she's been spotted, has she?"

Trying to ignore the terrible ache in her chest at the thought of the girl, Fable notched her chin high. There was only one thing in this entire stupid realm that she sometimes still felt a twinge of remorse over, and that was Snow White.

But the twinges hardly lasted anymore, and when they came, they were easy enough to ignore. Clenching her jaw, she pursed her lips and very quietly asked, "Are you sure, Mirror?"

She turned swiftly. The long, velvet robe of shadow and starlight she wore twirled around her ankles like a dark wave. Grabbing hold of the thick braid dangling over her shoulder, she played with the tip as she commanded her pulse to quiet.

In the decades since the King's death, Snow had turned Fable's name to mud. Turned her into a woman of utter darkness and evil. All in the Enchanted Forest feared their queen now, and it had grown far too taxing to make them believe she wasn't what they thought her to be.

Sometimes it was just easier to be exactly who others thought you were anyway. So yes, Fable killed when necessary. When the uprisings became too thick and wild and order could only be gained with a steel fist.

Curling her fingers into claws, she scraped it down the wood face of her worktable, causing a high-pitched squeal and curls of wood to flake off in her wake.

"I am, my queen," he said gravely. "The sentries you posted in the forest whispered it through the castle grounds not even half an hour ago. The girl plans a violent attack on the castle; she's got not only dwarves on her side but the rock trolls that live beneath hangman's bridge."

Flesh-eating dwarves were bad enough but very little could survive the brute strength and sheer violence of rock trolls on the hunt.

Snow White had always had the capacity to make herself loved by creatures incapable of loving anyone or anything else; it was one of her strengths. But had also become one of Fable's pet peeves.

Hanging her head, she stared at her book with unseeing eyes. For years, she'd strengthened her magick to the point that should the day ever come where Snow tried to make the ultimate power grab she'd be strong enough to defend herself and her stronghold, but Fable had never wanted things to get to this point.

46

Not with the girl.

Though a part of her now hated the child she'd once called her own, there would always be that side of her that couldn't help but love her too. Fable would no longer blame herself for everything that had happened that fateful night in this very tower, she'd only been defending her right to live, but in a small, still place in her heart, that was still capable of feeling pain...she knew that had she not thrown that killing curse, Snow's path might have turned out very differently.

"How much longer do I have?"

"The Ravens say she will strike at the witching hour once the castle is asleep and all is calm."

Knowing exactly what she would do, because Fable had been preparing for just such an inevitability ever since the day Snow had run away, she clenched her jaw and steeled her heart.

It was either her or the girl.

Fable hadn't come this far only to lose now.

"Then so be it."

Feeling as though the weight of the world had just come crashing down on her shoulders, she turned and looked at her only friend left in the world.

"You know what to do, Mirror." She lifted her chin, giving him the silent command to begin the enchantment over the castle. "Put them all down."

"My queen," he intoned, then faded in a fog of ethereal blue.

Walking over to the mirror Uriah had briefly abandoned, Fable studied her image. She was beauty personified that had never been in question.

There were few in all of Kingdom—either the above or the below—who boasted features such as hers. Skin as dark as deepest night, eyes as golden as the dawn, and hair that hung in soft, billowy waves down her back.

She was a product of true love. It was why she was as beautiful as she was, but her heart had turned dark, had been fouled by the spite, ugliness, and vanity of this realm.

Clenching long fingers against her robe, she turned her face to the side, studying the long, swan-like profile of herself.

Recently though she'd discovered something terrifying about herself. Something that had happened quite by accident. Mirror had been studying her silently as she'd dressed for her yearly royal ball.

The one time a year when she tried to actually be kind to her denizens and show them that their queen wasn't such a cruel, heartless witch as they thought her. And quite without thinking, she'd simply asked mirror, "how do I look?"

That was when it had happened.

Mirror had shown her not a stunning, vivacious beauty who looked as nubile and exquisite now as she had decades earlier, but instead there'd been another picture given her.

That of an old, withered hag with long drawn out features and aged flesh covered in sores and spots. There had been very little hair on her bald head, and what there'd been was thin and wild. She'd looked like a monster, like an evil crone from one of those blasted fairy tales the damned fairies liked to skew.

She'd shrieked at the vision, demanding Mirror tell her why he'd shown her that image, and that was when her world had been rocked.

"That woman," Mirror had said softly, "is no accident, my queen."

"Then who is it!" She'd screamed and railed, wanting to use her magick to shatter him into a thousand slivers so as to make that goddess awful image vanish, but knowing that if she did she'd lose her only friend forever.

Mirror had looked baffled like he couldn't fathom that she hadn't figured it out on her own. And even now, three months later, she still trembled when she recalled the hushed whisper of his gravelly voice as she'd said, "Why, it's you. You asked me how you looked, and this is who I see when I look into your heart now, Fable. You are no longer sprite, young, and lovely. You have been twisted by madness and black magick, this hag, my queen... this hag is you."

Shutting him up had been the only thing she'd known to do. She'd sealed his lips with magick and slowly backed away, shaking her head in denial. But as the days, weeks, and now months passed and every day she asked Mirror the same thing, the vision had gotten no prettier. In fact, mirror Fable had deteriorated worse.

Swallowing hard, she searched the pretty eyes looking back at her. To the rest of the world, this might be what she looked like, but Fable had seen the real sight, and it had been burned into her brain.

"Mirror," she whispered slowly, "how do I look today?"

Even when Uriah wasn't actively in his mirror, the magick held true. And just as before, the woman staring back at her was a befouled, disease riddled thing. Now, not only was the flesh aged, but also decaying in spots. The skin around her nose was turning gray. But that wasn't the worst; the worst was around her mouth, where the flesh had rotted so badly she could see through her cheek to the teeth inside.

Trembling, and inhaling rapidly, she shook her head but could no longer deny the truth.

Like a cancer, the black magick was twisting her, changing her.

Fable hadn't known the effects of such terrible magick until it was far too late. Galeta the bitch hadn't ever bothered to share it. That little fae had hightailed it away from Fable after the incident.

At first, she'd thought that perhaps it was just the reflection that was twisted, but a deep-seated root of worry had gnawed at her belly for days, she'd not wanted to speak to Mirror of it because she didn't think a mirror would care nearly as much as she did. Also, it had felt far too private to admit that she was scared. Which she was. She was petrified.

So one night, two weeks ago she'd consulted with the dark elf of the forest. A being far more twisted and deranged than Fable was. Where Fable only looked vile in her reflection, the dark elf appeared as that.

The elf had required payment first—the heart of an unborn babe.

Wicked, Fable might be, but even she had balked at the notion of stealing the heart of an unborn child. So she'd slaughtered a pregnant swine and had butchered the unborn piglet still in its womb. Pig hearts and human hearts looked remarkably similar.

And with a sprinkling of magick she'd stripped the essence of swine off of it, replacing it with that of a human child. Fable's magick was powerful; she'd known the elf wouldn't note the difference, and she'd been right.

The gray-skinned being hidden deep within a cloak of shadow, cackled as she brought the bloodied heart to her lips and suckled on it, moaning in sheer, perverted ecstasy.

"One answer and one answer only will I'll give to thee," the elf had said in a voice that sounded of rusted chains.

Fable tried to make out the elf's face; rumors abounded surrounding it. A being of such perverted looks that it appeared as though one of the walking dead, with an eyeball in its palm used for second sight and divination.

Truthfully, Fable wasn't sure, and she rather thought that not getting to see the dark elf might yet be a blessing in disguise. Swallowing the ball of disgust and fear, she'd clipped a nod.

"I only need one."

"Then asssk, dark one," the elf's voice sounded like the fluttering cadence of a snake's tongue flicking in and out of its mouth.

Grabbing hold of her stomach, Fable glanced around at the hauntingly quiet enchanted forest. With its thick-trunked, and towering trees covered in green moss, and rolls of fog curling up from the ground, fireflies dancing like drunken fairies in flight...it had all looked like a dream. A strange, surreal dream that she'd desperately wished to wake from but couldn't seem to.

Gathering what little strength she had left to her, she'd asked.

"Black magick has twisted my reflection into something hideous."

A low, curling kind of laughter began to echo through the trees. The sound came from the elf.

48

Stuttering, as her pulse skyrocketed in her chest, she pressed on, "it...it has turned me hideous. What...what will happen to—"

Fable couldn't keep speaking as the low sound soon turned high-pitched and terrible, like the wail of demon cries.

The elf, who'd been shorter than Fable—or so she'd thought—unfurled like a beanstalk shooting up into the sky.

Backing up, because the elf now towered over her, Fable stared in wide-eyed horror as the cloak was tossed to the side revealing the emaciated, deformed frame of the dark elf to her view.

The creature stood nearly as high as the tree behind her and had a wasted, withered frame full of bone and knots covered only in a thick layer of gray flesh. Her chest cavity was concaved and heaving like a bellows as she cackled with laughter.

Blond, matted hair covered in brambles, weeds, and spider webs whipped back and forth like skeletal branches in a stiff breeze. She was completely naked, but it was almost hard to tell.

Her breasts which were pointed and tipped with black nubs that she could only assume to be nipples dangled nearly down to her belly button, but the skin was so mottled and ruined that it appeared more like elephant skin than that of a humanoid.

Long, razor tipped blackened nails curled menacingly toward the ground like twisted twigs, and eyes as red as magma gleamed back at her malevolently.

"Will ye look like this, then? Is that what ye mean to ask, oh dark queen?" She said the words cruelly and dripping with scorn.

Stepping closer, she cocked her head to the side and grinned, revealing rows of stubbed and blackened teeth.

"Did ye think, ye little witch, that ye could dabble in black magick and not be affected by it? That it wouldn't demand it's due? That it wouldn't sink its claws into you and make you vile to one and all, forevermore?"

Her words were a breathy, lilt of madness that seemed to choke the life out of Fable. She gasped, clutching at her neck, desperate to take in a breath that didn't hurt, didn't ache.

But the madness in the elf's eyes only continued to burn brighter. Lighting up the night and casting long, malevolent shadows everywhere it touched.

"Once, I was a beauty too—"

"No," Fable shook her head. "No, this can't be."

The elf tossed her head back, and the wind howled, bowling through the leaves in the trees and scattering them in every direction. The stench of rot tickled Fable's nose as the dark elf continued to move in closer and closer.

Her heart twisted with a sick violence because she'd never tasted darkness so powerfully perverted before.

"Oh, yes, yes, yes!" The elf practically screamed.

And then, like magic, the wind ceased. The world grew calm, and where once stood a twisted, deformed, and monstrous perversion now stood a being of such stunning and ethereal beauty that it brought tears to Fable's eyes.

The dark elf's skin was still gray, but now it glowed like moonstone. The blond hair that had once been twisted up with twigs and weeds hung long and lush down to the backs of her knees.

Her eyes, which had earlier glowed like hellfire, were now a stunning, clear blue that even in the darkness sparkled like a gem. On her crown rested a gold dipped laurel wreath, and poking out of her hair on either side of her head were two large elf-shaped ears.

Her smile was radiant, and when she spoke, it sounded as clear as bells.

"Once, I looked like you. Beautiful. And all things lovely."

The cadence of her voice caused goose bumps to rise on Fable's forearms, and she had a difficult time comprehending that this lovely creature and the hideous monster could truly be one and the same.

"But my heart was twisted and blinded by love, a terrible kind of love. The love of power. I let it consume me, I should have fought harder, but I always thought just a little bit more*eee*."

49

Her voice trembled, deepened, and filled with the dark resonance once again. The pretty façade began to waver, and Fable thought she might be sick.

"What you see in the reflection, Fable of Seren will become who you are in truth if you do not fight the blackness."

And like a switch had been flipped, the night raged once again. The beauty of before had vanished, and in her place stood the twisted evil. The dark elf leered at Fable and in her eyes, she read the truth. That if she didn't stop soon, if she didn't stop what she was doing, this too would be her future.

Grabbing hold of her chest, the frantic beating of her heart thumped wildly against her fist.

"It can't be. This can't be."

"Oh, but it can and it will, darkness! It will!"

The sky erupted with bolts of lightning that tore through the heavens, the ground shook, stones—caught up in the gale force winds—ripped into Fable's cheeks bloodying her.

And then...it was all gone.

The dark elf.

The storm.

All of it.

Fable had stood in that forest alone, and knowing deep in her soul that this could never be her fate. That she'd fight it, tooth and nail. That she'd do whatever she had to do to make it end, to reverse the damage she'd already done.

Studying her reflection, she promised herself that this night would be the last night she used such evil magick.

"Just once more," she said, and then frowned.

Wondering if that strange demonic echo she'd just heard could have really come from her. Clamping down on her lips, she ignored the incessant beating in her skull that she should not use anymore black magick.

"If they think me a witch, then a witch I shall be."

And muttering the incantation beneath her breath, she turned her beautiful self into the image of the woman in the mirror.

Holding out her hands, she studied the grotesque flesh of her hands for only a moment.

But the moment she felt the quiver of powerful magick roll through the air, she turned her mind to what she must do next. Mirror had finally enacted the curse she'd whispered over the castle some years ago.

A sleeping curse. A deep, and unwaking sleeping curse. One only she could break. If Snow White cared so much for the people of this land, then she would know she could not kill Fable, because without her to recant the curse, the people would never rise again.

Uriah's face filled the mirror a second later. He took only a moment to study her, before nodding. "It is done, my queen."

She grinned, which, with this face looked more like a hideous pull of lips and gums.

"Good. Now I have only one task left to complete."

"You will see, Snow," he said without even asking. Mirror knew her well by now.

She nodded. "Yes. I will go to Snow White, and I will end this once and for all."

Turning back to her table, Fable picked up the uneaten red apple she'd placed out for her dinner earlier. Walking slowly, since this new withered frame demanded it, she moved toward the cauldron of liquid curse she always kept handy.

Holding the apple firmly by the stem she slowly dipped it in.

"Now any bite shall be your last," she murmured.

The apple gleamed prettily back at her, looking more perfect than any apple had a right to look. Smirking, she hugged the deadly weapon to her chest with one hand, while with the other she lifted the hood over her bald head.

"I will see you soon, my mirror," she looked at him, having the queerest sensation of a sudden.

Like she wouldn't see him soon at all. Like after tonight, everything was going to change, and not necessarily for the better.

Frowning deeply, she blinked and shook her head. Because just as oppressively powerful as the mood had come over her, it now scattered.

"My queen?" he asked, clearly noting her temporary distress.

Holding up her hand, she shook her head. "It is nothing, Mirror. Be well."

He clipped his head.

Fable turned and whispered, "Time to find the little brat."

# Chapter 8

*Fable*

She stepped into the camp invisible to all. The stench of troll and dwarves was a nasty scent on the back of her tongue and made her stomach heave.

How Snow could walk and live amongst them, Fable would never know.

Moving as quick as this stupid, old body could, she walked through the camp, peeking through the tent flaps and moving on when all she found was one farting or snoring dwarf or troll after another.

But finally, finally, and just at the center of the camp, did she find Snow White. And for a moment, the old love came flooding in.

She recalled the little girl's hugs. Her songs. The paintings she'd gift to her. Paintings that even to this day Fable still held onto, kept tucked in a safe place in the castle where no one could ever find and destroy them.

The girl was still heart-achingly beautiful.

Skin pale as snow, lips red as blood, and hair black as ebony. The legends had always gotten her right. In description at least. What the stories had failed to mention time and again was Snow's capacity to hold a grudge, or the brat's willingness to hold fast to the memory of an evil, cruel, and violent father and lay all the blame of his death at Fable's feet alone.

Snow was hardly the puritan the legends had made her out to be. Two months ago, Snow White had been solely responsible for the death of one Fable's most cherished and prized possessions.

A unicorn she'd found years ago. She'd found the poor, starving little creature whimpering pitifully beside its dead mother's carcass. Fable had been moved to tears at its plight and had spared the creature its own inevitable death.

If there'd been anything in the above she'd still shown any kind of kindness too, it had been Sterling. He'd been a good friend back to her. Unicorns were shy, ghostlike creatures. So rare that to spot one in one's life rarely, if ever, happened.

All within the realm had known of Fable's beloved pet. But she'd kept Sterling hidden from prying eyes. Wanting to protect him from those who'd wish to hurt her through him.

Fable had never discovered how Snow had learned of him, nor how she'd gotten into her heavily warded stables, but she had.

Sterling, used to his master's loving touch had come trustingly up to Snow. Who'd stabbed a sword through his heart. Her poor beast had dropped to his knees, foaming white at the mouth. Not even dead, before Snow White had pulled a grotesquely large sword from a sheath at her side and in one smooth motion, severed the horn from his head.

Sterling might have recovered if Fable had found him in time, but not without his horn, the very seed of his light magic and his soul, rested within it.

Fable had only seen it happen in her mirror after the fact, and what little love she'd still harbored for Snow had turned to ash after.

Snapping her fingers, she murmured a sleeping spell, and immediately the roll of powerful magick snapped through the air.

Snow White, who Fable had made certain would not be affected by the spell, jumped to her feet, looking into the darkness and spotting Fable immediately as she'd walked out of the shadows and into a small circle of moonlight.

Long, tense seconds passed between them as they studied one another. Finally, it was Snow who spoke first.

"What have you done to my Army?" she asked low, but her words shook with steel. Even in crone form, the girl had recognized her.

If Fable hadn't hated her, she might have been proud at the woman Snow White had become.

She shrugged. "They merely sleep, little one. As will you soon."

Snow White scoffed. "If you'd really wanted me asleep, you'd have done it at the same time as you did them. Why are you here?"

Fable grinned, and couldn't help but grin wider still when Snow shuddered. She knew just how hideous her grin was, it was good for a change that someone else got to enjoy it for a bit.

"To talk," she said as she slowly moved toward the girl. "To discover why it is you planned to attack my castle tonight?"

"Your castle!" Her face curled into a mask of hate. "It was never your castle; you killed my father. I am the rightful ruler of that—"

Fable rolled her eyes. "Keep telling yourself those lies, Snow White. Keep imagining that your father was some sort of hero. He wasn't. He was a cruel, terrible man who murdered his own mother so that that witch, Brunhilda could pose as her."

"Shut up!" Snow screamed, clapping hands over her ears.

But Fable was done keeping quiet.

"Did you know it was also he who ordered the execution of your mother? Did you know that, little Snow?"

"Stop it!"

"And you wish to know why?" She pressed on, undeterred by Snow's hate and violence. Fable was tired of shutting up; it was time this little bitch knew the kind of man she was so keen on defending.

"Because she didn't give him an heir. A male. A boy, Snow White. You were never going to be queen. Ever! Why do you think he locked you away in your own keep? Why do you think he raped me each and every night? So that I would produce his male. He didn't want me. And he didn't want you!"

With a deafening roar, Snow came at her.

Fable had expected it. Fighter she wasn't, what Fable was, however, was crafty and smart. To get Snow to eat the apple she had to be close and to be close meant forcing the stupid girl to come at her first.

Snow White jumped her, taking her down to the ground and getting atop of her. Her face was a contorted mask of rage and spittle flew from her lips when she said, "I'll kill you and take back what rightfully belongs to me!"

Fable reached into her pocket just as Snow White reached into her own. She'd had it all planned out. She'd known she'd take a beating tonight, probably gain a few bumps and bruises, and it was just fine by her.

What she'd not expected, however, was for Snow White to be reaching into her pocket to pull out Sterling's severed horn.

Eyes wide, fear beating a terrible rhythm in her skull, it all suddenly clicked into place as she finally realized why it was that Snow had killed her friend.

Unicorn's were comprised of nothing but white light. White light was a natural enemy to black.

"Snow White, don't!" she screamed.

But it was too late; Snow's arm came down with the type of force that could only be built up through years of hate. Fable had barely enough time to roll to her side, just far enough to escape the killing chest blow. Instead, the horn pierced her side, and immediately she felt the roll of its magic wash through her.

The pain was exquisite and terrible. Her entire body lit up like flame, making her feel as though she was being burned alive. Snow White reared back once more, and in her eyes, Fable knew that this time, the girl would not miss.

Gathering whatever shreds of power she still had left to her, she swallowed the scream of pain trapped in her throat and yanked the apple free.

Snow opened her mouth to say something else, but there'd be no more words from her.

53

Shoving the apple so far into her mouth, that the girl had no choice but to bite down in order to spit it out, Fable didn't have to wait long for the magick to take effect.

With a gasp of surprise, the girl then dropped like a sack of stone on top of her.

"*Oomph.*" Fable's breath came out sharply, and her entire body ached, only adrenaline kept her going.

Forcing her withered arms to work though they didn't want to, she finally managed to roll Snow's dead weight off of her. Snow White flopped over like a fish, long strands of hair mostly covered her face. The clothing of stitched deerskins she wore was stained by blood.

But it wasn't her own. It was Fable's. She touched her side and winced, then grimaced as her hand came away tacky and sticky with blood. That was when Fable noticed Sterling's horn lying on the ground.

Snow's hand had unfurled its death grip on it.

Stooping, Fable retrieved it, then closed her eyes as she cried for her precious pet who'd lost his life so that Snow could finally exact her revenge.

And it all came to a head.

The past, the present, even the future, it all collided into one giant ball of rage and Fable opened tear stained eyes, looking at Snow White with the same kind of malevolent and twisted hate the girl now felt for her.

The curse laced upon the apple was nothing but a sleeping curse. It wasn't true death. Fable could still wake her.

But she wouldn't.

Delicately strumming her fingers along the tip of Sterling's horn, she decided that the only way to end this war between them, to truly end it was to end her. Kneeling, she steeled her heart against what she was about to do and lifted her arm.

"STOP!"

The voice, so full of power, blasted against Fable's body, tossing her onto her arse violently. Nature was suddenly in chaos. Rain poured in great big bucketfuls from the sky which had boasted no storm clouds just seconds ago. Trees groaned—massively large trees with trunks as thick as a house—as they fought to remain standing in the suddenly hurricane force winds.

Groaning, body still on fire from where she'd been stabbed earlier, a sense of dread and fear filled Fable's body, because though she'd not heard the voice in years, she knew instinctually whose it was.

Only one woman had the power to control water as she now did.

Fighting to a sit up position, Fable stared at her grandmother. A towering vision of crystal clear water that raged like an out of control tide. Her beautiful face was twisted into a mask of pain and hurt and also anger.

Deep-seated anger.

"This is not the way, Fable! This is not how we taught you to be. Who we taught you to be."

And she felt such shame. Such horrible, horrible shame that she could no longer stare at Calypso. Could no longer see the wounded look in her eyes. When Fable had finally broken free of her captors, she'd told her family to leave her be.

She'd felt too full of evil and darkness and so rotten to the core she'd not wanted their censure, their judgment, but most especially to ever have to see their disappointment in her.

She'd known all along that if they'd seen Fable for who she'd really turned out to be, they'd hate her. Hate her like her grandmother did now.

"I do not hate you, my little flower. It is impossible."

Grandmother, who'd been standing a fair distance away from her, was now kneeling beside her, and wrapping her arms around Fable's waist and crying.

Crying.

Calypso—elemental goddess of all water and so ancient as to be nearly immortal—had never wept in all the years Fable had known her.

But she did so now. And she shook violently with it.

"Oh, my baby. My precious, precious baby. I should never have stayed away, even after you demanded I do it. I knew you weren't okay. I knew it, I just knew. My fault. This is all my fault, oh my beauty. My precious and beautiful, dark beauty."

And Fable wanted to remain aloof, wanted to throw her grandmother's arms off her and leave, wanted to vanish and hide and shake and be miserable and hope that she died of the heartache after a while.

But she'd not been held with such love in so long that she was helpless against her grandmother. She wielded her love like a blade and had skewered Fable straight through the heart.

So she stayed, and she squeezed her eyes shut—still wishing she could die and not have to witness the hurt, pain, and remorse in Calypso's eyes—but she held fast and sank into the cool depths of her grandmother's form.

When they finally pulled apart several minutes later, they were both tear stained, and heaving for breath, but the sky no longer shook.

"Grandmother, what are you doing here?" she finally asked, shocked by the little girl voice that had naturally come out of her.

She was a woman who'd done bad things. A lot of bad things, but she still felt small and inconsequential compared to her grandmother.

Calypso's face, which was now in elemental form, nothing but a cool sheet of water in the form of a stunning woman's face, looked at her with a mixture of love and terrible sadness.

"I'm here for you, my darling. To save you."

Fable's gaze flicked to the still sleeping Snow White, and she twisted her worm lips into a tight frown. "Save me from what? From killing her? She would have done it happily to me. She tried."

Caly's hand slid down Fable's waist, and wrapped around the wound in her side and instantly Fable felt the cool wash of her grandmother's powerful magick undulate all throughout her body, stitching her flesh back together. Not even a unicorn's horn was enough to stop the magick of a god.

"I know she did. But if you had done it, if you'd stuck that horn through her chest, then you would have been locked in this form in truth all the days of your life. And I did not want that for you, my precious."

Fable's lashes fluttered as Calypso then caressed the side of her face, and another powerful wave of magick rolled through her. And she saw that she was back to who she'd been. Her skin was taut and smooth and dark as the blackest night.

A fat tear splashed onto the tip of her nose as her heart ached, knowing she'd almost taken the dark path in truth.

"Look at me, dark flower." Calypso tipped her chin up, forcing Fable to meet the electric blue glow of her grandmother's eyes.

And seeing that love shining as bright as a beacon, even still, even having witnessed the depths of Fable's depravity firsthand, it was almost too much to bear. She tried to turn away again, but Calypso wouldn't let her.

"No, my dear. The prodigal has run long enough. It is time to heal you, Fable. It is time to rid you of this disease now infecting you. You are coming with me."

"Where?" her voice sounded broken and scratchy to her own ears.

"To a place far away, where you can heal, if you'll let yourself. Where no one expects you to be anything than what you truly are. Where you can relearn what it means to be you again. Will you come with me, my love?" Calypso gently, but determinedly took the horn from out of Fable's death grip, setting it down on the ground gently.

Snow's curled fingers were mere inches from it now. Sterling's horn, which had once been a symbol of great love for Fable, now turned into a weapon of ultimate destruction. It sickened her to see it.

She swallowed hard, tempted beyond imagining. But she also knew her scheming grandmother well, and though she sensed nothing bad, she did sense that Calypso was hiding something from her.

"You're not telling me everything, though, are you?"

A corner of Caly's lips tipped up. "No, my darling. I'm not. But you're going to have to trust me. Can you do that?"

She was tired.

Deeply.

To the very pit of her soul. Tired of the politics. The power. The darkness in her heart. Tired of fighting Snow White, tired of trying to get the people to—maybe not love her, but not fear her either. In short, Fable was tired of the life she lived.

Closing her eyes, she nodded as silent tears trekked down her cheeks. "I'll come. Wherever you want me to go, I'll come."

"Then stand up, my love, and follow me."

# Chapter 9

*Owiot*

He stood before the enormous man.

The Greek Lord of the underworld—Hades himself.

The god was an imposing figure dressed all in black, and standing before him with his arms crossed and glaring heatedly down his nose at Owiot.

For his part, he had no idea how he'd wound up here. All he knew was that he'd been walking amongst the stars one second, and the next he'd been snatched away by magick. Extremely powerful magick at that.

He'd expected maybe to find brimstone and madness surrounding him, but he stood instead in a forest full of shrieking screams and towering trees. Surrounded by several other men all blinking around in wide-eyed shock and wonder.

Hades clapped and the world shook. Even the shrieks ceased.

"Welcome," Hades boomed.

But his welcome had hardly sounded welcoming at all.

"You're here for one purpose. To find your forever mates. I don't care if you don't want to be here, my bride says you're destined to be here, and that's an end of things."

A few of the men blustered at that, several were gods themselves and puffed out their chests with hubris and disdain at Hades' high-handed treatment of them. But they were all lesser gods, like Owiot himself was, and when it came to a battle between lesser and greater, greater always won.

Well, all but one was a lesser god. The blond haired male looked Viking or Nordic. With his ice blue eyes and ruddy complexion he was definitely some form of Scandinavian god. Owiot vaguely recognized him as some sort of fertility god, but considering they were a dime a dozen, it didn't really pay to keep close attention to who was who. The only one that really mattered was Aphrodite, and he'd already had the distinct pleasure of meeting her face to face.

The Viking didn't seem as put out by the idea of being forced to play a game the way most of them were. He had his massive arms crossed over his massive chest and wore the type of secretive smile that said he found all of this more amusing than annoying.

"In a few moments, I will cloak you all in shadow. You will not get to choose your women; they will choose you."

"Oh, come on!" One man snapped. There was something about that male that was very off-putting to Owiot.

Not in his looks either. He had blond hair and green eyes with a skin tone much like Owiot's own—a burnished shade of umber. But every so often, when the light would strike him just so, there'd be a flicker of something very dark and very wrong in that male's eyes.

Hades lifted a brow. "You have something to say, Syrith?"

Syrith gave a cocky grin, shrugged, and said, "No. Nothing at all."

Hades narrowed his eyes, clearly not believing the male's easy acquiescence. "And how are your parents? Ragoth and Zelena? Still good I hope, so much catching up to do."

Syrith went instantly still, narrowing his eyes into razor-thin slits. Something about the mention of his parents had done it. Owiot couldn't help but wonder why.

"Fine. Just fine," Syrith practically hissed.

"Good. Happy to hear that," Hades said, and somehow Owiot had a feeling the Greek god had just won a small victory, though he couldn't fathom how.

"Now, as I said," Hades pressed on, "the women will be here shortly. They will choose you, guided by their inner muse. Do not flinch. Do not try to approach the women in anyway, if you do, I will kill you. And that is no bluff, trust me."

This time, when he said it, he looked directly at Owiot. And in his eyes glinted something dark and violent.

Owiot hadn't even known he'd be coming here in the first place, let alone that he'd be paired up with some female of unknown origins. But he'd always been quick to learn the world around him first before making any snap judgments. First impressions weren't always the right ones; they were simply the ones that stuck with you longest.

"Any questions?" Hades asked, looking and sounding bored.

Syrith raised a finger.

"No one. Good." Hades smirked because clearly he'd seen Syrith raise his hand. "Then go away."

And so saying, a thick veil of shadow descended on all of them. Shadow so deep and impenetrable it wasn't natural, but concocted by dark magick.

There was another side effect of the shadow; it canceled out any noise outside of his own sphere of it. Owiot could see the vague shapes of the other males, but could no longer hear them.

He was just noting that when he sensed, he was no longer alone.

"I wanted to speak with you privately, Owiot."

Turning, recognizing the voice of Hades, he dipped his head. "About?"

It would do no good to demand Hades release him. The major gods of any pantheon were always capricious and willful; it was never smart to get on the bad side of any of them. No, instead he'd wait this out knowing that eventually he'd uncover the truth of things.

Hades, tall and imposing, had scaled himself down to size, so that he no longer towered over Owiot, but instead stood only a few inches taller. He was attempting to be approachable, a tactic Owiot himself was familiar with as his god form was far too imposing for most anyone to gaze upon long.

"It is against the rules of this infernal game to reveal the female who's been chosen for you."

Owiot set his lips, waiting to hear the god out.

"But"—Hades inhaled deeply before steepling his fingers—"there are mitigating circumstances near and dear to my heart with your chosen mate. Circumstances that force me to break my woman's rules, and should she learn of this, she'll no doubt try to drown my bubble butt arse." He snorted, sounding amused, but then quickly turned serious again. "Your chosen mate is my granddaughter, Fable."

Why did that name sound so familiar to him?

Being of the Native American pantheon, Owiot wasn't as familiar with other smaller pantheons, but the Greeks and Romans were extensive and hard to ignore on a bad day. He'd heard her name before.

Something to do with curses and death and violence—none of it, had been good. Which made him wonder why they thought pairing her with him would be a suitable idea.

Hades closed his eyes, and Owiot was taken aback by the raw honesty that the Greek god revealed in just that simple gesture. His granddaughter meant a great deal to him, and Hades was worried. Very much so.

"Why have I been chosen for this...game?" Owiot asked slowly, taking his time with framing the question, knowing that sometimes you didn't get more than one shot to learn something.

Hades eyes glowed with hell flame, and Owiot knew it was well within the god's power to shield his emotions from him, but he wasn't doing it. It was that small reveal that had Owiot finally curious about his "chosen mate."

"Because you can mend her." Was all Hades said.

Owiot thinned his lips. "I'm not certain that you truly know who I am, Lord Hades—"

He held up his hand, stalling Owiot's words. "We know exactly who you are and what you do."

"So if you know, then you understand that I bring nothing but sorrow to whoever I'm with."

He gave a bitter chuckle. "Oh, believe me, I'm aware. But feeling sorrow, keenly, it is not always a bad thing. Sometimes it's only through accepting the sadness that we can start to heal."

No one had ever told him that before. When his brothers and sisters would go on their great hunts, Owiot was never asked to attend. They loved him, but no one liked him, not really. No one liked to be reminded of all they'd lost, of all they'd once had. No one liked to feel the blade of sadness pierce their soul; constantly reminding them all the mistakes they'd made throughout the entirety of their long-lived lives.

Even Owiot himself grew weary of the suffering.

"It is a cruel fate you've inflicted upon your granddaughter."

"No." Hades smile was soft but sad. "No. We've chosen correctly, for you both."

"If you feel you've chosen correctly, and yet still you come to warn me, then I can only imagine that your next step now is to threaten me if I don't make your granddaughter happy. Am I correct?"

Chuckling under his breath, Hades winked. "Something like that. Brimstone. Fire. Hail. Cerberus ripping your heart out."

Being threatened with bodily harm shouldn't have made Owiot chuckle, and yet it did. Despite the fact that he didn't want to be here, and wasn't sure he was ready to meet the *fable* herself, he liked the Lord of the Underworld more than he might have imagined.

"Just be good to her, Owiot. Treat my little flower kindly; it is all I ask."

The promise sprang readily to his lips. "I vow it."

No sooner had the words left, than Hades vanished and suddenly Owiot grew aware of the females. Standing before the group of them was Calypso and Aphrodite, it didn't matter which pantheon you belonged to, everyone knew of those two wild women.

Calypso's temper was legendary, and Aphrodite's ability to create a true love match was equally so.

But for once Owiot didn't care what the goddesses were saying, no, his attention had been drawn like magic to the dark skinned beauty standing off to the side alone. Dressed in a cloak of midnight and starlight, her form was covered, but her face was revealed to him.

Her eyes reminded him of the golden pelts of the buffalo that roamed his planes. Her lips were painted both dark and ruby red and split right down the middle—so that one side was a vibrant red and the other a bottomless black. She was unique in looks, and different than the women of his land, but something inside of her called deeply to something inside of him.

Because it was evident to him, even from this distance, that sadness and misery were her constant, and probably only, allies. She'd lived so long with the emotions that it clung to her like second skin, a living, breathing entity of gloom and bitterness.

Owiot watched only her. No longer caring why he'd been dragged down here because all he knew was that he had to know her. He had to meet her. He had to talk with her. And deep in his soul, he knew she had to be none other than Hades' little flower.

Meanwhile, Fable herself seemed completely caught up and mesmerized by the blue fairy who flitted a few spaces over from her. The fairy, no doubt aware of Fable's special attention, was chewing on her bottom lip with a nervous, anxious type of unsettled look on her face.

If looks could kill, Fable would have ended the little fae, which made Owiot wonder what their history might be.

A little while later the goddesses cried out that it was time for the women to "fetch their man meat," goose bumps rose up on Owiot's arms because the time had finally come.

She stood by like a shy, timid little mouse. But he sensed she was not normally so. Her intelligent gaze looked intently at each and every one of them, reminding Owiot immediately of the same sort of look in her grandfather's eyes—smart, cunning, and able to see beyond the mere superficial.

Other women ran forward quickly, snatching up their men with a touch of their hand, causing both to vanish immediately to parts unknown.

When he looked back at her, it was to note her looking squarely at him. Her gorgeous, golden eyes roved the shadows of his face as if trying by will alone to pierce through the veil Hades had poured over him to discern his true form.

His heart thundered like wild stallions in his chest, his mouth grew dry, and his ears rang as he waited with bated breath for her to come to him. One step. Two. Three. Four...and then.

She stood before him, and he was blasted by her overwhelming presence and beauty. She wasn't simply pretty. She was heart-achingly lovely. Her features chiseled as though by a master sculptor. Vision breathed to life by the gods. She had high, slashing cheekbones, full lips that on anyone else would look far too big, but fit her face exactly right. A slender column of a throat, and skin so dark it blended near perfectly to the shadow covering him. The combination of such dark skin and equally light, golden eyes made it hard to not become enthralled. She reminded him of something...

And then he knew. The black god of the Navajo people. He was the god of the nothingness of night. An endless form of pure, ebony black. If the black god had had a female antithesis, Owiot could only imagine she would be it.

"By the gods," he whispered, and she twitched, blinking prettily back at him.

She said nothing, only cocked her head, causing a pitch black curl to slip out from behind her hood and dangle provocatively over her shoulder. Teasing him, tempting him to touch. He swallowed hard, knowing he'd never seen such perfection in his life.

The air was laced with her scent, darkly lush and intoxicating. Like honeysuckle dipped in shadow and swirled in starlight. It was all he could do to keep his hands to himself.

"Forgive me, male," she said.

And her husky voice wracked his flesh with a deep-seated yearning and need to be touched. She took so long he began to worry that she might never touch him at all. To go from being an unwilling participant, to now, actively desiring she reach out and take hold of his hand was astonishing. Owiot had always heard of the power of a true love match in Kingdom. How it could literally shake mountains and uproot foundations, but he'd always thought the tales nothing more than silly fluff meant to titillate the weak-minded. Now though, standing before her, and feeling the slickness of his palms, the rapid beating of his pulse, and the powerful shivers wracking his flesh he knew the stories were all true.

Standing before him was a stranger, and a woman he was desperate to know. Only two other women besides Fable remained. The witch, Baba Yaga, and a centauress with a flowing crown of honey-wheat colored hair. All three women passed each other a hard glance, as though they spoke silently to each other of their misgivings and Owiot shook his head.

He was about to tell her there was nothing to forgive and urge her to please hurry, but the moment her hand landed on his arm he was tossed violently through the sands of time and into utter and void darkness.

*Fable*

She'd not known what kind of land to expect. Grandmother hadn't shared much in terms of what the games even looked like.

Only that they'd each land in their own little section of it, apart from the other contestants. Fable could only reason it was so that the couples would get an opportunity to learn each other in a more private setting. Possibly.

She wasn't sure.

So when she stepped through the veil of time and into her new and temporary realm, she was stunned to silence.

This land was nothing at all like what she'd expected.

The sky was a lovely shade of soft lavender—like the sky right before a cloudless sunset. Birds of every shape, color, and size flew breezily through the air. Air which smelled richly of flowers and ripe, sweet fruit.

In the distance, she could hear the gentle roar of a waterfall. And the trees that surrounded them on all sides were the most gorgeous kinds of conifers she'd ever seen. The needles were a green so brilliant they almost sparkled like gems. The red trunks were neatly corrugated and thick.

Woodland creatures—deer, squirrel, rabbits, and more scampered to and fro.

The sky was full of the type of fluffy clouds that made one want to lie down and imagine that they were, in fact, moving pictures—a dragon, a castle, a handsome knight on his handsome steed—

A very masculine clearing throat cut through her musings, causing her to gasp and twirl. She'd completely forgotten about her "chosen male."

It was on the tip of Fable's tongue to tell him not to try and get close to her. Not to even speak to her. That she cared not a whit about finding a mate, or a future King. That she'd come to escape the horrors of her life and nothing more.

Until she saw him, that was.

His face looked to be chiseled from granite. There was nothing soft about him. He had a strong jaw, high cheekbones, a wide—but not too wide—nose. Ridiculously full lips for a male, and eyes the color of melted, dark chocolate.

He also had a head of hair that could almost rival her own in length. It was long, coming to rest nearly at his waistline and straight as a board. It was dark, but not black—sort of a mixture of amber and mocha, so that when the weak sunlight hit it just right it gleamed with strands of deepest red.

His chest, which was incidentally also massive, was bare. Showcasing his corded abdomen and small, circular brown nipples that poked out just a tad. He wore animal skin leggings that clung to his strong thighs like second skin, leaving nothing to the imagination, and moccasins on his feet.

This male, this...man—for he was definitely that—was the complete opposite of her once king in just about every way.

"*Hahh*," she mumbled, pretty sure she'd not said an actual word, but unable to form anything more coherent than that.

He grinned, and her heart trembled. Her stomach quivered, and she knew that if she tried to walk now, she'd probably fall flat on her bum.

Breathing hitching as she struggled to string words together that made any kind of sense, she caught herself backing up a step when he began walking toward her. He might be gorgeous, but she didn't know him. Fable had learned a hard lesson years ago.

Sometimes beauty hid a wealth of evil.

"Don't...don't come closer," she said weakly. Sick at her stomach now because of the way his eyes had flashed with hurt.

"Okay," he said.

And again her flesh prickled tight with goosebumps when he spoke. His voice wasn't as deep as her grandfather's or father's, but it was soothing and melodious and entranced her all the same.

She cocked her head and her brows lowered. "That's it?" she asked confused. "Just okay?"

He spread his arms and hands wide in a semi-circle sort of gesture. "Just. Okay," he said again, and she was confused.

She'd not detected the hint of fear or hatred she was accustomed to back in her world when he spoke to her. His tone had been even, and gentle.

But also sad.

Very, very sad.

And what she'd assumed at first had been caused by her, she now wondered whether it was more inherent to him after all.

"What is your name, male?"

Closing his fingers into a fist, he gently touched it to his chest and good goddess, she couldn't explain what that simple little gesture had suddenly made her feel.

Hot. Cold. Excited. Giddy. Curious. All of it, and more.

"I am Owiot."

The way he pronounced his name, like "Ow-e-ot," gave her shivers. It was lyrical and beautiful to hear, like ear candy, it tasted delicious. And she realized with a bit of a shock, that she was actually smiling at him.

Once she noticed that she immediately stopped. Smoothing her features back into the tightly controlled mask she'd grown accustomed to over the years.

"You are a god, aren't you? Native American, if I'm not mistaken."

One corner of his delectable mouth curled up at the edge and again, it felt a lot like getting punched in the solar plexus. It was growing considerably harder to breathe right all of a sudden.

She nervously placed the tips of her cold fingertips to the corner of her jaw, needing some sort of tactile sensation to drag her back from the heated curls of anticipation and excitement she felt just gazing upon him.

He nodded. "I am."

She shivered. "Hm."

Fable really hoped it wasn't going to become a habit of hers whenever she was around him now to mutter nothing but incoherent nonsense.

"Hm," she mumbled again and then wanted to smack herself. She was a queen. A feared and respected queen—well, not respected at all, but feared was true enough. She needed to remember who she was.

Squaring her shoulders, she took a fortifying breath and then forced herself to say, "Interesting. And of what exactly?"

It was fascinating watching the play of shadow and lavender sunlight dance upon his firm flesh. Good gods, when she'd seen his image in shadow earlier, she could never have imagined that the male would be so...so...appealing.

Yummy.

Gorgeous.

He'd been tall. And slightly wide—which made her think he had to have some sort of musculature to him. He'd also been chosen by her grandmother and aunt, which meant he was going to be her physical ideal.

Only thing was, Fable had never realized that her physical ideal wasn't blond, and with clear colored eyes. She was, frankly, stunned that she liked looking at him so much.

Her playthings had always fit a certain mold before. Young. Dumb. And vigorous in bed. But one thing they'd all had in common—no long hair. She detested the look of long hair on men.

But especially if they didn't at least tie it back or up. She'd shuddered every time she'd seen a man walk past with his hair hanging long.

But with Owiot, she couldn't help but wonder what his hair might feel like.

He grinned again, as though he knew what she'd been thinking, and she cleared her throat, eyeing him angrily.

"What?" she snapped, crossing her arms over her chest and notching her chin high in her imperious manner, mostly because she was mortified to think that he possibly had heard her thoughts.

Some gods could.

Though she'd not heard of Owiot before, she could only assume him to be a lesser god; it didn't mean he didn't have the capabilities of the greater gods too.

When he spoke, he showed off a dazzling array of straight, white teeth. He really was exceedingly handsome.

"Only that," he said affably, "I answered your question, but I am not sure you heard it since you continued to stare at me in dazed wonder."

"Dazed wonder. Pft." She rolled her eyes. "Give me a break."

That ever-present grin grew wider. "Am I wrong?"

"Pft." Was all she had to say to that. Because there was no way in Tartarus that she was going to own up to the fact that he was right. "I was thinking of something important."

Namely, how delicious it would be to peel those leggings off him and get a look at every square inch of him. But again, none of his business.

"Now, repeat your answer back to me."

Yes, she knew she sounded like the evil queen again. But it was her fail-safe way. When life got out of control, it's who she became. The hard-nosed, power hungry, bitch everyone knew and hated. Fable had lost what it meant to be vulnerable.

She'd been so once and had very nearly died because of it.

Vulnerability was a weakness and a disease she could not afford to entertain.

His brows rose. Very thick, very beautifully formed dark brows that framed those gorgeous, sort of slanted eyes of his.

Good gods, she was in so much trouble.

"Are you so high-handed and imperious with everyone, Fable, or am I simply the honorary recipient of it?" He didn't sound angry, merely curious.

She gasped, mouth-hanging open. Because no one, *no one* other than her own family had ever called her on her bluster.

Feeling suddenly foolish and even slightly mortified, she didn't know what to do.

"What?" she muttered.

But he flicked his wrist. "It's okay. I merely wished to know. My answer was, I am the Native American Children's god. Though some have also called me the broody son of the Sky god. And still others simply call me sadness." He shrugged as though it made no difference to him what she thought of the terms.

Her cheeks heated with shame; thankfully her skin was so dark that he'd never know he'd actually gotten her to blush. She could count on one hand the number of times she'd blushed in her life.

"Oh," she said softly.

But he no longer seemed engaged with her; he was looking over her shoulders. Squinting up into the distance.

"I see a castle. I can only assume that is to be our home while we are here. Perhaps we should journey there before the sun sets?"

He was brushing her off.

And she didn't like that.

He wasn't even being mean or malicious about it either, which would have made it so much easier on her because then she could have cursed him to be a newt and be done with it. But it was impossible to hate someone who seemed ridiculously, impossibly kind.

Of course, this was simply her first impression of him. He might be an ogre, a monster, and the worst kind of villain. But deep down she sensed that what you saw with Owiot was what you got with Owiot. He'd not pulled any punches with her yet.

She wiggled her toes, feeling strangely anxious and unsure.

63

He looked like he was about to head off in the direction of the castle, and she suffered a very strange case of not wanting him to leave her just yet.

Thrusting out her arm, she grabbed hold of his elbow in a firm grip. His skin was warm, addictively so. And he smelled amazing. Like the cosmos...full of stardust and night. He glanced down at her hand, then up at her with an obvious question mark shaping his brows.

"We do not need to walk, male. I can take us there."

"You can?"

"Mm." She nodded, and then feeling the strange need to show off for him, she snapped her fingers and vanished them both in a plume of thick shadow. It wasn't black magick she used, only that inherent to her own nature. It was magic, plain and simple.

A second later they stood upon the stone landing of the massive castle, staring out at the lovely expanse of forest before them.

In her dreams as a young woman this had been what she'd imagined the above would look like. A fairy tale fashioned of dreams and white magic. Somehow, it was almost as if grandmother had plucked the idea from her head and had fashioned it to life just for her.

Reluctantly she dropped Owiot's arm, but not before brushing her thumb along the tight skin of his forearm. Her finger tingled when she pulled it back.

He looked down at his arm, still wearing a frown, before looking back at her. "Thank you, female."

She shrugged. "It's what I do."

This was the man she was supposed to find true love with? A part of her could almost believe it. But another giant part of her wasn't sure she deserved any sort of happiness.

Her life was so dark, so tainted, and ugly, and Owiot...he seemed anything but.

# Chapter 10

*Fable*

They were about to head into the castle proper, to explore it when she spied something dark in the distance. Dark, huge, and moving with great speed toward them.

"What is that?" she asked quietly, not afraid, but more than just a little curious.

No bird she'd ever known flew quite so fast. And though it appeared as little more than a black spec now, it was so far away, that she knew whatever it was, was actually massive.

Owiot stood very still, looking to where she pointed.

As it flew faster, the spec began to take on shape. It grew longer, more sinuous, and with an exceedingly broad wingspan.

It also began to change in color. From dark, to a dazzling white—like that of freshly fallen snow glinting in the sunlight.

A minute later, she knew exactly what they looked at.

"I am not certain—" Owiot began to say, but she shook her head.

"I do. It's a dragon."

Dragon's were dangerous. Territorial. And downright pissy at the best of times.

Gathering her considerable power to herself, she vibrated like a tuning fork as her body swirled with shadow and the thickening swell of her dark magick.

She was just about to blast the interloper with a bolt of it when the coloration changed once more—to one far more familiar to her.

Golden.

The dragon roared.

And there was nothing in all of Kingdom that sounded quite like the roar of a dragon. They could move the heavens itself when they roared, but when an Earth Shaker roared, why...the earth itself would rip open.

The castle heaved mightily, causing her to stumble a step.

It was Owiot's turn to latch onto her elbow, to steady her. And though she'd wanted nothing more than to feel his touch, she had far more pressing matters on her mind now.

Like why in the name of all that was holy had Button suddenly decided to make a showing in her realm?

Squashing her power to just the merest of trickles, she glared at the growing shadow, which was now massively huge and could no doubt destroy half this castle with one swipe of his golden tail should he be of a mind to.

She'd not seen Button in ages, and yet Fable recognized the ice blue of his eyes. Dragons, who'd been taken in as pampered and cherished pets, became what was known as familiars. Meaning they took on aspects of their keepers.

In Button's case, he'd taken on Galeta's blue coloration in his eyes.

"Damn that filthy fae to the very depths of the River Styx," she spat heatedly.

If there was one thing in Fable's life she was sure she'd never forgive, it would be Galeta's cruel treachery.

Button landed gracefully on a turret that was, coincidentally enough, the proper size and length to handle the weight and mass of a dragon his size.

Ice blue eyes drilled intelligently into Fable's heated ones.

"Well," she snapped at him, knowing full well that the blasted creature hadn't shown up here by coincidence at all.

Turrets weren't made to support dragons. Which meant, grandmother had had a hand in this too.

She felt Owiot's quizzical look on her face, asking without asking what in the world was going on. But it was never wise to turn one's back on a fully-grown dragon. They tended to take the action as an insult and had been known to eat men for less.

"I come bearing news, dark queen," he said in the thick dragonish burr of his kind. Like rolling sandpaper and the roar of a shifting tide all at once.

Owiot flinched; clearly he'd not expected the beast to talk. She wondered if in his realm they even knew what dragons were.

"Then, speak," she snapped. "I've no time for your games today."

He chuckled, and the tops of the mighty trees shook violently.

"Oh, come. Come. Queen. It was never I that had a grievance with you. Can we not be at least a little civil? We will be working together for quite some time."

She curled her upper lip into a snarl. "Yes, and how is your bitch of a keeper today, eh? Dead, I hope."

His chuckle caused the winds to slap against her face, pushing her back on her heels. She had to wrap her and Owiot in magic to hold them in place.

"Galeta the Blue," he stressed, "is fine as ever. Thrust into the games with you, as I'm sure you know."

"Oh, I saw her." She rubbed her palms together menacingly. "Give her a message for me when you see her next, will you, darling?"

He lifted a scaled brow, ice blue eyes dancing merrily. Button had ever loved his verbal spars with her. "Anything for you, dark one."

Her answering smile was full of hate and malice. "Tell her; I've not forgotten. And I look forward to my time with her in the ring."

He chuckled. "I'll make a note of that. But sadly, I am not here to chit-chat," he said, snapping his corrugated and sharp as knives teeth back at her, "I come on higher orders today."

"Indeed. Well, spit it out," she huffed, crossing her arms and glaring hotly at him. Far as Fable was concerned, whether she and Button had ever shared grief was a moot point, he worked for the enemy, which made him her enemy too.

The way the lavender sunlight dappled along his scales was terribly pretty, though she'd never tell him so. Button gleamed like a polished marble of fool's gold, casting radiant prisms along the stone walls of the castle and grounds.

"You know how the games work, so I am not here to lecture you further on that. What I am here for is to give you your own riddle to solve. Every contestant within the games has a quest particular to them. Yours is simply this, remember."

She snorted. "Remember what?"

He shrugged massive shoulders. "That I cannot tell you, queen. Simply that you must decipher on your own what that might mean to you."

"And if I don't remember that nonsense?"

"Then you'll be doomed to be apart eternally."

She frowned. "What? Owiot and I? How is that punishment? We hardly know one another?"

*Owiot*

He looked at her curiously. She was still as beautiful as before, but there was an implacable coldness to her that he'd not seen while alone with her. A razor-edged hardness that she wore like a steel mask.

66

If he'd not witnessed the transformation with his own eyes, he'd have thought he'd gone insane. But the moment Fable had recognized the dragon; there'd been a subtle shifting in her appearance. Cold, foreboding, and...dark. He tasted that darkness in her now, like a disease of the soul it infected every inch of her.

Though he wasn't afraid of her.

He was a god. She wasn't. She had the blood of the gods running through her veins, and he tasted the strength of her will and power, but she could not harm him if he did not allow it.

But this woman...he did not like her as much. There was a cruelness to her that settled uneasily in his bones. He much preferred the woman he'd been with back in the Glen.

When they'd been alone, and she'd been unsure of the world around her. When she'd allowed a tiny sliver of innocence and pain to peek through the tightly controlled shell, she was used to wearing.

Why was she like this?

Owiot, because he rarely mingled amongst others, had become very good at one thing. Studying and seeing beneath the veneer others presented to the world. Even amongst the gods, he could recognize truth from lie easily.

And this...who she was right now, this was a lie.

But why?

The dragon chuckled deeply and again the very earth shook with the sound of it. Owiot had never been around such majestic creatures before, though he had heard of them, monsters that roamed the other realms. Intelligent, but deadly creatures that would raze an entire town to get at their treasure.

There was clearly history between Fable and this dragon, and none of it sounded good.

"I do not know why things are as they are, dark queen. I am simply the messenger."

She snorted. "Well, message delivered. You may go now."

He tsked. "Not yet, though I am sure you'd love nothing so much as getting me out of your hair until I deliver my entire message I cannot leave."

Fable rolled her eyes. "Then get on with it and spare me further grievance."

The dragon released his grip on the turret and held up one large clawed foot. Extending out each claw as though they were fingers, he proceeded to run through the litany of what would be required them in this race.

"The game is set to last a month. The only way to end your time here is to confess to true love. It cannot be a false confession as Aphrodite will know. If you do confess falsely, you'll be penalized. Every few days you will be placed into a life or death match, pitted against one of the other queens trapped in this realm. The rules to winning are simple. Do whatever needs doing to stop your opponent."

"Kill them? Is that what you're saying?"

"If needs be." He shrugged as though he didn't care.

"Whatever. What else?"

Owiot frowned at her blithe and easygoing manner with which she'd said it. As though life meant very little to her.

"As you already know, though I feel I should stress the saying of it, the last couple to remain in the games will face severe punishment. So do not be the last. Fall in love, which is the entire purpose of the games."

Again she rolled her eyes and muttered something softly under her breath, something that had sounded suspiciously like, "whatever."

He pursed his lips.

"The only other things of note is this," the dragon pressed on, "when the day comes for the trial, it will be I that takes you there. And all familiars have been swapped."

She cocked her head, looking truly concerned this time. "Mirror?"

The dragon nodded. "Yes, he is here."

"Who is he with?" she asked quickly.

"That I cannot say."

"Is he safe?" she rushed on, sounding almost breathless with fear.

It was the first time he'd heard such a sound come from her. And here...here he knew she'd let that hard shell crack just a bit to show the true woman once again. She was anxious, scared really, for someone or something other than herself.

And he couldn't help but drape his arm over her shoulder and give her a soft squeeze, responding immediately to the pain in her voice.

She gasped, going completely still on him and glancing at him from the corner of her eye.

Intrinsically, Owiot understood Fable wasn't used to contact. Probably of any sort. So he was surprised that rather than step out of his arms, instead, she rested her weight upon him just a very tiny bit. Though she hadn't relaxed, she was giving him the cue that his touch wasn't wholly unappreciated.

"No familiar may be harmed during the trials. Mirror is safe," the dragon replied directly.

And she released a shaky breath. But then that armor went back up into place, and this time, she did step out of the circle of his arm. Leaving him to stare quizzically at her.

Her moods were as mercurial as the winds.

"You have two days time before the first trial takes place. A chance, no doubt, for all the couples to learn one another. When the time comes, I will return for you. Until then, you have this."

He extended his neck, and for the first time, Owiot realized the dragon wore a necklace. Dangling off the necklace was a delicate looking, red glass pendant that gleamed like flame.

Fable snapped her fingers, and immediately the necklace had transferred from him to her. It rested on the palm of her hand and was in fact much bigger than it had at first appeared on the dragon's neck.

Her lips set into a thin line. "A looking bauble, is that it?"

How she'd figured that out so quickly was beyond Owiot. He'd simply thought it jewelry.

The dragon nodded. "Aye. That it is. If you wish you, you may look inside of it and study which queen it is that you'll be facing next. Though if I'm not mistaken, rumor has it you'll be paired off with Baba Yaga first."

"That witch," she said with a clipped voice. "Lovely."

And that lovely had definitely sounded anything but.

Owiot was almost tempted to chuckle at the pained look in her expression. He liked it when Fable dropped the mask; there was so much more to the woman than merely a beautiful façade.

Chuckling again, as the dragon often seemed wont to do, he shrugged. "Blame your family for that; I am simply the messenger. Now, I must bid thee adieu. Enjoy yourselves," he said the last in singsong, and then with one final mighty roar that caused both he and Fable to grimace in response, the dragon jumped into the sky and flew off.

Leaving him and her alone.

Again.

And this time when she turned to look at him, her mask had fallen once more and instead of the imperious, frightful queen...what he saw on her face now, made him open his arms to her.

She didn't say anything to him. Simply walked into them, buried her face in his chest, and curled her fingers tight to his back. And he knew then; he'd been right. The Fable the world saw was nothing but illusion; smoke and mirrors cast by an exceptionally talented witch, but one that seemed to drain the very life out of her each time she did it.

Owiot could hardly fathom the many sides and faces of this woman, all he knew was this...he was desperate to learn her.

All of her.

"This is not good, Owiot," she said softly, "this is very not good."

# Chapter 11

*Fable*

They explored the castle quickly.

Moving from room to room with alacrity. There'd be more time to go in-depth later on, and for some reason, Fable felt the need to play hostess to him. Though she knew about as much of this place as he did. But the truth was, she needed this tour to end soon.

She needed to get away from him for a moment. She needed solitude, a place to hide and gather her thoughts without his eagle-eyed gaze following her every movement.

They'd barely gotten to half the castle when the need to flee overwhelmed her, and she rudely announced, "Pick your room. I've picked mine."

Fable didn't wait for him to respond. She snapped her fingers, and vanished to the one room she'd known from the start would be hers.

The tower. And this tower, it was identical to hers back home. Built of gray stone, with one tiny window, to let in sunlight, a small bed, a rug, hearth, and a workbench.

Stepping through was almost like coming home. The small space was comforting and familiar, and the shakes that had gotten hold of her while touring the damned place began to slowly ease.

Gripping the edge of the table until her knuckles blanched, she hung her head, closed her eyes, and tried to breathe.

Owiot was disrupting her equilibrium.

And that was happening with him doing nothing at all.

Except he had, hadn't he? He'd touched her. Placed an arm around her when Button had appeared, and when the beast had left he'd opened his arms to her and held her tight.

Why?

Why didn't he sense her capacity for violence and darkness? He had to; evil leeched from her very pores. She'd become one with it now.

She looked to the far wall, where Mirror would have been if this had truly been her home. But he wasn't there. The corners of her lips turned down, feeling a strange, disquieting ache in the center of her heart at his absence.

Ever since coming to the above she'd never been long without her friend. Her only friend.

Moving to sit on the edge of the straw-filled mattress that would be her bed for however long it took before she could escape this nightmare, she gazed out the window with unseeing eyes and wondered if she'd made the right decision to come to this after all?

And as she wondered that, her mind inevitably returned to what she'd done. To Snow. To her people. All of them locked in the sleep of the dead, forever and permanently frozen in time should she never utter the incantation to break their curse.

She'd been justified in her actions.

Hadn't she?

Sitting in this tower, looking out at the lavender skyline, she was no longer so sure of herself. Of anything anymore, really. She squeezed her eyes shut and tried to forget about Kingdom, about all the people who'd betrayed and hurt her through the years. She sank into the darkness she always retreated to when life became too much, but this time, the darkness wasn't comforting her...this time, it pricked at her soul, trying to force her to acknowledge an unpleasant truth about herself.

69

But, just as she'd done countless times before, she quieted that still, small voice. Ignoring it's unsettling truths, burying them deep in her consciousness, to a spot so black and void within her that she could get lost in it.

"Do not think," she whispered, "do not think of this."

And like she'd done so many times before she was finally able to let it go. But like a crowded closet, she knew that she was quickly reaching the tipping point before the doors were shattered and all that she'd hidden within came tumbling out. The day that happened, she had a horrible, sinking feeling that she might not survive it.

Fable had no idea how long she sat there in a trance-like pose until suddenly she grew aware of his presence. Owiot's energy rushed through her like a shock of bright, white light. Scattering and clearing the dreck and shadows that lived within her and just as it had when she'd first seen him she took in a breath that didn't hurt, that made her feel...free.

White magic didn't mean the wielder was pure and faultless. What it did mean was that the practitioner tapped into the powers of nature rather than the forces of darkness.

She looked up, and his gaze was steady and oddly comforting. Even though she saw him, he rapped gently on the door as though to announce his presence without startling her.

"May I come in?" he asked in that same calm cadence of his that made her flesh tingle and her bones feel soft within her.

Twisting her lips, she waged an internal battle with herself. She wanted to send him away, demand he leave her alone. Because that's what she always did. When life got too confusing or hard for her, she withdrew into her tight shell. Never letting anyone in.

So why weren't the words coming to her now? Why couldn't she seem to form the sentence together and say it?

Frustrated with herself and tired of always being so guarded, her shoulders drooped, and she muttered, "Whatever."

He padded softly toward her, his footsteps so silent that had she not been watching him move, she'd have thought he hadn't budged yet. His loping graceful manner reminded her of a wolf almost—predatory and powerful, but curious.

Her damned traitorous heart began to pound rapidly in her chest. Completely against her will, she found herself fascinated by this male.

Stopping only once he'd gotten to within a few inches of her, he knelt. So that he came eye level to her and cocked his head, causing his razor-straight hair to slide like a graceful mahogany wave across his naked shoulder.

"Have I done wrong, Fable?"

She frowned hard. "What?"

His deep chocolate eyes never flinched at her cold reply.

"Why did you run from me?"

She chuckled darkly. "Run? From you? You must be mad."

"Stop that." His voice was intense and serious. "Do not hide behind that mask with me. I won't allow it."

Gobsmacked, breathless, and also chagrined—all emotions she never handled well—she straightened her shoulders, giving into the rage that always simmered just below the surface with her.

"How dare you! You don't know me. You know nothing of—"

Grabbing her wildly, flailing hands he jerked them toward his chest. Covering her cold fingers with his warm ones, almost like a hug. And the touch of him...by the gods.

Her mouth parted just slightly, words completely lost to her.

"You are right, Fable. I do not know *you*. But you are wrong too. For I do know you. I know your kind."

"My kind?" She lifted a shapely brow, saying the words far sharper than she'd intended to. "And what exactly does that mean?"

If he was scared of her tone, he didn't show it. Instead, he chuckled warmly. "Do you think that I've lived amongst gods all my life and haven't learned a thing or two in that time? Do you think that I cannot see that beneath the sharp tongue and spine of steel is a woman unsure of herself and who she really is?"

She gasped a tiny inhalation of sound because he was stripping her bare, exposing her worst fears and bringing them out into the light of day by simply speaking the words into being.

If anyone within her realm other than Mirror had ever spoken to her thus, he or she would have quickly been reduced to ashes. And though Owiot was a god, there were ways to hurt even him.

Ways she knew well. She could defend herself by might, by power, demand he take it all back. But all she could do was shake and tremble and damn the silent tears sliding down her cheeks.

"How?" she asked, the only word she was capable of speaking in that moment.

She'd expected him not to understand, but he smiled gently, thumb stroking the inside of her wrist and making her feel crazy, wonderful, confusing things.

"I've told you my names, Fable. But not what I can do, or who I am."

She sniffed, yanking one hand out of his grip to wipe up her stupid tears. "You like kids, and you make people sad."

A bitter laugh escaped her.

"Sort of like you're doing to me now," she said softly.

His eyes—so soulful and penetrating and lovely to gaze upon—finally did flinch. And immediately she felt like an arse, wanting to take the words back, wanting to say it wasn't true, simply to spare him.

Which was a first for her. She wasn't exactly known for sparing the feelings of others often, if ever.

"No. Though I am not surprised you think so. The truth is, that when I'm around others, I do not make them feel what they don't already feel in some shape or fashion. Humans and even gods bear a great capacity to hide from their darkest, most troubling parts of themselves. But the sentiment is always there it's simply buried so deep that most times they think it does not exist."

The hand that had released her earlier, he now placed against her breast—which should have elicited one of two responses from her. Either an enraged and indignant gasp of outrage followed by a satisfying slap to his handsome face. Or a kittenish mewl of pleasure and a subtle drifting in toward him to let him know she wanted more. And though in some ways she felt both emotions, the way he held himself absolutely still and stared at her like he was actually peering into her soul, she couldn't seem to do anything other than look back at him. Owiot wasn't feeling her up; instead, he was covering the wild beat of her heart with his palm and forcing her to listen to her sadness.

His intense gaze literally seemed to swallow her whole, and she found herself falling into a web of stars—an infinite string of them that lit up the vacuum of night with winking pinpricks of silver dust. And as she fell she *saw*. Saw herself as a child. Happy, carefree, and much loved. Then as a young woman. Idealistic. Naïve. But still happy, still sure in the goodness of others.

Then she saw herself step through the portal between the above and the below. Saw the sparkle of joy dance through her lioness gaze, the rapturous smile take over her face as she tipped her face up toward the sun for her first inhale of air.

Her heart trembled to see that girl.

So young. So sure of herself and the world she moved in. Sure that she'd made the right choice. Even when that damnable driver had accosted her. She'd just known she'd been made for this world.

That she'd finally found the place where she belonged.

Then she saw him.

George.

Come galloping up over the hill. Wearing his crown and riding his white stallion. So handsome. So virile. Literally her knight in shining armor. Reaching a hand down to her, and inviting her to stay with him forever.

71

She'd been so smitten, so immediately drawn into his web that she'd never noticed what she noticed now.

The hardness to his lips. The calculating gleam in his deep blue eyes. Or the tortured gleam in his guardsman's eyes. Charles sat astride his own mount and shook his head once. An instinctual type of movement that spoke volumes without saying a word. He'd tried to warn her off. Tried to make her leave.

But she'd been so silly, and young, and trusting.

And the moment she took George's hand was the moment she'd sealed all their dooms.

Fable wanted to scream at Owiot to make it stop. But she was falling, falling, falling...unable to halt the perpetual slide into that darkness she'd bottled up for years.

Tearing through more images and memories.

Feeling the heavy weight of the crown upon her head the moment she'd said, "I do."

How George had squeezed her hand, near to the point of pain, and deep in her soul, she'd known that her white knight had just become her tormentor.

The visit from Brunhilda, where under the guise of lavishing wedding gifts upon her, she'd fooled Fable into putting on that cuff. And then the slow descent into madness and pain.

Being smacked in the face by the dowager for not dressing appropriately, or saying the right thing. Brunhilda telling the rest of the castle to never approach the queen, or even so much as speak to her, upon pain of death.

Losing any potential allies she could have had. Seeing the noose slowly tighten around her and knowing she could do nothing to stop it, until finally she'd been locked away.

Discovering the truth of who George and the witch really were. Being repeatedly raped, night after night. Learning her dark craft at the hands of a wicked fairy. Growing in power and rage.

Until finally...she killed them all.

Seeing Snow's eyes and knowing any love she'd been given by the little princess had been dashed to ribbons forever.

And then her rebirth into evil.

Fable hadn't realized until now how even the outer had exposed the inner. When she'd first arrived at the Enchanted Forest she'd dressed in pale, light colors. But slowly her style had evolved into shadow and darkness.

Her harsh and unflinching look as she'd smite an entire village for threats against her crown and right to rule. Her cruelty.

"Stop." She was finally able to mumble miserably; voice cracking as she pleaded with him. "Please, goddess, stop this."

And then she was back. No longer falling through an endless parade of stars, but staring deep into molten eyes that saw far too much.

His palms came up to her face, and she waited for him to look at her in disgust. With fear.

He'd seen the very worst of her soul. Exposed it completely.

But instead, he glided his fingers down her cheeks, drying her tears as best he could.

"I see you, Fable of Seren."

She swallowed painfully, almost too afraid to move, afraid that if she did the kindness in his gaze would finally turn to recrimination, to hate. Like it had done with so many others.

She circled his wrists with her far smaller hands, not able to close the circle. She wasn't sure whether it was to hang onto something, or push him away. All she knew was that touching Owiot grounded her back to the present.

"I'm not worth seeing, Owiot. I fear I never have been." There. The truth she'd buried down deep, the one she would kill to never let anyone know of it. She told it so easily to him. Fable tasted the bitter tang of self-loathing on the back of her tongue.

He shook his head, and then in a move that surprised her. He pulled her toward him. He was going to kiss her.

He was...

And then he did.

The press of his firm lips to hers rocked through her soul. Not because there was passion, or intensity, or even longing—though there was for her—but because he'd opened himself to her too and let her taste of the divine.

Of the godhood within himself.

Of the healing white light of his own soul and that of the world that surrounded them. And she *remembered*. And suddenly the words that Button had whispered to her made so much sense.

It wasn't a point in time that she needed to remember. Rather, it was the sweet, innocence of her youth. The burning memory of what it was to be pure of heart and happy again.

The carefree joy and radiance of that light washed through her, and where the light touched the darkness fled.

Not permanently, or even forever. Not if she wouldn't allow it. But he was showing her another way. He was showing her who she could be if she'd just let it in.

He pulled back, and the light was gone. She whimpered, wanting more. Wanting all of it.

"Look at me, dark queen."

She did. No longer able to fight her pull to him.

And she gasped, because the sadness, the pain that had been inside of her, was now reflected in the depths of his chocolate eyes.

"What did you do?" she breathed, touching her fingers to the corner of his eyes as she watched her terrible memories play through his gaze like a rolling image.

"I took it inside of me, Fable."

"No. Give it back. You cannot handle what I've done, it will hurt you, it would ruin—"

His smile was gentle. "I did not take it all, Fable, but I wished to give you at least a little peace."

"Why?" she asked again because she was so very confused by him. He did not know her, and yet he'd done this for her. He'd taken out her darkness. He let her breathe again. "Why, Owiot? Why did you do this?"

"Because," he said after a moment, "we all deserve to be happy sometimes."


*Owiot*

Gritting his teeth against the unbearable pressure of her demons waging battle inside of him, Owiot had no choice but to leave her there. He'd sensed he'd pushed her as far as she was capable. She sat on that bed, bathed in shadow and beauty, and staring unblinkingly at the wall ahead of her and his heart ached to stay by her side.

Owiot could not understand his irresistible draw to her, or his need to save her from herself. He'd promised himself after the last time that he'd never do this again. Never again allow his emotions to gain the upper hand on his common sense, but when she'd abandoned him to flee like a terrified rabbit from a prowling coyote, he'd had no choice but to follow.

Fable's sadness was such a tangible, terrible thing that he was helpless but to respond to it. Though it was more than that. More than the call of that emotion that played havoc with his soul, it was the woman herself.

Once, many moons ago there'd been another woman. One who'd made his soul long, just as Fable did now. Weary, aching everywhere, he forced himself to not think about Aiyana.

Walking painfully slow down the winding staircase, he made his way gingerly toward the exit of the castle itself. He needed to rid himself of her demons soon.

It was never pleasant hanging on to the sins of another, but Fable's sins were far darker and deeper than most. By the time he took the last step his body ached like that of a broken and aged elder not long for this world.

The moment he stepped into the weak rays of sunlight, he tipped his face toward the Great Spirit—in any realm, tribe, or incarnation, his peoples never changed. The names might be different for all, but they were all one and the same.

"I call you Sister Mountain Lion. Brother Coyote. Sister Crow. And Brother Eagle," he intoned, feeling his insides began to quake and tremble as he prepared to shed this weak mortal form for that of his true one. "I ask you to accept my sacrifice. Take of me. Cleanse me. Purify my heart, mind, and soul to do what it is I've been called to do. Show me truth."

Raising his hands toward the sky, he spread his fingers wide, dropped his head and felt the call of the Great Spirit descend from above.

As breath left him, the wind rolled and gathered to the four corners of this land. A great cry sounded from the sky above, as the spirit form of Brother Eagle and Sister Crow fell upon him.

Eagle—a screen of clouds and starlight—landed on his shoulders. Hooking sharply curved talons into his flesh.

He grunted, beginning the chant of release.

Crow—came not as spirit, but in true animal form. With feathers, gleaming like polished obsidian and emeralds as his large wings fluttered gracefully, and with each flap thunder rolled. He rested upon Owiot's head, cawing loudly.

Owiot's body shook violently. Fable's demons inside of him screamed, clawing at his innermost self, demanding he not do them as he was about to do. Biting down on his back teeth, he accepted the pain as his own, becoming one with it and sliding deeper into the spirit world.

"To me, Coyote...and, and Mountain Lion," he stuttered with the last vestige of strength he still possessed.

And then he knew they were there. Even without turning, he felt the sly, trickster pad through the woods behind him, slinking in shadow and chuckling softly to himself.

Mountain Lion was not too far behind her brother. She came at Owiot from the front, her tawny-eyed gaze piercing through the veil of Owiot's mortal form into the god beneath.

Coyote pounced from behind, and Mountain Lion from the front. Slamming him to the ground and sinking their claws into him.

The touch of the four released his soul. He erupted from the shell... a god.

*Fable*

She was drawn to the window. Knowing, without knowing, that he was out there.

Moving like a thought, as though in a trance toward it, she got to the casement in time to witness the majesty of Owiot's transformation from man to more.

Her eyes grew wide as the animals—who were clearly not true animals at all—came to him. An eagle built of stars and clouds. A crow with feathers beyond the scope of imagination. A mountain lion more regal and lovely than any feline she'd ever seen, and a laughing coyote, they surrounded Owiot in a tight circle, and before she knew it the beautiful, beautiful man who'd touched something deep inside of her soul exploded outward like a supernova.

The sky exploded with lightning and thunder, turning from lavender to pitch black. And now bursting with stars.

But the stars, they did not remain just within the sky. The stars were everywhere.

In the trees. On the ground.

Even, in her room.

Gasping, she reached for one of them. An impossibly bright jewel of white that winked and twinkled and beckoned for her to touch it.

The tiny star landed on her palm, and she couldn't begin to describe the emotions that assailed her then.

Glory.

Wonder.

Awe.

But so much more too.

"Owiot," she whispered, somehow understanding that this, all of this was him. Caressing the tiny gem a moment, she then curled her fingers around it and brought it to her chest.

Warmth spread throughout her body. She closed her eyes and was once more falling into a net of stars.

But this time, it was different.

It didn't hurt.

It was so lovely. And though she stumbled, she knew she'd not be harmed, because the stars were so much more than just lights. The stars were him—Owiot, and the wind whispered his chant to her, "*you are not alone, Fable. Not ever alone.*"

# Chapter 12

*Fable*

She blinked her eyes open, confused for a moment where she was. Back in her tower in the Enchanted Forest, everything looked the same and yet it was somehow different too.

But then slowly the memories of the night before came back to her. The games. A man bathed in shadows. Warm, chocolate eyes. A gentle touch. Coyote. Crow. Mountain Lion. Eagle. And stars.

With a gasp, she tossed her sheets aside. Wondering when she'd gotten into bed. When she'd fallen asleep. But the thought was fleeting.

Had he left her forever?

What had happened yesterday?

Really happened?

She'd felt him take of her darkness. Extract it from her. And though she still sensed a wellspring of it deep within her, she also felt freer, lighter than she had in forever.

"Owiot," she breathed his name like a benediction.

Taking less than a minute to brush her teeth, and pull on a robe of whatever color—she didn't even care— from the closet, she bounded down the steps as fast as she could. She could snap her fingers and escape, but she wouldn't know where to. So she had to settle for searching for him the old fashioned way, by using the two legs she'd been born with.

Panic beat heavy wings in her chest as she looked inside one empty room after another. Had this all been a strange, wonderful dream? Had she imagined the god? Had he never even been real at all?

And if it had, then why did she suddenly feel so empty, sad, and lonely? That was her life on a daily basis. She never got to sit down to a nice spot of tea with a friend talking over the day's events, never knew what it felt like to be invited to a ball she did not put on, she never even got the chance to simply sit and have a conversation based on nothing with a stranger.

Because in the Enchanted Forest all knew her, and knew to stay well clear of their "Dark Queen." Owiot had been the only human since she'd assumed the crown who had ever treated her—not even as an equal—but as simply another woman. He wasn't scared of her, and never acted as though she was above him in stature or rank, to him she'd simply been Fable and not the Evil Queen.

It was that epiphany that had her running faster. He couldn't leave her now. Not when she finally knew what it felt like to be *normal*.

Tripping over the long belt of her robe, that she'd forgotten to tie up, she would have fallen flat on her face except for the fact that a pair of strong arms suddenly caught her.

Strong, and very human looking arms.

Clinging tight to them, she glanced up and squeaked, "Owiot! You're here."

His grin was brighter than the sun, and literally filled every crack and crevice of the castle with its light. Anywhere he moved, he obliterated the darkness.

Beautiful brown eyes ensnared her. "Yes, *darkness*, I am."

The way he said that word made her shiver. She swallowed hard, still gripping tight to his arms, unable to peel her fingers off him.

Up until now, Owiot had been the epitome of gentlemanly. Looking at her with respect, and difference. But he was looking at her very differently now. His gaze was hot, smoldering as he straightened them both and slowly perused her body at his leisure.

Her knees shook under the weight of his intense stare. She'd been looked at with lust many times in her life, but this was more than mere lust. This was something else entirely.

It was visceral.

Raw.

Carnal.

Need.

She gulped. Owiot looked similar to what he had yesterday. But his leggings were painted with red clay markings. His moccasins gleaming with beads of turquoise and cobalt, and his chest was painted with black slashes down his ridged and tightly corded abdomen. His hair was still free and long, but a lone eagle feather had been braided into it.

"I thought you left me," she whispered, digging her nails in deep. Not realizing her actions, until he looked down at her hands, still wearing his ever-present and patient smile.

With a start she released him, tasting her pulse on the back of her tongue.

"I'm...I'm sorry."

He tipped her chin up. "Don't be. We have one more day before the trials."

She knew what he was saying. She nodded. "Spend the day with me, Owiot."

Not since first meeting George had Fable felt this kind of soul deep need, and honestly, it scared the life out of her.

She'd made herself weak once before, and had nearly paid with her life for it. She'd sworn she'd never do it again. But when she'd woken up this morning without the weight of the demons bearing down on her, and fearing that Owiot had fled, she'd known the choice was no longer her own.

"Always," he said in a steady voice.

*Calypso*

If Calypso's jaw could have hit the floor, it would have hit the floor. Turning her gaze off the sea orb she watched her granddaughter and Owiot through, she looked at her lifelong friend, Aphrodite, with a stunned expression.

"Holy. Tartarus," Dite squeaked, looking much the same way Caly felt.

Hades, who rarely participated in the games, except for an occasional update on his only granddaughter grunted, cleared his throat loudly and said, "I'm going for a walk."

"Mmhmm," Dite chortled after he'd left. "Because he knows those two are gonna get their bow chicka wow wow's on real quick. Did you see the way he looked at her!" She clasped her fingers together and squealed again, before tossing herself back on Caly's clamshell bed with a delirious smile wreathing her pretty face.

But Calypso couldn't speak.

Because the tears that had been lodged in her throat the day she'd found Fable standing over Snow White were about to break loose.

It took Dite more than a second to realize that her normally gregarious friend still hadn't said a word.

Frowning now, looking concerned, she jerked to a sitting position. "Cals?"

And that was it. The proverbial straw that broke the camel's back. Calypso sobbed.

But rather than turn the waves into a choppy tsunami of fury, her tears were happy and grateful and so damned relieved that the waters began to glow an ethereal blue.

The sea animals within joined in their goddess's joy, chattering and swimming happily.

Understanding immediately touched Dite's brows. "Oh, Cals. It's okay, sweetling. She's okay. She's going to be okay. I told you, you'll get her back. Love may not be able to build a mansion of gold, but I've found that love can often do wonders to heal a fractured soul."

Then tugging on Calypso's shoulder, Aphrodite pulled her in for a tight hug, and the elemental goddess who never cried now cried for the second time in so many days. Tears of absolute and incandescent joy, because deep down she knew her granddaughter was truly going to be okay now.

Aphrodite looked back at the sea orb with a bright and happy smile on her face. "I am going to do something for your granddaughter, something I rarely do, my sweet Calypso, but only because I love you so much."

Caly frowned. "What?"

"I am going to meddle," she said sweetly, and then touching the very tip of her finger to the sea orb, she closed her eyes and glowed with love.

The waves of that powerful emotion filtered through her very pores, pouring into the sea orb in rushing, pulsing waves of incandescent mother of pearl. The light show last less than a minute, and when it was done, and Aphrodite no longer glowed, she turned to Calypso and smiled wide.

Her big blue eyes practically gleamed in her stunningly, beautiful face.

"What did you do, Dites?"

Themis, who was mostly a wraith in this games, stepped through into Caly's room just then. Dressed in scuffed jeans at the knees, barefoot, and wearing a Def Leppard t-shirt that cut off at her belly button smiled brightly, her lambent milky white eyes gazed upon them—it was no small thing to be stared down by Justice, only the few with nerves built of steel could endure it, but even Caly got fidgety about it if it lasted too long. Themis had also recently dyed her naturally silver-white hair to a shocking shade of fire-engine red. In short Blindy looked hawt.

Themis was the goddess of justice, and one of a very few on the short list of besties she had.

"I believe I can answer that," she smirked.

Aphrodite rolled her eyes. "Don't start with me, Thems. You'd better not tell me that was breaking any rules because you and I both know—"

"What in holy Tartarus did you do!" Caly snapped, feeling anxious and nervous for her granddaughter.

Themis crossed her arms, glared hotly at Calypso, but then realizing the elemental was about to completely lose her mind, finally sighed deeply and said, "Aphrodite pumped their realm full of love juice. Basically shot them up with a speedball of love, lust, etc., etc," she said as she rolled her wrist.

Calypso frowned. "But weren't they already well on their way to—"

Aphrodite pinched her brows, rubbing them as though she were tired. "Yes. They were. But I wanted to help not only Fable, who I love deeply but you and Hades too, Cals. Their partnership is a true one, no matter how much I might wish I could, if the hearts aren't meant to be joined even I cannot make it so. I simply ensured that the match was accelerated."

"But why?"

Calypso frowned, having a difficult time piecing together why Aphrodite had done that. Fable and Owiot were a true love match, and would have gotten there far sooner than later—as seemed to be the case with a few others in the games, i.e., the Pied Piper and Baba, both stubborn mule-headed women if you asked her.

Themis plopped down beside Calypso and crossed her legs. "No doubt because she knows the prophecy, same as I."

"Prophecy?" For an ancient, Calypso was feeling wholly stupid at the moment. "What prophecy? Why do I not know of this prophecy?"

Aphrodite cringed and hunched her shoulders, and then speaking rapidly said, "Thems and I didn't want to bother you with trivialities, we knew how stressful these games would be on you and didn't wish to worry you."

Calypso glowered. "The Fates spoke with you two?" she snapped, growing increasingly vexed by her besties. The waters around them began to churn.

Blindy gave a snuffling sort of laugh, "Oh, tone it down, crazy. More like I consulted them, you know it is sort of part of my gig. Justice and all." She popped her t-shirt and gave Calypso a soft eye roll, as if to say—you annoy me, but I love you dearly.

One of these days, Calypso was sure she was definitely going to drown their asses. She thinned her lips. "And, what did they say?" she finally snapped after they both sat staring at her like dumb baboons.

"Two will die."

Caly's jaw dropped. "What? Two? But, but...not by our hands. You, yourself told us we couldn't kill any of them, Thems."

Themis shook her head. "You're right. It won't be by any of our hands. But there will be two deaths in these games."

"Can't we fix this?" Caly asked she'd never wanted any of the contestants to perish. Not even the damnable Blue, who she hated with the fires of ten thousand suns.

She'd merely wanted the Blue to taste the pain of regret and sorrow, but not the permanent stroke of death.

Both women shook their heads, but Dite was the one to answer.

"We asked, we even considered stopping the games, but the deaths have been prophesied now, there can be no going back."

Themis sighed. "Our only hope of saving whoever they are is to actually let the games run its course, with us here and monitoring closely; there is the possibility that perhaps, and just maybe, we could somehow work a miracle."

Finally, Calypso understood why Aphrodite had interceded. Looking to her friend, she said softly, "You're trying to make sure it won't be them, aren't you?"

Dites shrugged, looking adorably embarrassed. "For your sakes and hers, I may have cheated just a little. I want them out as quickly as possible, Caly. Surely, you can understand why now?"

While it didn't exactly break the rules of the game, it was definitely a gray and questionable area. But this was her granddaughter, and Calypso would break any rules in heaven or in Tartarus to ensure Fable's safety.

Sighing deeply she nodded. "How much longer until they leave then, Dite?"

Spreading her arms wide, she shrugged. "At a guess, I'd say a few hours to a day or two tops."

If Calypso could stop these games, she would. But there were limits to even what a god could do. They'd enacted the games, and now for better or worse, they had to let the blasted thing run its course.

Crossing her fingers, she looked back at the sea orb and whispered with all her heart, "Fall in love, little darkness, and do it quickly. Grandmother's heart can't take this..."

*Owiot*

The Great Spirit had revealed the truth to him.

Just as he'd asked.

Owiot had known that the immediate pull and draw to Fable couldn't simply be chance. Nothing happened in life without a cause behind it. It wasn't just a quirk of fate that had brought them together.

Fable was his in truth.

The female crafted just for him.

The female he'd waited his whole life for.

In this strange land full of strange peoples he'd finally found her. But now she had to learn the whole truth of him, a truth she would probably not like.

The thought of losing her now was crippling, but he knew he had to be honest with her above all else.

"You look beautiful today, darkness."

Long lashes brushed the tops of her cheeks as she smiled shyly. "Thank you."

When she'd raced down the stairs earlier in the morning, she'd worn nothing but a translucent robe of sheer white dappled with exotic, colorful flowers on the fabric.

She looked like the rare jewel that she truly was and he'd lost his breath for a moment, overwhelmed and dazzled by her beauty.

Now she was dressed in white slip dress that fell to just past her knees and had a peekaboo opening at her shoulders, showing off the gleaming ebony flesh that beckoned him to touch. His fingers twitched helplessly at his sides. The collar of the dress was modest, but also very appealing. It was ruffled and showed just a hint of the tops of her luscious breasts. He wet his lips. Her hair had been twisted up, which should have made her look severe, but she'd placed a wreath of sheer white flowers upon her crown, which had softened her features tremendously. On her feet, she wore dainty slippers that showed off her colored toenails prettily.

Fable was like a breath of fresh air and so different from the woman he'd first met, she looked young and oddly vulnerable, and he found he liked this side of her tremendously.

Last night when he'd opened his *sight* to her, she'd not been the only one to see a vision. He'd seen one too. Of her.

Of the life she'd led. The trauma she'd faced. How she'd clawed her way out of it, turning herself from the trusting and caring person she intrinsically was, into a woman chiseled by iron and forged in steel.

It had made Owiot sick to know the pain she'd felt, the violence that had been done to her. To see her at the end of her rope and so desperate to never be hurt again that she'd turned toward black magick to make her feel safe and strong again.

He now understood why Hades had talked to him as he had.

Taking her swinging hands in his, he squeezed them gently, and then in a moment of need brought them to his lips and tenderly planted a kiss on the palm of each lovely hand.

Her mouth slightly parted and her eyes rounded into tiny saucers of surprise. But his heart was too full and too happy to continue to pretend with her. Hanging tight to her one hand, he crooked his arm for her and slipped her hand through it. His smile grew wider as he felt the tremors course through her.

It was satisfying to know she was as affected by him as he was by her.

He'd not slept much, if anything, last night. His thoughts had been solely consumed by this gorgeous, broken woman.

When he'd returned to his mortal form, he'd asked Sister Mountain Lion and Sister Crow for advice.

As females themselves, they'd given him unique insights into the mind of his paired female. He'd spent the better part of the morning crafting his gift for her.

So far as Owiot understood it, within this sheltered realm built just for him and Fable he retained all of his power. Only once they were in the games would he be crippled and deprived of it.

Taking advantage of that fact, it had been simple enough to reshape and reform this oasis into the one Fable had always imagined she would one day be in.

He'd plucked the images straight from her memories last night and while he'd been excited building it for her, now that he led her toward his surprise he had to admit to a fissure of doubt eating away at his insides.

What if she didn't understand his gesture, or worse, did and simply hated it? He chewed on the inside of his cheek as his stomach twisted with nerves and feelings of idiocy.

"Where are you taking me?" she asked, and his flesh shivered at the husky, morning quality of her already dulcet voice.

Glancing at her, he noted the confused twist of her lips and brows. Such full, kissable lips. Lips he'd just barely touched the day before, but that he now wished he had the right to lean down and claim with authority.

But he couldn't. Not until he told her everything.

Giving her a secretive smile, he led her toward the front of the castle. "It's a surprise."

"Surprise?" She thinned her feline eyes at him. "What kind of surprise? You know not all surprises are the good kinds."

He chuckled. "My jaded, little darkness. What you must think of me. I am not a wolf."

She chuckled. The sound was deep and throaty, and again only reinforcing her feline nature to him. "Are you sure about that? Because I'm fairly certain that you a—"

That *are* quickly switched to an *ahh* when they stepped through the archway and out into the open. Because no longer were they simply a castle in an abandoned forest. The forest had been temporarily transformed into a bustling, fairy tale cosmopolitan of sorts.

There were stores and stalls everywhere. People dressed in exotic garb, some of them pale skinned, but others as dark skinned as his own female meandering about as they smiled, chatted, and shopped.

The buildings themselves were an architectural wonder of stone and wood masonry. Polished facades that climbed into the heavens seven, eight, and sometimes even twenty stories high. But all of it built in a haphazard manner that made it reasonable to believe one strong gust would knock them over.

Women looking like exotic flowers in spools of wildly colored fabric dotted the landscape, while men in slightly tamer versions of the clothing accompanied them.

Chimney stacks set atop each building belched out differing colors of smoke. Some red as molten lava, others blue as the cool waters of Seren itself. In short, this place was a fairy tale wonderland of magic and wonder.

"How did...you?" She turned to him. Unable to even finish the final words, because her eyes gleamed and her jaw trembled.

He cleared his throat, hoping that was an excited reaction and that she wasn't upset.

"These are all my memories?" Unspoken was the word *how*.

Her long fingernails dug in tight to his chest, but he didn't flinch at the feel of them carving crescent moon shapes into his flesh. Instead, he lifted his hand and lightly brushed a loose curl back behind her ear.

She shuddered, and her eyes were like twin magnets holding his own gaze fast. Gods, she was the prettiest thing he'd ever seen in his life.

None of the parading females around them could hold a candle to his female.

"Last night," he said deeply, "I saw your memories."

Her breathing hitched, but he didn't want her to be nervous or scared of him. So he shook his head and rushed on.

"I just wanted to give you a day, Fable, a day where you could live in truth the reality of your dreams. A day where—"

An inarticulate little cry was the only warning he got before she tossed her arms around his neck and tugged him down with a powerful little yank. His brows lifted high on his forehead in shock, but then he surrendered to her unpracticed charms when her gorgeous, full red lips stole a kiss from him.

And this one was far from chaste. Nothing at all like what he'd given her last night.

Her hot, little tongue traced the seam of his lips, demanding he part to her, which he did. Gladly. And a powerful grunt spilled from his throat when he finally tasted of her.

She was sweet.

Like raspberries dipped in sugar—tart and addictive all at the same time. Her kiss didn't last long, but when she finally pulled back, he was shocked to note that he couldn't seem to take a steady breath.

She bit her bottom lip, and he moaned, wanting badly to return the favor.

Thankfully, she was distracted already. Like an excited, young girl she slipped her fingers through his and tugged him forward.

"Oh my goddess, this is amazing," she squealed.

Seriously squealed. Her features were giddy and youthful. Not at all like the woman he'd left back in her room the day before who'd looked weighted down by the cares of the world.

Fable had been choking on the darkness. And though he'd not taken nearly half of it from her, she seemed like a different woman already.

"Look at this place!" She picked up the pace. Looking in awe through one window storefront after another.

There was a hat maker's shop. The glass in front was stenciled with thick white letters boldly declaring "Clara's Milliner, the best hatmaker in all of Kingdom!" And the samples on display seemed to agree.

They were a delight to the eyes—hats in every shape and size and fashion was inside, some were in the shape of fantastical creatures or inventions. Like dragons, ships, and even a typewriter. But there were other more feminine ones, pretty delicate things covered in flowers and spools of gossamer fabric.

It was those—but especially one in particular—that had Fable pressing her nose up to the window with a delighted, feminine gasp. It was a deep purple satin color, with a pearl white netting that covered the face up to the nose. Glued onto the hat itself were crystal clear flowers that almost looked carved of gems the way the twinkled in the light. Her tawny eyes were rounded and entranced, and Owiot grinned. Wanting to give her anything and everything her heart desired right now, even if it was the moon.

"You should take it," he said softly.

She shook her head, and he could practically read the denial sitting heavy on her tongue.

Standing to the side, so that she could look at him, he nodded. "Fable, this day won't last. It's not built to last. This is mostly illusion. Very good illusion. But illusion nonetheless. I created this day for one purpose. So that you might enjoy it. So that you can build a new memory of what your first day should have been like."

Her nostrils flared, and a lone tear slipped from the corner of her eye. But she made no move to brush it away. Instead, she shook her head. "Oh, Owiot. No one has ever done anything like this for me. You have no idea how much this means—"

Twisting his lips, he nodded. "I think I do, beautiful one. Do not thank me. All I ask is that you and I enjoy this day. Tomorrow we fight, today we—"

"Play!" She finished for him. Then with a cheeky grin, she ran, tugging him along with her and shoving into the door.

Immediately a human sized frog dressed in a rich gold gown of brocaded silk hopped forward. She was pretty, if not alien and unusual looking. With big, blue colored eyes, smooth skin, brightly painted red lips and impossibly long eyelashes.

*Ribbbbbit*, her throat pouch bulged as she smiled.

"Hello," she said in a smooth, silken voice. "How might I help you?"

Owiot had been a bit baffled by Fable's dreams when he'd first seen them. Creatures that walked and talked and dressed like man. But he'd soon realized that as a little girl in the below, she'd had no real idea what Kingdom could or would be. She'd simply dreamed dreams any ten-year-old girl might if she lived in a land brimming with magic.

So now, standing in front of the frog clerk, he grinned indulgently at his woman's fantasies, delighted and entranced by the world and scope of her imagination.

If Fable was shocked that a frog lady was attending to them, she didn't show it. Instead, she hooked her thumb unerringly toward the hat resting behind her shoulder.

"That. I want that." She beamed.

Frog girl's grin grew wider. "Excellent choice, mistress! Let's see if we can't also find you a few more while we're at it. Come with me." She gestured, turning and beginning her hop over toward the hat racks.

With a delighted squeal, Fable squeezed his hand one final time and followed the sales clerk.

"My, you have such lovely skin," Frogina—as he now thought of her in his head—said toward a still beaming Fable.

Owiot chuckled, finding an empty spot on a bench to sit and wait. Glancing over at another male, dressed in tweed and holding onto a newspaper with legs crossed and reading with a bored expression, he nodded.

Said man glanced at Owiot side-eyed, "Just got here?" he asked.

"Mm." Owiot nodded.

82

Tweed guy grunted. "Be prepared to be here at least two hours, those damned sales girls know exactly how to turn our females heads."

Owiot chuckled.

Tweed guy was right. Fable was in there almost four.

*Fable*

She couldn't believe how much fun she was having. At first, Fable had worried that the people in this place, whether imaginary or not, would know her by sight. By reputation. Would scream and flee the second it dawned on them who they were dealing with, but no matter how many times she mentioned her name, or even that of Snow White they'd just give her one of those pleasant, but vacant smiles letting her know they had no idea who she or Snow was.

Eventually, she'd settled into a happy rhythm, moving from store front to store front without a care in the world as she shopped to her heart's content.

She knew she'd not get to keep any of this once the day ended, but it was so much fun pretending.

For his part, Owiot was the best company she'd ever had. He'd encourage her to try on one gown after another after another, all the while sitting there and emboldening her each step of the way.

The day was over half gone at this point, and it was suddenly overwhelmingly sad to her that this day should ever end. It had been the best one she'd ever known in her life.

She had bought over twenty items of goods, which they had neatly stacked in boxes around their bench as they sat down for a much-deserved break of tea and cookies.

The tiny café was decorated in nothing but flowering vines. On the walls, on the floors, even wrapped around the legs of the tables, so that one almost felt like they'd fallen through Alice's hole into a world of fairy wonder.

Fable had no love lost for the damned fairies of the tales, but she rather enjoyed her time in this strange and wonderful café.

"Did you have fun?" Owiot asked gravely, as he took a small bite out of an earl gray scented scone.

Setting her petite four down onto the delicate china bone plate painted in pearl pinks and blues, she nodded. "More than I could possibly tell you. I loved every minute of this place, Owiot. And now you also know my deep, dark secret."

He twitched a brow, as though to ask, "what?"

She grinned. "I love to shop."

Her laugh was light and carefree, and she couldn't begin to describe the relief she felt in not feeling tied down to the woman who wore the crown. In this magical place, she was simply Fable—a young woman of Seren, who had just discovered the beauty and wonder and magic of the above, and it was more than she could have ever imagined.

"That's okay by me." He grinned. "I like to watch you shop."

Blushing fiercely, she glanced down at the table full of teas and cake plates. That comment had felt weirdly and wonderfully intimate, and her stomach couldn't seem to stop twisting and turning on itself. She'd hardly touched her tea or cookies, but she was too nervous to eat.

A feminine malady that hadn't overcome her...well, ever. Even when she'd "fallen in love" with George her appetite had always remained intact. But now, she couldn't seem to find it in her to want to do anything other than stare at him. All day long.

Wondering each time she put on a gown...not whether it would fit right or look right, but whether he'd like it. How he'd look at her in it. And each time she'd walked out for his inspection, and his eyes would turn both heated and soft, a region of her heart melted.

83

Fable was beginning to fear that this affliction wouldn't lessen but only continue to grow in intensity with time.

She'd not overthought it when she'd decided to take off her already pretty gown, and replace it instead with a soft lavender slinky dress with a heart shaped bodice and a pile of ruffles that fanned out around her hips and back. There was a long vertical slit on each side that showed off her supple and smooth calves. Her shoes were a deep, royal purple and velvet, which matched the hat she'd spied at the milliner's earlier in the day.

Leaving her hair down, so that it hung soft and loose down her slim shoulders, she'd felt entirely different from the woman she typically was. But she liked that. Loved it in fact, because here she wasn't the evil queen. Not once had Owiot ever made her feel that way, and it was easy now to recall the memories of the young girl she'd once been and view those recollections, not with bitterness and self-loathing, but fondly and happily.

Flicking a glance toward his face, already knowing he was looking at her intently, she still shivered all over again at the quiet intensity of the man. Never once in her life had she thought this of anyone, but Owiot was simply perfect.

Not just in looks, but in his heart.

He was kind and sweet and gentle, and so damned thoughtful that she felt almost overwhelmed by him. Expecting for him to show his ugly side at some point. Because everyone had one. No one was perfect.

Not even her beloved mother and father, and definitely not her grandmother or grandfather. But that was why she loved them because they were flawed. Maybe not as badly as she was, but they were real and tangible.

With Owiot she almost felt overwhelmed because it wasn't possible for someone to be this kind and gentle and well...bloody, damn perfect.

She scowled, which he noted immediately.

"What's the matter? Is the food—"

Holding up her hand to stall his words, she shook her head. "No. It's nothing. Don't mind me. I'm simply too far into my head for my own good sometimes."

"Want to talk about it?" he asked, setting down his napkin and sitting back in his seat in a relaxed posture.

A woman dressed in a skimpy and sheer dress that fell to her ankles sauntered past. She had buxom breasts and hips and skin nearly the complexion of Owiot himself, with sultry cat eyes and full red lips. In short she was gorgeous, and Fable froze, waiting to see him turn his gaze toward her. Or even just a flick of movement to show he saw her just as George would often do on the rare occasions they'd dined in the banquet hall together. But not once did Owiot turn away.

And rather than feel relieved by that, she got irrationally upset. "You're too bloody perfect."

"What?" he frowned as if confused by her statement.

Growling beneath her breath, thinking this might have all been a bad idea after all, she flicked her fingers. "Nothing. Don't mind me. I'm in a weird mood all of a sudden."

"What do you need me to do, Fable?"

And that was exactly the problem. He'd done too much already. More than she could ever repay him for. None of this was his fault either. How awful was it that she was growing upset because he was perfect? How fair was that? And yet kindness such as he'd shown her had rarely been done in her life, it had been so rare in fact, that she didn't trust it. Wasn't sure she knew how to either.

"Just talk to me, Owiot."

"About?" he asked, shrugging and looking upset that she was unhappy which in turn caused her to get upset about the fact that she was going to self-sabotage like she was prone to do, but not knowing how in the world to stop it either.

Searching for something, anything, she latched onto the first idea that popped into her head. "Tell me a story. About your people."

Blinking, and still looking at her strangely—like he was confused—but also wanting to please her, he nodded. "Okay. Anything, or was there—"

"Anything." She rolled her wrist. "I don't know. It doesn't matter."

He grinned and her heart threatened to tear from her chest it beat so hard. She wanted to reach over to him and tell him she was sorry, ask him to forgive her for being like this. For being her. For being so incapable of accepting kindness as a reality that she was going to wind up pushing him away.

This day had been utterly perfect.

Why couldn't that be enough for her?

"Okay. How about the story of how the worlds began?"

Her lips twitched, curious despite herself. She and Owiot came from far different realms. She already knew the story of how Kingdom began.

The Ten made it so. Fairies of such power that the strength of their combined wills created all the magic and creatures that inhabited this world.

"Sure," she said softly. "Tell me your story."

Instantly Owiot transformed. His eyes took on a sparkle and a radiance of light lit him up from within so that he gently glowed. It wasn't an overt glow, she had to squint to really see it, but he did, and her stomach grew warm. Gods, he was gorgeous.

"Long ago a great island floated in a giant ocean. This island hung from four thick ropes at each end of the sky." He held up his arms, demonstrating for her the ropes.

She sighed. Couldn't help it. Owiot was in his element and misgivings or not; she was helpless to resist his lure. "Mmhmm," she mumbled, "go on."

"There were no peoples, and it was always dark. The animals could not see, and so they grabbed the sun and set it in the sky so that it would move from east to west each day. Then the Great Spirit told the animals and plants that they must remain awake for seven days and not to sleep. But not all the animals and plants could. Those that did like the pine and cedar were rewarded with staying green all year long. But as punishment all the others were made to lose their leaves. The animals that stayed awake, such as the owl and mountain lion were rewarded by being able to see in the dark. Soon after First Man and First Woman appeared and with them came the first children, Changing Twins—"

Fable was entranced by his storytelling ability, his natural ease, and rhythm with which he told his tale. How his entire body got into the act of the telling of it. He moved his arms, and his smile never wavered. All around onlookers gawked at him, immediately drawn to his innate charm that oozed from his pores, and she was unable to keep her thoughts to herself any longer.

"You're amazing. Do you know that, male?" Her words sounded far sadder than she'd meant them too.

Slowly he lowered his arms, looking at her intently. "I hear a 'but' in there."

She shrugged, not bothering to deny it.

His finger was under her chin, tipping it up again and forcing her to look back at him. "But what, darkness? Do you not care for my stories?"

Swatting at his hand, not hard, but not gently either she clamped down on her tumultuous emotions at the flash of hurt that crossed through his dark gaze.

"That's just the thing, Owiot. I care too much. I love it. I love everything about this place..." *I even think I love everything about you...*

She clamped her lips shut. She'd never tell him what she'd just thought. Ever. She'd trusted once before and nearly died because of it. She was a fool, a fool, and idiot to think she could afford to do it again.

A muscle in his jaw ticked as he clenched down on his back teeth. "I am pushing you away as I do everyone else. I've tried hard to tamp down my magic around you, Fable, tried hard to—"

"Goddess!" she snapped, unable to bear it another second. "It's not you, okay." And the laugh that spilled off her tongue sounded frantic and slightly crazed to her own ears.

She was falling. Too fast and too hard and she was terrified. That was the truth.

"Look. I know when people say it's not you it's me they don't mean it."

His nostrils flared, and he looked away, and it killed her. Killed her. She hated it. Wanted to stomp her foot in disgust at herself for doing what she always did. He didn't deserve this. Didn't deserve her craziness, it wasn't Owiot's fault that George had ruined her so completely.

"Then if not me, what is it," he asked, and she could sense he was holding back his own impatience, still being horribly and wonderfully perfect to her.

And she could no longer conceal it. "You're perfect. Too damn perfect. And it's killing me, okay. If that's what you want to know. No one is totally perfect. But you created this beautiful world for me, and these gowns, and this beautiful hat," she flicked at the veil and sniffed, fighting back the stupid tears she was so tired of crying, "he ruined me, Owiot. George ruined me, and I don't know how to trust people anymore. I'm a horrible, bad person, and you shouldn't want anything to do with me. I hurt and destroy anyone who gets too close to me."

His fingers were so strong and warm when they found hers. And though she was breathing heavy and fighting the damned tears with all she was worth, she looked up at him, miserable to the very root of her soul.

"I'm not perfect, darkness. Not by a long shot."

She swallowed hard. "You're just saying that. Trying to make me feel better, it won't—"

His lips twisted into a painful scowl. The first time she'd ever witnessed him looking anything other than calm, and the words died on her tongue. Instantly she wanted to ease his suffering, his pain. She squeezed his fingers back.

"Owiot?" she asked softly.

And when he swallowed thickly, she knew he fought his own tears. "Fable, I did not want to tell you this yet, but...I killed my wife."

# Chapter 13

*Fable*

First, she went cold, and then a strange buzzing filled her ears. Snatching her hand back from his, it wasn't Owiot she stared at now, but George. George with his blond hair and blue eyes and wicked heart who promised her the world and stole her soul instead, crushing it to powder and turning her bitter.

Closing his eyes, he shook his head. "This is all wrong. I want to show you something."

Her nostrils flared. Because though her brain told her over and over that this was Owiot, not George, her heart was a mangled ruined mess and the only thing she could focus on was the fact that he'd killed his wife. Just as George had.

Owiot snatched up her hand, brought it to his lips and kissed her knuckles tenderly. And though she still ached from his words, her body couldn't help but respond, and that terrified her.

Terrified her that it was far too late for her to back out of this now, even knowing he was the devil come to snatch away what last little parts of her were still good.

"Trust me, darkness. Though you do not need to, I ask that you would. I ask you to have faith in me. Will you?"

And though it was the hardest thing she'd ever done in her life, she swallowed her pain and fears and simply said, "Yes."

His lashes fluttered closed briefly, and then he flicked his wrist and instantly the beautiful world he'd created for her vanished. Disappeared like it had never been. He still gripped her hand as they floated through a canvas of impenetrable sky.

Tugging her tight into his body, he held her easily against his form. As though shielding her, hugging her, and she sighed from the contact of him along the length of her. He pointed over her shoulder and whispered in her ear, "Look at that star and see my sins for what they are, beautiful darkness, and then you can decide whether I'm worth saving or not."

He was gone. And the world that had been nothing but void was gone too. Fable stood in a grassy plain full of rolling wheat and surrounded by majestic snow-capped mountains on all sides.

The sky was a beautiful lavender-orange, and the sun was barely a dot left in it.

And that was when she saw them.

Owiot and someone else, a stunningly beautiful woman with nut-brown hair that fell past her waist dressed in a beaded deerskin dress that stopped at her knees. Her lips were a pale shade of mauve and pink. Her facial structure was delicate and extremely feminine.

Not sharp and slashing like Fable's own. Where Fable had a strong jaw line, this woman had a soft, heart-shaped one. Fable's cheekbones were high; hers weren't. Fable had a strong nose. This woman's was small and rounded.

They were opposites in every way.

Painted beneath her eyes was a striking thick strip of turquoise blue that caused her warm brown eyes to look even deeper and more mysterious.

Walking beside her was Owiot, strong, gorgeous, and wearing a frown. The sadness in his eyes was striking and caused Fable to place a hand on her chest, curling it in tight.

87

She wanted to take that sadness from him. Wanted to hug him. To fix him.

"Aiyana, what are you saying?"

Her eyes flashed stormily back at him. And heavy black clouds began to gather overhead.

"I do not want you, Owiot. I never have. And I never will."

"But you said that you lo—"

Rolling her eyes heavily, she crossed her arms over her chest and sneered. "Did you really think anyone could love you? You!" She laughed, and the sound of it was cruel and biting. "When I am with you, you make me want to slit my throat. Your touch sickens me. Your kisses make me want to retch. I could never be happy with you."

Every word was like a dagger to his heart. Fable could see the pain written in his dark brown eyes. He stood before Aiyana, his wife, clenching and unclenching his fists and staring at her with desperation.

"Please, Aiyana, do not do this. You know what will happen to you if you choose this. It would kill me. I could not see harm come to you ever."

"Ha!"

Rain began to pelt the land around them, bringing fist-sized hail chunks down with it. But neither of them flinched as they were pelted by it, both of them far too angry to focus on the pain.

"Anything would be better than being forced to lie with you another day."

He blinked, looking stunned. "You don't mean that. You would never have married me if—"

Her lip curled. "I did it only to spare my brother's crops. His land is fertile now, thanks to my sacrifice. Let me go, Owiot."

"Please. Don't do this." He closed his eyes.

And Fable was confused. Because she was expecting to see a raging madman, bent on forcing his wife to remain with him. But he was pleading, begging her to not to leave him. The way the rain fell looked like tears running down his cheeks.

But Aiyana was fiercely cold and disgusted, shaking her head and laughing. "You don't have a choice, and you know it."

"You cannot leave me. You know what will happen if you do. I won't have a choice. You were a mortal; you would fade if you severed your soul from mine. I will never touch you again. Never come around you again, only do not choose this path. Please."

She snorted. "Yes, you would. And you know it. You'll come back like a scampering coyote, begging me to give you that family, those bastard children you've always wanted. But I am done. Through. My legacy to my family will be fertile land that is all I ever wanted. The only way to ensure I never have to see you again is to leave. And so I will. I have chosen, and there is nothing you can do to change my mind."

Closing his eyes, he looked like a man shattered. Fable's hands clenched, feeling the tight gathering of her dark magick crawl through her bones. Even knowing what she witnessed was nothing more than a memory of the past, she wanted to hurt Aiyana, kill her even. Destroy the woman bringing such misery to a good man like him.

"Is this truly want you want?" he asked softly, but his words echoed on the wind.

Hate burned through her eyes. "Yes. Untether our souls."

He nodded and moved like he'd just aged a thousand lifetimes in the span of seconds he called forth a glowing ball of blue light.

Fable gasped, recognizing the draw of soul magic. The sphere was a mix of dark and light blues that glittered like sapphire ash in the sunlight. And she knew that the light blue was Owiot's own.

Souls, like hearts, could be stained with darkness if the person was too full of sins. She knew because she'd seen hers before. Fable's was a blue so deep as to be nearly black.

Owiot's was pure and so lovely it brought tears to her eyes.

With each twist of the soul orb, Aiyana trembled, weakening before Fable's eyes. But each time Owiot tried to stop, she would shake her head and force him to continue.

Until finally, with one last tiny tug, he pulled their souls apart.

There were no theatrical death throes from Aiyana. She simply gasped and dropped to the earth, dead before impact.

And where once there'd been a beautiful and nubile woman, the husk that lay on the ground was withered and ancient looking, almost nothing but flesh over bones.

But Owiot didn't seem phased by it. With a great cry that rent the sky with lightning and thunder, he dropped to his knees, gathering the desiccated corpse to his chest and hugged her tight.

"I would have given you the world, Aiyana. Why was I never enough for you? Why?"

The broken shell of a voice coming out of the man broke something inside of Fable. No longer did she see him as too perfect and far beyond her reach, but as strangely human and in need of saving himself.

No one had ever wanted her to save them. Because that's not what she did. Fable destroyed. But she didn't want to destroy him, fast or no, magical or not...she didn't know how this was happening, all she did know was that Owiot was the male created in all the cosmos just for her.

Not George.

Not Charles.

She hadn't met her perfect match before and thus had been miserable. She'd forced the fates hands and had paid dearly for it. But lingering in the cosmos far away had been a male that would make Fable want to be more.

Be infinitely better than she'd been.

Owiot kissed Aiyana's brow one final time, and as he did so, the body turned to dust, sifting through his hands like sand in an hourglass. But her ashes did not scatter as they should. Instead, godlight from within his own form poured down into what had once been Aiyana, transforming her one final time, into that of a perfect and beautiful white flower painted with thick bands of turquoise blue upon its perfectly shaped petal.

*Owiot*

When the scene faded, and Fable stood before him, he waited on tenterhooks to hear what she'd say. Owiot had lost love once before and had survived it. He could survive this too, though he'd felt the type of instant connection and bond to Fable that only came around once in a lifetime.

He'd survive her leaving, but he knew he'd never be the same again.

She looked like an angel in spring when she finally turned toward him. The clothes she'd found in the temporary world they'd called their own for the day had vanished along with it. She was back to wearing what she'd been when the day had first begun.

Her hair was a wild halo of dark ebony flowing like a wave down her back. The wreath of wildflowers twined through the strands made her look youthful, almost fairy-like. In a word, she was stunning and stole his breath.

Without saying a word, she walked into his space, wrapped her arms around his neck and pulled him down for a kiss.

The kiss was as soft as a petal's touch, but her words whispered through his veins like fire as she said, "take us home, Owiot."

# Chapter 14

*Fable*

He returned them back to their castle. To the familiar environment, she'd come to know as her temporary home away from home. Rolling hills full of gorgeous conifers and majestic oaks. Sky still blazing that strange-hued orange and lavender color of perpetually encroaching night. Birds still trilling and singing their songs.

This place brought her peace, but so too did the man she still held hands with.

Owiot glanced down at her face, his eyes intense as though hoping to peer into her soul. She felt he was seconds away from leaving her again unless she stopped him first.

"Well, I suppose—"

Squeezing his fingers tight, she shook her head. "Walk with me. Please."

Tiny smile lines kissed the corners of his eyes. "Where?"

No hesitation, no stuttering...the fact that he seemed just as keen as she was to remain in his presence was telling and made her feel weak with relief. She shrugged.

"Outside? Maybe."

He nodded.

They'd yet to really explore the castle proper, but Fable was discovering that she rather enjoyed nature more than she'd expected to. A stone tower had been her home for so long, it was what she knew, where she'd always been most comfortable, but now the thought of going into that tower...alone, it made her anxious.

Owiot turned on his heel, taking her along with him, and walking them out the door. The moment they were back outside, she inhaled the rich scent of pine and damp earth deep into her lungs, feeling her soul settle within her.

They walked in companionable silence for several minutes before Owiot finally asked, "Tell me something about yourself, Fable. Something no one else knows."

"What?" She grinned, feeling ridiculously giddy and carefree. "What something?"

But she wasn't the only one feeling that sentiment; the same emotions were clearly scrawled across his handsome features as well.

"I don't know. What's your favorite color?"

She snorted. "Black. And that's hardly a secret."

He lifted a brow, studying her. "Black?"

"Yes. And? What's the problem?" She sassed him. Enjoying their easy, silly conversation. "And please don't tell me that white makes me look pure because I swear I'll stab you with a rusted knife if you—"

Turning toward her, his large palms settled on her slim shoulders. Owiot towered over her. Not a position she was generally fond of, but with him, it made her feel somehow comforted and safe.

"You would look stunning in whatever you wore. But you're a rare flower that should stand out, my darkness, not remain hidden in shadow."

*Oh my...*

She trembled.

He'd called her, *my darkness.* She wondered if he knew the proprietary stance he'd just taken with her and then realized that he probably had because he'd been slipping those little endearments throughout most of their conversations all day.

Fact was, everything Owiot had done today had cemented one very important fact for her. She liked it. Like, liked him liked him. Like, possibly even felt the first tingles of love liked him.

90

And yes, she knew how stupid and foolish of her it was to give into these emotions yet again. But she'd been without love for so long, been so starved for it, that sadly any sort of attention to her personage that was positive would have probably ensured her eventual downfall.

It was a sad fact, but Fable had been beyond lonely. It really wouldn't have taken much to make her drop her guard this way. Well, here anyway. In a land as far removed and distant from the Enchanted Forest as feasibly possible it was easy enough to do. Had she met Owiot in the Enchanted Forest she doubted she'd have given him more than a cursory glance, and certainly not a second of her time. There she wore her mask like a shield.

Leaning up on tiptoe she knew she was being reckless and imprudent, but she was so tired of fighting this.

"What color should I be in then?" she asked in her huskiest drawl.

His pupils dilated, taking up nearly all of his irises and she couldn't help but smirk. Enjoying the fact that she held such power over him already. And not because she'd tapped into black magick, no, this power was purely innate and made her giddy with joy.

A man she liked liked her back. It was as simple as that, and it was glorious.

He ran the pads of his fingers down her bicep, sliding it along the half sleeve of her dress and her flesh at the same time, breaking her out in a heated wash of desperate longing.

"White, my darkness. I love you in white."

George had also liked her in white. And for years, she'd learned to hate the color, but she didn't hate it now.

She pursed her lips, so close to his own that she shared breath with him. It would be nothing to lean up and snatch a kiss from him. He'd let her. She knew it.

But Fable wanted a lot more than just a kiss.

"I'll keep that in mind," she said, and this time, she didn't have to try to make her voice sound husky because it already naturally was.

It was his turn to shiver.

Unable to resist from touching him as she'd wanted to all day, she threaded her fingers through his silken hair, playing idly with the feather tied into it. His eyelids flickered with suppressed desire.

And that's when she made the decision.

She was going to make love to him.

Tonight.

No regrets. No matter what. Strong magic was at work here, ancient and primal magic that was the very solid basis and foundation for all of Kingdom. The power of true mates converging.

Fable had been around her Auntie Aphrodite long enough to recognize the taste and texture of it, and it was here. All around them, but it was delicate magic still. Just barely in its infancy. Like a budding bloom still young and weak on the surface, but it was just beneath the surface where the true power gathered. All it needed was a little spark, a little nudge to turn the ember into a flame.

But did she dare?

"You want to know something about me, Owiot?" she asked sweetly, softly.

He grunted in an adorable fashion, and she decided to take the leap, to brave the unknown and trust that just this once, she didn't have to fear her heart being broken.

"The last time I was really happy was the day I turned seventeen. I still lived in the below, in Seren, with my family. And though I had a good family, the reason why I was so happy was because that was the day that I finally got to fulfill my dream of going to the above. Stepping through that portal between realms was the very last memory I have of knowing true joy."

His gaze turned sad, and she took a deep breath because she wasn't done. What she was about to do now, it was either the stupidest or the bravest thing she'd ever done in her life. Only time would tell. Ignoring the razor tipped butterfly wings swarming through her belly she whispered the words straight from her heart.

"Until now, Starlight. Until you." Then she framed his face with her hands and waited, fingers twitching from fear and the silent recriminations that maybe she'd misunderstood his subtle cues, maybe she shouldn't have said—

"Darkness," he moaned.

Full on shivery moaned too. Like a mix between a growl and a groan of desperate need and she dug her toes into the thick carpet of grass.

And then they were moving, being whisked through a tunnel of stars. And she wasn't the one doing it. It was his magic that spirited them away.

Then they were there.

Wherever there was. A land brimming with starlight and fae light that twinkled through the dusky blue sky. Flowers with bright red and pink bulbs swayed as high as her hips and gave off an exotic perfume of Eastern realm scents—midnight jasmine and dusky patchouli.

The field of flowers stretched out as far as the eye could see in every direction.

She swallowed. "Flowers?"

His touch was firm, and sure as he brushed them up her arms, telling her exactly why he'd brought her here.

Her stomach flipped almost painfully to her knees, and her pulse couldn't seem to stop hammering through her veins.

"Because," he said in that same scratchy tenor, "this is how I see you, my darkness."

She frowned, but his fingers brushed at the lines, smoothing them out. "As my exotic flower. This is where you should lay your head every night, beneath the stars, in a field full of flowers."

Fable wasn't sure what she was nodding about, but she was nodding all the same.

"And this," he said, stepping so close into her sphere of space that not an inch of distance separated them now, "is where I'll make love to you tonight. If you'll let me."

"Yes," she squeaked. "Yes, oh goddess yes."


*Owiot*

She'd seen his darkest hour, witnessed the life he'd had to end, the life he'd loved then and even now, and Fable still wanted him.

Her enthusiastic yes had almost completely undone him.

Feeling the animal of the Great Spirit within him stir to life, he growled triumphantly and then proceeded to do to Fable as he'd dreamt of doing since the very first moment he'd seen her.

"I love this dress on you," he said, then dug his fingers into the square collar and with a firm yank ripped the fabric in two. Exposing a long vee of smooth, polished ebony skin to his greedy and voracious gaze.

She gasped, chest heaving, causing her beautifully rounded breasts to rise and fall sharply.

With a greedy groan, he cupped one breast in his large palm. Her skin was so soft, like the velvet touch of a rose petal. Her flesh puckered under his touch, and the constant heavy sway of her breaths was an erotic and hypnotizing sight. He squeezed delicately and then unable to resist the temptation of her any longer, he shrugged the tattered edge of her dress down to her waist with his free hand, exposing the fullness of her from the waist up.

The contrast of them together, it was a sight to behold.

He was mahogany. She was ebony. Reddish-brown and deepest black—like earth and sky when they met each night. Her nipples were even darker than the rest of her, and small disks the size of his thumb. Her stomach was flat, but toned muscle. Her neck was long, like a black swan's—a thing of regal and majestic beauty.

"My gods," he whispered in reverent delight.

92

She curled her finger beneath his jaw, forcing him to look into her golden, tawny eyes. Eyes that practically glowed in the moonlight.

With the fae light dancing behind her, and the swaying blooms all around them, it was easy to imagine that Fable was little more than a mirage. An image he'd conjured up from the deepest depths of his heart to fill the void there for so long.

But like fog over rolling waters, spirits always faded with the morning light, and he was terrified she'd do the same.

"Will you leave me, Fable?" he asked without censure, without thought, both panicked and nervous to hear her response.

She shook her head. "I'm here now, Owiot."

It wasn't the answer he wanted, but it would have to do for now. Sliding his hand down to where the fabric had bunched around her waist, he tugged at it, and she took the hint. She shimmied her hips as she helped him push it down. It slipped off her easily, puddling at her feet in a snow-white heap.

Taking a measured step back, he drank in the sight of her. Nude beneath the moonlight, wearing only a smile and a wreath of white flowers, he suffered the strangest urge to grab her and never let go.

"Stop thinking and just look at me, Starlight," she said it softly, and the words carried on the jasmine scented breeze like the toll of bells.

Then lifting her hands above her head, she began to sway. Her legs were long and lean, her center was neatly trimmed, and though he couldn't wait to go exploring, he was entranced by the glide of her hips. Broader than her waist by several inches, she was a voluptuous woman, and his entire body ached to join with her.

"Did you know?" she said, as she continued to sway. "That I am more than mere darkness?"

Clearing his throat to try and clear the fog of lust from his brain long enough that he could concentrate on her words, he said, "No."

Her rose red lips tipped up at the corners. "I am. I am shadow too. I am the deepest depths of the ocean blue. Black as the night and mysterious as the void."

And then her swaying became more powerful, quicker. Until her form began to blur, to become echo images of herself, and then finally...she fractured apart into banding swirls of pearly grays and black.

That shadow moved like a thought toward him, surrounding him in a tight embrace. He inhaled deeply, skin breaking out in a wash of heated need as he felt the flow and swell of her power, her presence move over him like massaging fingers. From the crown of his head to the tips of his feet.

The pressure at his cheek increased, and he knew she'd kissed him then, but she didn't stop. She continued to pepper his jaw, his nose, his forehead, cheeks, and neck until he was gasping for breath from her phantom kisses.

And all the while he felt her finger-like touch move all over him.

As quickly as it had begun, her power snapped back, and she was form once more. A woman of night and shadow, smiling up at him with a mischievous twinkle in her lioness eyes.

"Nice bum," she said in a husky drawl.

Frowning, he glanced down and then chuckled.

It was only then that he realized her movements hadn't been random at all, she'd undressed him and he'd never even noticed. His leggings had been tossed to who knew where. Away. Probably gone for good. But he didn't care. He could fashion another.

"Fable," he said.

"Yes, Owiot?"

Her scent of flowers overwhelmed his senses. He wanted to take her; to drive into her as was his nature. With primal abandon and enthusiasm. But he didn't dare until he got her consent. Deep down he'd always suspected that Aiyana's leaving had had everything to do with his strong sexual appetites. In life he was gentle, thoughtful, and caring, but when it came to sex his desires were claiming and even sometimes crazed.

93

"Can you accept me as I am?"

Her gaze traveled slowly down, landing on his rock hard and painfully aching penis and remaining there for several long, tense seconds as her grin slowly grew wider and wider. Wetting her lips, she finally said, "Oh, I think I can handle whatever you've got to give me, male."

That was all he needed to know.

Closing the scant distance between them, he yanked her to him. Owiot was a god, a god born of the sky god himself. A powerful and majestic spirit built of thunder and lightning.

When he took her, the sky began to rumble.

She gasped, but not with fear. Slamming her form tight to his, he hooked a foot behind her knee and twisted, causing them both to tumble to the ground. He shifted, to take the brunt of the fall.

A startled laugh dropped off her tongue, but that laugh soon turned into a moan when he rolled her onto her back and cupped both her breasts in hand.

"Oh goddess," she whimpered.

Lowering his head, he took one tight bud into his mouth, suckling and laving his tongue along the turgid bit of pebbled flesh. Her nails dug into his scalp as she began to writhe and moan beneath him.

But he wasn't done. He nipped at her nipple too. Biting down until he left a crescent mark, not hard enough to break the skin, but hard enough to let her know she was with him. Hard enough to leave his mark, his imprint upon her.

Her back bowed, and a keening noise crawled up her throat. "Owiot! More!"

With an animal growl, he forced himself off the one breast, and onto the other. Her skin tasted of salt, soap, and perfume—an intoxicating combination that he wanted to lick and suckle at all night long.

He could love on her breasts forever, but there was another area of her body that he wished to become more intimately familiar with.

Moving over her body, and trapping her legs between his, he proceeded to move slowly down. Taking his time as he meandered closer and closer to the heated core of her femininity. He pressed kisses onto her stomach, her ribs, nipped and suckled at her sweet belly button.

And the farther south he went, the more wild and jerky her movements became. Then he kissed her inner thigh, and she tensed up.

"Holy Tartarus!" She grunted, halfway sitting as her stomach flexed and her nails dug in deeper to his scalp.

She took a fistful of his hair in hand and tugged.

Her eyes were aglow with lust and desire. Her full lips looked swollen and bee stung, as though she'd been biting down hard on them.

"You don't waste any time, do you, big guy?"

His only answer was a throaty chuckle. With a flick of his head, he jerked out of her grip, and spread her legs wide, exposing her to his greedy gaze.

She was pink and flushed down there. He'd expected every inch of her to be as dark as the rest, so it was shocking—almost hypnotizing—to see such vivid color.

"Fable, my Fable," he murmured, incoherent with desire.

She'd sat up and was resting her weight on her hands. Knowing exactly what he wanted, what he needed, she nodded.

Moving one of her hands, she set it on the crown of his head and pushed gently. The sky exploded with lightning, streaking across the navy blue canvas with violent veins of silver and gold.

Then she laid back, and he settled in to feast.

# Chapter 15

*Fable*

The man—god—was as gorgeous nude as he was dressed. His skin gleaming like polished cherry wood.

His cock had been more than adequate in size and beautifully veiny and plump at the tip. His abdomen as hard as granite and both smooth and rippled as she'd wandered her fingers over him. With his long hair billowing behind him, she'd felt like the luckiest girl in the world.

That was until he'd decided to start their night off between her thighs.

When Owiot had asked for permission, she hadn't exactly expected him to go down there so soon. She'd had plenty of lovers in her life, and eventually, they'd gotten around to oral intercourse, but never on the first time. It had always been something they'd had to work themselves up to.

But this god was voracious and hungry, and she was more than glad to oblige.

She curled her fingers into the long stalks of jeweled colored grass and stared up at the nighttime sky that looked ready to tear itself apart with its fury and waited for the first touch of him.

Fable didn't have to wait long.

His hot tongue slid from top to bottom in one long, smooth, cat-like stroke.

"Holy gods," she squeaked, nearly dying from the electric caress of that velvety tongue.

But then he was latching onto the jewel at the very center of her and sucking in hard as he swirled his tongue, and she swore that she'd suddenly forgotten how to breathe.

The world was splintering apart around them, and she could have cared less if she'd died in it. All she knew was she would die without his mouth on her bringing her to a type of frenzied climax she'd never experienced in all of her days.

"Owiot. Owiot!" she moaned his name incoherently over and over, tossing her head from side to side as she screwed her eyes shut and chased the little death threatening to kill her.

But then he brought his thumb into play as well, and that was her undoing. She climaxed so violently and brutally that she shifted into shadow against her will, clinging tightly to his body with all her might, terrified and afraid that if she didn't she'd never find herself whole again.

When she finally felt safe enough to open her eyes, Owiot was grinning down at her, and lightly rubbing circles onto her back. He looked content, but she was far from it.

With a hungry cry, she shoved against his chest, tossed him down and then said laughingly, "Did you really think you were done?"

His eyes were wide but laughing. "What did you have in mind, my darkness?"

"More. More. More."

She slammed her mouth down to his, violently, shivering as he accepted that aspect of her so easily. She clawed, bit, and knocked teeth with him, and he was right there with her. Raking his fingers down her spine, making her bow her back in almost pain but all of it mixed up with so much pleasure.

His hot, hard length poked her in the arse, making her squirm with delicious need. He grunted, gripping her lower spine and holding her still.

"Keep it up, my feral one, and I won't last much longer." He grunted.

"Oh, but you will." She singsonged. "You are a god after all."

He chuckled. "Not of fertility, even I have my limitati—"

95

"Ssh." She nuzzled his nose, then stole a kiss, swiping her tongue along the seam of his mouth until he automatically opened to her. "Too much talking," she mumbled, before dipping in and tasting of the starlight he was made of.

Kissing Owiot was like sucking in the cosmos. It was infinite and unfathomable—stars, and planets, and the never-ending delights of creation itself, a beautiful universe of chaos and shifting lights and colors. She was addicted to his taste. Needing him inside of her now, she rose up just slightly on her knees and then impaled herself.

He howled. Literally tossed his head back, elongating his neck—causing the cords of his tendons to stand out—as he gave into his animal form. He did not shift into an animal, but he was more than merely human now.

Owiot bristled with the divine. His skin glowed, his hair gleamed, his eyes burned, and he was all hers. Every last gorgeous inch of him.

He broke away from her kiss then, staring her in the eyes and she felt herself falling, sliding into that tunnel of stars, but she wasn't ready to lose herself just yet.

Fable grabbed his head and forced his mouth to her left breast. Like the good boy he was, he knew exactly what she wanted and sucked her nipple into his moist heat.

"Oh gods," she groaned as his tongue swirled around and around, "I'm coming, Owiot. I'm coming."

Just a little bit more, one last swivel of her hips would get her there. He slammed his hips up just as she slammed down and then she could no longer fight it. This time, Owiot didn't give her a choice. This time, he grabbed her face.

"Look at me, darkness," he grunted.

And it was the tone of his voice that forced her to open her eyes. Because when he spoke she heard the eagle, the coyote, the crow, and the mountain lion shiver behind each word.

She was fracturing, splintering into a thousand tiny pieces of herself, but he was right there to catch her. Even as she slid into that endless, yawning chasm of starlight, he was there. He was everywhere.

And Fable knew, deep in her soul, that what they'd done tonight...there'd be no coming back from that. Ever.

Owiot, was sadly, not a fertility god. He'd only managed to make love three more times before he'd been forced to collapse from exhaustion.

Though she couldn't really complain. Her body was nothing but jelly and ached in places it had not ached in for years, but only in the most glorious way, of course.

They still lay in the field of night and flowers, curled around one another. The sky had settled back into a peaceful, quiet solitude full of ethereal white clouds.

He was strumming her back, staring up and wearing a small smile.

"Owiot," she said after watching him in silence for ten minutes.

Finally, he turned to her, and she returned his grin to see the starlight dancing through his milk chocolate eyes.

"Yes?"

"Why do they call you the god of children?"

He chuckled. And the sound was nice.

Actually, there wasn't anything about her male that wasn't nice. He had a sexy voice, a hypnotic voice, and smelled great. Amazing really. Like musk and wood smoke and earth and woodsy cologne mingled with something a little more exotic, though she wasn't sure what. All she knew was she couldn't get enough of him.

Snorting, he shrugged, watching as she leaned up on an elbow to run her fingers across his smooth chest. No hair. None at all. Most men she'd been with had at least a little, some had a lot. But not Owiot. He even had very little leg hair. It was like all that hair had decided to grace the crown of his very gorgeous hair instead; she'd never seen a man with such thick head hair.

God, she had it bad.

"It was Aiyana's doing."

Fable frowned. "Your wife? But I thought she was human. How was she able to give you a—"

"No." He shook his head. "She did not bestow the title upon me. She visited Mother Buffalo, who told her that I was the god of children."

She lifted a brow. "That's it? Just like that. Oh, by the way, Aiyana, your lover, he's the god of children. So go make babies."

He laughed heartily at her words, and she couldn't help but chuckle too. She felt so carefree and easy with him, so unlike her normal self. This was a side of her few rarely were privileged to see, a side she thought she'd never reveal to another. The fact that the Evil Queen actually had a sense of humor would likely have rocked the Enchanted Forest to its very foundation and caused many to die of shock.

"She wouldn't go deep into details about it." The laughter slowly faded from his eyes and his mood turned pensive.

Fable sensed the shift in him immediately and stilled, wondering if she'd said or done something wrong.

"I believe that in my heart, it was that conversation exactly with Mother Buffalo that caused Aiyana's heart to turn from me."

He was staring broodily off into the distance, and the sadness that he always kept wrapped so closely to himself, began to disperse to the winds. And suddenly everything looked a little more sad, a little more gloomy and melancholy. The burden of carrying that emotion all alone, it must have been horrible for him. She couldn't help but wonder if anyone at all during his life had ever helped share in the pain of it.

"Look at me, Owiot," she murmured, lightly trailing her finger along his chin, noticing for the first time that he had a silvery scar that ran from the base of his neck to the very tip of his chin.

It was thin now, and not very wide, but based on its length alone she knew it had to have been extremely painful when he received the wound.

He looked at her, holding none of his anguish back from her and all she could do was smile softly, letting him know she was here, and he wasn't alone.

They stared at one another for several long moments, neither speaking, simply content to be exposed and vulnerable to each other as they'd never been to anyone else before.

Owiot framed her left cheek with his callused palm, and she cuddled into his touch, body growing hungry again for more of him.

"Did she not want children?" she asked softly. Thinking of her own situation, and the potion she'd drunk when the Blue had revealed George's plans to her. It wasn't that Fable hadn't wanted children, she just hadn't wanted them with him, and now she was doomed to never have them at all.

And it had never bothered her before meeting Owiot because there'd never been anyone she'd wanted children with. It was a terrible thought to bear, the burden of knowing he was the god of children, and she could never give him any.

She frowned, but he still looked away and hadn't noticed.

At some point, she'd have to tell him. And though she worried he might not like it, might even decide she ultimately wasn't worth the hassle, he deserved to know the truth.

"No. She did not. Aiyana was vain and feared losing her beauty to childbirth. She began to resent my coming to her, and eventually refused to lie with me at all, fearing I'd trick her somehow. Though I vowed that was not my way, and I would never do anything to her she did not want, Mother Buffalo's words haunted her till the day she died."

His hand had dropped and was now casually resting on her hip as his thumb rubbed idle circles on her flesh, making her tingle down low. But this conversation was important to her.

"Do you like children?"

He blinked, staring at her as though trying to understand the strange turn of her questions. Though he seemed clearly confused, he answered her anyway. "I suppose I do. They petition me frequently. What I like most about them is their innocence. Their laughter and verve. There is no deceit in a child; they simply are who they are. And that is refreshing."

She swallowed hard, feeling a knot of unease gathering in her belly. "Would it bother you if you could never have any?"

Realizing that she was slyly trying to ask him a roundabout question, he sat part way up, resting his weight on his forearm. His eyes were thinned and looking at her with a question burning through their depths.

"Darkness?" he asked softly.

She was going to be sick. She knew he knew; he had to know. No woman asked a man if he wanted children, especially not after such a fun and fierce tussle, unless there was a reason for it.

"Yes," she squeaked, hearing her word echo through the canyon like a death knell to her heart.

"Do you have a child already? One I do not—"

Blowing out a relieved breath, because he hadn't sounded so much terrified of her asking him those sorts of questions, as confused, she gave a bitter laugh.

"No. Well, I mean...I don't know. Maybe." She tossed up her hands and then chuckled at the perplexed expression on his face. "Did I confuse you? Let me start over."

"A little," he grinned. "And I'd like that. Do you or don't you have a child?"

"I do. And I don't." She shrugged, holding up a hand when he opened his mouth. "Let me get this out before you ask more questions. Otherwise, you're liable to confuse me." Taking a deep breath to steel her nerves with, she pressed on. "George and I never had any children."

At the mention of her husband's name, Owiot's jaw clenched tight. She'd known when he'd taken some of the demons from her soul that he'd seen her memories of George and Brunhilda. The only good thing that came of that was that she didn't have to explain to him just what kind of a tyrant her husband had been.

"I took a...potion"—she wet her lips in a nervous gesture—"to ensure I could never bear his children. Or anyone else's..." She clenched her back teeth, hating how reed thin her voice had sounded just now.

"Ah. I see." Was all he said.

Her heart squeezed like a fist in her chest at the thought that he might be disappointed that she was sterile and unable to give him children, no different than Aiyana choosing to do the same to him. Because ultimately Fable had chosen her fate.

"But...but you have to understand," she held up her hand, "he was a monster. A horrible, evil man who would have ruined our children the same way he ruined his Snow White."

"Snow White," Owiot murmured, saying her name slowly. "The child who wishes you dead."

There was no censure in his words, but she flinched all the same.

"Yes. Her."

Drawing a knee up, so that he could rest an arm over it, he sat in a casual pose, looking as regal and majestic nude as he did with his leggings on.

"You love her still, don't you?"

She said nothing, only turned her face to the side and stared at the blades of grass curling like delicate stemmed jewels along her ankles. Mixed in with the hate was love still, he was right. But she couldn't forget the fact that she'd also had every intention of ending Snow White's life just a few days ago, so disgusted and heartsick over what the girl had done to her throughout the years—the lies, the constant threat of war and attacks on her person, not to mention the people under her employ, and worst of all...the death of Sterling—that at some point along the way all that love had turned to hate.

His thumb brushed against her cheeks, wiping up the silent tears. "I saw the truth of it all when I tapped into your soul. You do still love her, though she's wounded you deeply."

Closing her eyes, she leaned deeper into his touch. "Yes, but she hates me now. And blames me for the death of her father. She cannot see reason, cannot see beyond that night, refuses even to try and see things from my point of view."

"My darkness, I wonder if you've ever considered the fact that just as the witch cursed you, she too may have cursed the daughter."

Her eyes snapped open. "I have considered it, many times. Always hoping to find evidence of my suspicions. But I have studied her at length and have never noticed a cuff on—"

He shook his head. "Fable, you should know better than most that magic can take on many forms."

She snapped her mouth shut, heart beating like thundering hooves in her chest. Was it possible that Snow White had not only been cursed by Brunhilda, but that she was even now still under the witch's influence? Was it really possible that even in death Brunhilda haunted them?

"I would have noticed. I would have—"

Gathering her flailing wrists in his hands, he squeezed tight. Centering her thoughts back on him. His gaze was steady and sure.

"We sometimes fail to see the truth of things closest to us. The daughter's hatred has cut you deeply, far deeper than you might even suspect."

Her nostrils flared. "What do you mean?"

"Fable, it was only the night of George's death—the night that Snow saw you kill him—that caused your heart to turn dark."

"No." She shook her head hard. "No. I was studying the black craft before that night. That's when—"

"No," he said again, his voice steady. "No, learning the arcane arts does not make one's soul dark. It is only the gleeful invocation of it that does it."

"I killed George and Brunhilda with a killing curse."

"To defend yourself. Again, you did not call upon the darkness with avarice."

Her brows dipped as she began to think back to when it first started for her. When she'd begun to employ the black arts with willful deliberation.

Back, back, back her thoughts spun until the very moment of inception. The moment that dark seed sprouted deep in her soul, the moment she decided to step completely into the void and embrace her baser instincts.

The moment she'd looked up at Snow and the girl's eyes had burned with hate. It had been that precise moment that the small tether of Fable's humanity had snapped. That had been the moment she'd decided that love was a weakness, a blight, and a disease of the soul. The moment she'd stepped away from the light and into the darkness.

And all of that had happened because she'd lost the love of a little girl she'd cared for as her own.

She shook her head. "I'm a weak, selfish, awful person, aren't I, Owiot."

Fable didn't phrase it as a question because it wasn't a question. She knew it was fact and she felt an emotion she'd not felt in a long, long time.

Shame.

But rather than fight it as was her instinctive reaction, she allowed herself to feel the full weight of it for the first time in her life and what she saw made her sick.

Her breathing grew harsh. Her thoughts focused on all that she'd done, all she'd been about to do. It was never easy coming to grips with one's ugliness, and it was doubly so for her because her sins were far greater than most.

"Breathe, darkness. Breathe." He was there, holding her face in his strong hands and she startled, looking at him as her beacon, her focus.

He nodded. "Good. You're going to be okay, my beauty. Simply breathe."

"But...but, I'm a—"

"You were."

She shook her head, curling her fingers around his wrist. "And now I'm not? In just a matter of days, I'm not, is that what you're telling me because we both know that's nonsense. My sins are plenty; I've done so much. So much, how can I ever make this right? How can the scales of justice and balance ever be righted?"

"The choice is yours, Fable. Whether to continue on this path or go back to the one you know. The familiar twisted one full of thorns and weeds. Alone and forever battling the weight of your own demons."

"How do I stop, Owiot? Here, I am a different woman because here no one cares who I am. But back there, in the Enchanted Forest, no would believe I'd turned over a new leaf. It's impossible."

"The journey of a thousand miles begins with the first step," he said gravely. "You are right; some may see you and not believe. But all it takes is one to light a spark of hope. You can make them see you've changed, you only have to be patient."

She bit her bottom lip, wishing she was brave enough to tell him that she didn't want to do it alone, that she wanted him to be by her side through all of it. That he made her feel safe and not afraid to be vulnerable. But those words were far too heavy to be spoken so soon.

"And Snow? Do you know what I was about to do to her before I was brought here?"

He nodded. "I saw."

"You did?" She swallowed hard; saddened that he'd seen that side of her. Disgusted by her own actions, disgusted that she'd let her hatred of George destroy all that had been good within her.

"But you didn't kill her. In fact, you didn't kill any of them. When you get back to your land—"

"If I get back. You know the last ones in these games can't leave."

His lips twitched like he knew a secret she didn't yet. And the look made her feel warm to the tips of her toes.

"You will get back, Fable. In fact, I wouldn't doubt if you were the first to leave."

Her heart thudded almost painfully in her chest. Was he saying what she thought he was saying?

That was impossible, right? True love, the kind that sonnets and poems were written about, it couldn't possibly happen so quick.

Could it?

"When the time comes, you'll know exactly what to do about Snow White."

She wished she could believe him. Wished she had as much faith in herself as he seemed to have in her. It wasn't that she didn't want to change. She did. Even before she'd come here, she'd grown weary of the life she'd led, the lonely never-ending cycle of hate and war that had become her existence.

It had been so easy to let it go here. But what would she do when she returned home? How would she act?

Fable wanted to be a better person. And not because of him either, but because she was tired of being who she was never meant to be.

Leaning over, he kissed her gently. But just that simple ghost of a touch was enough to ignite the embers of passion.

"Mm," she moaned, pressing her breasts tight against his chest. "I like that. Do it again."

His lips twitched. "You're changing the subject."

She shrugged. "Yes, because I'm tired of thinking of all of that. I want to forget, help me to forget, Owiot. Please."

And he did. This time, when they came together, it wasn't animalistic or rough, but sweet, gentle, and full of unspoken and heartfelt confessions.

By the time they finally finished, Fable keenly felt the lapse of time and the knowledge that in a little while she was to face her first trial. A trial where she was given the freedom to not only wound but possibly even end her opponent.

The child eater. She shuddered just thinking of the infamous Baba Yaga whose powers, it was said, came from the very devil himself.

"In just a few hours I have to battle," she whispered, cuddling in tight to his warm body.

Laying with Owiot was a lot like snuggling against a hearth on a blustery winter's night, he was so warm and wonderful feeling. He kissed the crown of her head.

"I know. And I won't leave your side, woman. I vow it."

# Chapter 16

*Fable*

Waking up in the morning was exceedingly difficult to do. Today was the start of the "games." It was also one of the rare times that she wanted to swear at her grandmother for creating something so dastardly.

Stretching her arms high above her head, she became suddenly aware that Owiot watched her.

Rubbing the sleep from her eyes, she smiled up at him. "Good morning."

"Morning," he said, as he tenderly brushed a curl of hair out of her eyes.

He suddenly frowned.

"What?" she snapped, instantly aware that something was wrong. Touching her face, wondering if she'd finally turned into the vision of the hag she'd seen in Mirror, she shook her head. "What's wrong?"

"Your eyes, Fable."

She blinked. "What's wrong with my eyes?"

Terrified that they were now milky white like a crone's, or something else equally hideous, she called a looking glass to her.

Instantly a small, pewter colored handheld mirror rested in her palm. Biting her bottom lip, she held the mirror up and then froze.

Gasping.

Because the eyes staring back at her were eyes she'd not seen in ages. They were the very same texture and color as that of her mother's, Nimue. Aquamarine—like the cool glassy color of the Caribbean's.

"My eyes," she whispered in awe as they filled with heat. "My eyes have changed. Why?"

Owiot pushed her hand away, forcing her to look him in the eyes. "I can only assume it's because you are changed, Fable."

"Is this permanent?" She touched the corner of her eyes.

For so long her eyes had been bronze-gold that to see them so different now was beyond startling. Her heart raced in her chest at the sight of a woman she did not recognize. Oddly enough, though it scared her to see the blue, it also warmed her down to her very soul. Because it truly was like gazing upon the pretty, aquamarine eyes of her mother. Seeing them now fill with tears, it was easy enough to imagine that it was mother looking back at her.

"What is this magic?" she asked with awe in her voice as she lightly danced her fingertips beneath her eyes and shook her head in wonder.

"I don't know." He shrugged. "Only you can determine that. What it does mean is this. You are changing, Fable. You've begun to solve the riddle Button gave you—"

"...Remember who you are," they both said at once.

Feeling sexually sated, and stupidly happy, she laughed. From deep in her belly, the type of laugh that was full of wonder and light and eased the anxiety she'd felt upon awakening.

"My gods, you're beautiful when you do that," he said, and she grinned.

"Then maybe I should do it more often."

He nodded. "Maybe you should."

Fable was just about to suggest that he come lay down beside her, and maybe they could get back to what they'd been doing all through the night when she spied a looming black shape winging in the distance.

She groaned.

Owiot, attuned to her own emotions, turned to glance over his shoulders. "The dragon returns," he said.

And immediately she sensed the light-hearted mood was gone. The time for war was now, and she was so not ready.

Normally she'd prepare. Have spells ready. Would have an active plan of attack. But she'd been so consumed by her time with Owiot that she'd firmly shoved Baba Yaga to the very back of her mind.

Well, now Baba was in the forefront in a very real way, and she knew she was in big trouble.

Owiot stood. Button drew ever closer.

Holding out his hand to her, he helped her to stand too.

"Get us dressed, Fable," he said quickly.

And she obeyed without question. Waving a hand first over herself, then him, she willed clothing back upon their bodies. For Owiot, she wove a pair of leggings from supple tanned leather she'd had stored back in her true castle in the Enchanted Forest.

For herself, she'd fashioned a gown built from her own innate ability to draw on shadow and smoke. The dress was a thing of beauty, curling like billowing fog around her long legs, and leaving her arms and chest-line bare for easier mobility.

But it wasn't simply a fashion statement. If say, grandmother transported them to a land of perpetual sunlight—like what Auntie Fiera's home world was—then Fable would still be able to tap into the power of shadows and darkness by drawing on her dress.

As far as plans went, there really wasn't much of one. She was winging it and cringing and praying to the gods that she didn't do something stupid, like get her and Owiot killed in the process.

Knowing she'd screwed up so royally with her preparations made her anxious and that anxiety made her furious with herself.

"She's going to try and kill you, Owiot."

He shook his head. "Don't worry about me, Fable. I need you to focus on getting out of there alive."

Nothing more could be said, because that was the moment that Button decided to land. For such a massive creature, he could be exceedingly light on his feet when he wanted to be. The blooms barely stirred in his wake.

He looked far more massive this morning than he had the previous one. Button took his time tucking in his large bat-like wings tight to his body.

"Miss me?" he asked in his sibilant and throaty growl.

She glowered. "Hardly. Is it time already?"

He nodded his regal neck. "Mm. Indeed, it is, fair queen. But I must warn you, Baba has planned most exceedingly well for this meeting. To be honest, I hardly think you stand a chance."

His laughter caused the ground to shake.

Fable clenched her fists tight. Owiot hugged her to him.

"Relax, Fable."

"How? How can I? I was a fool, Owiot, a stupid, silly fool who lost her head and thought only with her heart instead of focusing on—"

He kissed her. Stealing the very breath from her lungs. When he was done moving those sexy lips over hers, she could hardly think straight anymore.

"Uh," she exhaled heavily, swaying into his body, "what was I—"

He grinned, showing off his straight white teeth. She framed his face lovingly, the time for pretending how she really felt for this man was long overdue.

Rubbing the tips of their noses together, she breathed against his mouth. "I'll protect you, Owiot. With my life."

"It's not me I worry about, my darkness."

On the ride over Fable had asked Button to make sure Baba felt his landing. The dragon had laughed, but promised to do his best.

And when they'd finally sailed through dimensions, and she spied a world full of sandy islands, and waters overflowing with predators, she'd grinned. Good as his word, when Button landed, he sprayed the Magic Queen with large blasts of sand.

It wasn't easy sliding off of a dragon's back, even one that was willing; Button was easily two stories off the ground. But he crouched low and with the help of Owiot's waiting hand, she managed to slide off without looking too awkward about it.

She turned, and that's when she finally spied the infamous child eater herself.

Baba was dressed in boots, a thong, and a ridiculous looking vest that covered an exceedingly lumpy chest.

Fable frowned, idly curious, but then Baba Yaga was known as the crone too and certainly the three breasts could be an extension of her more unpleasant form. She shuddered.

Baba was having a conversation it seemed.

With herself.

She was laughing, snorting, and swearing. She was a gorgeous woman—three breasts aside—with long, flowing brown hair and such pale white skin with nary a mar to it that she was like the yin to Fable's yang.

The witch was also clearly mad as a hatter and Fable didn't think it could have been possible, but she grew even more nervous. Where was the witch's mate?

Try as she might, Fable couldn't see hide nor hair of the male. The humid, and horribly hot land they were in was nothing but a flat stretch of interspersed islands with no trees, animals, or otherwise. If he were here, she'd have seen him by now.

Gritting her teeth, she tried to reason with herself that Baba's male had to be around; it was in the terms of the foolish games. Each cycle gave each combatant a chance to permanently end the other's mate. Which seemed a silly way to go about making a love connection, but it was what it was.

And she'd be damned if she let Baba steal Owiot from her now.

Owiot slid up to her side, grasping hold of her hand. "He is here somewhere. I can sense another male's presence."

Whipping around to look at her own male who made her heart tremble with the powerful stirrings of love and lust, she shook her head. "Yes, but where? Owiot, I won't let her harm you. I have to find him first."

"Ssh. Ssh." He rubbed a soft curl of her hair between his thumb and forefinger, and she felt the touch of him roll like magic even across her scalp.

She sighed, beginning to lose herself to his calming influence.

"If you're done playing kissy face with ugly over there, let's get on with this already," Baba yelled, practically cackling it in her pretty, grating voice.

Already wound up far too tightly, those words caused Fable's energies to explode. She snapped.

"I will end you!" She twirled toward the witch, feeling her darkness begin to gather and coil like a tight band around her.

Terrified of losing Owiot. Upset that she hadn't prepared more thoroughly, Fable became a living ball of power.

"I'd like to see you try!" Baba chimed, cackling like all witches were prone to do, and that was it.

Fable didn't feed off the black magick. Instead, she tapped into the power she'd been born with. She was the daughter of the Sea King and the granddaughter of the Water Elemental, Calypso.

Calling to the seas surrounding them, she beckoned them to heed her cry. Instantly the waters began to thrash and roil. The skies above grew thick with black clouds and jagged streaks of lightning and rolls of thunder. And then she pulled at the shadows from her dress.

Obscuring both her and Owiot from that damned witch's sight. Baba could not kill what she could not see.

"Owiot," she called, holding out her hand to him.

The sounds of nature blasting itself apart concealed their voices from the crazy witch on the opposite island. Owiot's hand slipped into hers easily. "I'm here, Fable."

Assured by his touch, she again tried to ground and focus herself and not get lost to the rage. What she was doing, she knew wasn't going to be good enough. Not against a witch of Baba's caliber.

Fable might stand a chance if she tapped into her black arts, but she wanted to prove to herself that she was different. That she wasn't the same awful woman she'd once been.

That she could be a better person. So she'd fight this fight handicapped by her own dubious desire to prove herself as worthy and good. Damn her black soul.

She growled, causing a bolt of lightning to strike the island where Baba stood.

"Missed me!" cried the witch, and Fable lost it.

"Where's your male!" she demanded, shielding Owiot as best she could behind a thick screen of smoke and shadow.

But already she could sense the witch gathering her arsenal together.

"Find him if you want him so badly. I'm sure you'd be his type. Anything's his type. Probably even your male would be his type."

She said it without rancor, which caused Fable's lips to twitch, liking the damned witch a little bit better for it. That didn't mean she'd be deterred.

And then she felt the dark sucking pull of powerful magick shoot like a bolt through her shadow and landing square in Owiot's chest.

Fable's eyes grew as she imagined all sorts of horrors. Owiot imploding, exploding, turning against her, or simply just dropping dead to the ground.

Owiot grabbed at his chest, grunting.

"What have you done, you witch!" Fable cried, voice choked with terror and rage.

"Now, now. Temper. Temper." Baba wagged her finger.

And though Fable knew that the witch was inciting her to rage purposefully, no doubt to get her unhinged and unbalanced enough to screw up, she couldn't stop from walking right into that trap anyway.

Owiot meant too much to her now.

Everything really.

She should have bloody told him how she felt before this damned game started and spared them both this nonsense, but she'd always had a hard time owning up to her true feelings. And something of this magnitude was just a wee bit harder for her.

Angry, Fable directed another bolt of lightning to strike at the witch. But Baba was spry and jumped clear just in time so that the deadly attack only barely grazed the heel of her boot instead.

"Well, shite!" she snapped.

And that was the first time that Fable had put the witch back on her heels that she decided to go with the same attack again. More lightning, and more, and more, until the black land was lit with silvery-golden sprays of it.

"You will show me your male!" She cried again, assured for the time being that whatever spell the damned witch had tossed on her male, it wasn't a killing blow.

Not yet anyway.

Using a wee bit of magic to amplify her voice through the howls of the roaring winds, she said it again. "Show me your male, Baba Yaga!"

Flicking her wrist, she called yet more fog from her gown, swirling it tight around the witch. Without finding the male, though, this damned cat and mouse game could last for at least twelve hours, twelve hours she had no intention of being a part of.

Maybe the witch had hidden him in plain sight. Transfigured him somehow to appear as something else. A witch of Baba's capability could easily perform a spell like that.

"You seem to really have a hard on for my male, what's the matter, *ryba*, Owiot not man enough for you?" Baba taunted.

And despite herself, Fable growled. The first time it had been funny, but she was growing enraged by the witch's antics. And there was a strange chiming of bells in the breeze that couldn't possibly herald anything good.

Owiot stood just off to her side. Safe for now. But she knew Baba hadn't yet begun to fight back, and that was a scary thought.

She needed to end this now. If she was Baba, and she'd transfigured her male, the only smart thing to do would be to keep him as close to her as possible. Which meant, she had to get her and Owiot across this deep channel full of sharks.

Again tapping into her innate powers, she solidified a small bridge of water. She was nowhere near as powerful when it came to controlling water as her father or grandmother, but she was a Serenite and was at least capable of creating a bridge.

"Owiot, come on. We have to find her male. I know Baba is hiding him, which means the male has to be close to her."

Grabbing his hand, she tugged on him so that he'd follow. Which he did without a word.

Owiot in no way seemed nervous for himself, but he was constantly strumming her back with his fingers, letting her know that his worry was for her alone. It was sweet and wonderful and if she had more time she'd thank him in a very carnal way for being so wonderful, but there was absolutely no time for anything other than praying to the gods that they'd escape this wretched place in one piece.

The bell-like ringing of chimes had begun to grow louder.

Fable bit her lip when they finally stepped foot onto Baba's island; her gut instinct was screaming at her that she'd made a mistake in forcing Owiot to follow her. And yet, if she left him behind he'd be exposed and defenseless against Baba's magick.

In these spelled realms all males were stripped down to the very merest threads of magic inherent to them. Basically, they were as powerful as a level one witch, which was to say, hardly at all.

"Owiot," Baba called out, and she was close. Very, very close. "I think that maybe you and I have gotten off on the wrong foot, don't you think? I don't hate you. I just need to kill you. It's nothing personal, really."

Fable blinked, squashing her desire to slam her fist through the witch's nose for threatening her male, and instead choosing for once to be smart and think first rather than simply react.

Pointing to her left, she gestured at Owiot that she thought Baba's presence was just over there; they were going to get her. End her. Kill her and the male. She and Owiot were going to be free; they were going to—

Somewhere a baby cried.

Fable and Owiot froze, a greasy ball of terror slid down her throat into her belly as the child cried harder. The infant bellowed in terror.

Had the witch really brought a child into the games as a pawn? She wouldn't dare, even Fable wouldn't be so cold as that. She broke out in a cold sweat, thoughts churning with an almost overpowering need to save the baby.

Fable was praying and hoping she'd simply misheard, but the next cry struck terror into her own soul. She could not condemn an infant to death.

"A child, Fable! She's hidden a child!" Owiot cried, and Fable's heart sank because she knew that he'd just given away their position to the witch.

But they had to look for the baby.

And the only way to do that was to obliterate the one thing that was keeping them safe.

The veil of shadow.

With a sinking heart, she sucked the darkness back in, and she and Owiot immediately began searching for the little one. Baba was a witch. A powerful witch. One strong enough to create an illusion so real that she could trick a witch as powerful as Fable herself.

The more they searched, the more she knew her fears were valid, there was nothing and no one. The sound of Baba's cruel laughter rolled through Fable's veins like ice water.

"Oh, there's no child." The witch chuckled.

She stood before them, tattered, and bleeding, with lightning burns on her flesh and her hair a rat's nest that had tangled around her trim shoulders, but gloating and full of hubris and Fable knew they were in big, big trouble.

In Baba's hand was a small pewter vial of black death. Fable instantly recognized the dark roll of black magick.

"There is, however, death in here. I'm sorry, Owiot, I'm sure you're a perfectly nice—"

*Ribbit. Ribbit. Ribbit.*

An ugly frog poked its head out of Baba's vest, the source of that third breast and Fable wanted to smack herself senseless, disgusted that she hadn't put two and two together from the beginning.

The witch had transfigured her male. Into a frog. And she was harboring him.

She would kill him. With one strike. And she'd use black magick if she had to. Yes, it would stain her soul and probably kill Owiot's faith in her—the thought of which wounded her deeply—, but she'd be damned if she let the witch hurt her male.

Gathering her power to herself, ready to hurl it at that damned frog's head, Fable barely caught a glint of silver before Baba Yaga flicked it with unerring accuracy at her.

Or rather, at the spot just behind Fable.

At Owiot.

She heard Owiot's roar of pain a moment later, and Fable stopped thinking about the damned witch or her male, terrified that Owiot had been mortally wounded, she turned.

Only to note a moment later through the heart-pounding terror that he hadn't been dealt a deathblow. Instead, the ten-inch blade had been impaled into his foot.

Running to her male's side, Fable dropped to her knees, trying to pull the knife out, but she knew the moment she touched the hilt that the blade had been spelled to hold fast.

Owiot was stuck.

Furious, but refusing to leave his side, she wrapped her arms around his shoulders. Wanting to kill both witch and her mate if they dared to try anything now.

But rather than attack. The frog—who was no longer a frog but a handsome blond-haired, blue-eyed Viking male—floated in the air, laughing and crowing as he tossed a small leather pouch into the air.

That small pouch changed into a ship and with a hearty cry of, "To me, wench!"

He held out his hand to Baba, who happily took it and with her final parting words of: "It's been fun, kids, but my carriage awaits." The witch and her Viking sailed off into the clouds.

Owiot sat down, grunting and biting down on his back teeth; his face contorted in a tight mask of pain. The gloomy skies vanished the moment Fable muted her powers.

She was heartsick and upset that in the end Owiot had been hurt, and she'd been unable to stop Baba's attack.

"I'm so sorry, starlight." Her voice was a broken whisper. "It's all my fault. I failed you. I failed us. I should have—"

And even through his pain, he comforted her. Touching his thumb to her jaw, he pressed in lightly. "No, you didn't, darkness. She tricked us."

"I shouldn't have fallen for it. I knew it was a trap."

"Yes, but you still choose to save the child anyway. Fable, we've won a victory today."

She wanted so badly to pull the blade out but knew that trying anything would only increase his pain. There was a time limit to these things, the only thing they could do was wait it out. Which was less than ideal, but there was literally nothing more she could do for him other than sit beside him and hold his hand.

Which is just what she chose to do.

"I don't see any of this as a victory, Owiot."

His look was a mixture of pain and love, and it made her heart swell.

"I felt your call of black magick, felt your desire to use it, but you didn't, Fable. Not once did you battle with that darkness. And your eyes are bluer than ever."

His thumb lightly grazed the corner of her eye.

*I love you...*

The words were just there, on the tip of her tongue and ready to be breathed to life, ready to be spoken. But she was scared. So very scared. Not because she thought he didn't care for her, she knew he did.

But because the ghosts of her pasts taunted and mocked her, telling her she'd done this once before and was only setting herself up for yet more pain. That George had seemed like an angel until he'd turned back into his true demonic form. That she might be doing the very same thing with Owiot.

And just as doubt would threaten to suffocate her, hope would rear its bloody head and tell her just the opposite. That George had never taken such care of her. That George had never taken the demons from her. Taken a knife wound for her. That George had never shared any intimacies with her...and on and on and on it went, the battle for whether to tell him or not raged like a tsunami inside her heart.

Hope, however, was stronger than almost any emotion in all the worlds; hope gave her heart wings and told her to "just try one more time," that Owiot was someone worth fighting for.

She was going to do it. Just rip it off and say it and put it out there and if he didn't return her affections she'd understand, but for once in her life she wanted to be brave. She wanted to—

"Just hold my hand, Fable. That's all I need right now. Is just for you to hold my hand," he said softly and with a thread of pain laced behind it.

Like the coward that she was, she held his hand and said no more.

# Chapter 17

*Calypso*

"Are you sure, Dite? Shouldn't we stick to the plan and pair them in the order we chose?"

Aphrodite had thrown Caly a curve ball just now. One she wasn't sure about, and that truthfully made her sick to her stomach.

"No, I really think this is the route we need to go. We need to offer her the chance to battle The Blue next."

Calypso shook her head, glancing at a still brooding Hades. Her lover hadn't said much after today's match. It had been hard to watch Baba nearly destroy her granddaughter's mate, and if she hadn't been so sure of the outcome of these love matches, Calypso would have probably tossed the damned witch back to Kingdom and rescued her granddaughter and future grandson-in-law. It had been all she could do to sit back and simply watch.

Though she had chewed more than half of her nails down to the quick. Which sucked, but whatever, they'd grow back. Why hadn't the girl just said the words already? Or Owiot for that matter? Aphrodite had pumped so much of her love juice into their realm that even Calypso was affected by it whenever she stared through the sea orb. Frustrated and grumpy, she turned on her seat, staring at her husband.

"Hades, what do you think?" she asked.

"I don't know, Caly." He sighed deeply. "I'm beyond my element with this. All I know is this, if anything happens to Fable, I will personally end everyone in there."

And she knew he would too. Calypso looked toward Dite, who was pleading with her eyes and clasping her fingers tight.

"You have to trust me, just as you did before."

"But why!" she snapped, then rubbed at her throbbing brow. This was no fun, not the way she'd hoped.

Calypso was too close to Fable. She should have known that going into the games, but she hadn't expected it to be so hard to sit back and watch her granddaughter suffer as she had.

"She's almost done, Dites. It's just a matter of hours, possibly even a day before she and Owiot admit how they really feel. If you throw Galeta at her as her next match, she'll stay. For a chance at retribution, and rightly so."

Aphrodite, who'd taken to watching Baba Yaga's child—Phlegm—through the entirety of the games, rocked his cradle as the little green flesh ball began to stir awake.

Immediately the goblin child settled back down into a deep slumber.

"Okay, say she does choose to stay. What's so wrong with that? You saw what she did to Baba in there. If the witch hadn't tricked her, Fable probably would have won that match."

Calypso set her jaw, glancing off to the side. How could she put into words what she was feeling? The pain that felt like a stab to the chest each time she saw her granddaughter get hurt. There were very few things in life Calypso loved more than her family.

"She's not a child anymore, Cals, you don't have to protect her. She's strong, and she's—"

"She cast us out for years!" she snapped, frustrated enough that she finally allowed herself to speak the words that had haunted her from the beginning. "She thought she was too dirty, too repugnant for us to love and she had no one, Dites. No one! And I can't...I can't watch that happen to her again."

Her voice cracked, and the seas rolled.

Hades stood up, coming over to his bride's side and reaching down, he helped her up and gently embraced her. Kissing her temple as she shuddered into his strong, powerful body.

"It won't happen, Caly." Aphrodite spoke softly like one would to a spooked animal.

"How do you know?"

Her friend's smile was dazzling as she said, "Because I just do. Because I know how love works, and I know that this is the final step to getting her there. She has to willingly walk away from the one thing she wanted most for all those years. Revenge on the Blue. When she does that, she'll choose Owiot with her whole heart and soul and have no regrets, but she needs that chance."

"But what if you're wrong?" Caly squeaked, praying with all her might and soul that Aphrodite was right. That Fable would walk away from the darkness this time, that she'd choose love. Choose life. But she was so scared that her granddaughter wouldn't, because she and Fable were so similar in so many ways.

If Calypso were in Fable's shoes, she'd choose revenge and love. But if Fable did, the chances were very good her granddaughter might not walk away from this alive.

"All I can say is trust me, Caly. But I won't push you on this, if you're not—"

Curling her fingers into her husband's dark collar, Calypso buried her face in his chest and murmured, "Then do it. I'll trust you."

*Fable*

Button landed back in the verdant rolling valley of pines and lavender-tinged skylight.

Owiot had healed almost instantly the moment he'd slipped from that realm and back into this one. His powers had returned when they'd parted through the shimmering veil between worlds and he'd breathed a heady sigh of relief behind her.

She was grateful that he was okay. But she was also upset by how close they'd come to losing everything.

Why hadn't that witch killed him? She'd taunted them with death. And Fable had even seen the surety of it in Baba's moss green eyes when she'd tipped the vile toward them.

But at the last moment, it was like the witch had changed her mind and decided to merely pin his foot instead.

In short they got lucky. Very lucky. Whoever came next might not be so generous.

Button was shaking his massive head and flexing his membranous wings like a dog shaking water loose. Owiot grabbed hold of her hand, squeezing gently and refusing to let go—which she was completely fine with as she had no desire to go without him tonight—the very trying, very long ordeal was finally over, and she was going to tell him everything. It was foolish to waste another minute in this place when the keys to freedom were literally at their fingertips.

She'd decided it was time to be brave. Time to stop hiding her head in the sand when things got too frightening or unsure and simply fess up.

"I have something to tell you," Owiot whispered in her ear a moment later and a delicious shiver coursed down her spine.

Leaning into him, she wrapped her free arm around his bicep and squeezed. "And I have something to tell you too, my starlight."

He was looking directly at her when she'd said that and his eyes blazed with silver fire.

"Oh, by the way," Button said before they got too far down the path.

She groaned, knowing in her gut that anytime that bastard of a dragon sounded so blasé and amused, nothing good ever came from it.

Twirling on her heel, she snapped. "What, Button? What now?"

The massive, golden-scaled dragon chuckled heartily, causing the ground beneath their feet to gently sway.

"Don't shoot the messenger, Evil Queen. I'm merely to tell you who you're next opponent will be."

Rolling her eyes, and awash with relief she held up her hand. "No need, I'm not—"

But he pressed on as though he'd not heard her.

"It's none other than my own mistress, Galeta the Blue."

The words died on her tongue. She gasped, suddenly suffused by rage, by a desperate desire to confront the villainous, evil fairy disguised as something made of light and goodness, when in fact she was the epitome of all that was wrong and corrupt within Kingdom.

Button lifted a regal brow. "Now, what was it that you were saying, oh dark one?"

She glanced at Owiot, who'd gone unnaturally still beside her, awaiting her answer.

And though she shouldn't know his thoughts, she did. She could read them clearly on his face.

He wanted her to tell the dragon that there'd be no meeting. No need for it, because she'd found her mate in truth and she was done with this blasted world.

Five seconds ago, she'd have been able to utter those words in truth. But the need for vengeance was an insidious thing. Through all the years since Galeta's leaving, Fable had tried in vain to conjure the demonic fairy again, to bring her forth so that she could extract her revenge—but the Blue had never shown.

Now, not only was she here, but Fable would be pitted against her next. The Fates had handed her revenge on a silver platter. How could she walk away from that now?

"No? Nothing?" Button chuckled, stirring the breeze. Unfurling his wings, he unfolded his body to its long, majestic length. Ready to set sail. "I'll make sure to let the goddesses know."

Owiot's eyes practically bore through her skull; she felt the heavy weight of his stare like an anchor tied to her soul.

He wanted her to choose him. To choose him over her revenge. Over her need to hurt and kill. Over the darkness that had pervaded her mind these past centuries. To become a new woman, the type of woman he could proud of—*she* could be proud of.

This was a test.

She knew it.

Clenching her fists, she opened her mouth, but no sound escaped. She swallowed hard, trying to find the right words, searching her heart for that tiny kernel of goodness still left to her...

Button smirked. "I'll be seeing you then, Dark One."

And with a chuckle, he burst from the ground with one powerful flap of his mighty wings.

Only once he'd become a spec did the words come tumbling out. "No, wait! Button, come back, wait!"

But it was too late. The beast was gone.

Tears choked her vision as she twirled toward Owiot, lifting out a hand to beg him to understand, that she'd simply suffered a moment's weakness, but her male too was long gone. And where he'd stood rested one lone beautiful flower with petals of white and thick bands of turquoise across each.

With a cry torn from her heart, she dropped to her knees, and plucked the pretty flower up, hugging it tight to her chest.

"Owiot," she breathed, knowing in her heart that she'd wounded him as deeply as his Aiyana had. She shook her head, and cried alone.

The flower trembled in her hands.

*Owiot*

Her look of unfiltered greed for revenge against the Blue had nearly shattered his heart. Aiyana had chosen to die rather than to remain with him; he'd hoped after they'd shared of their souls with each other that Fable would not do the same to him.

Call him a coward, but the moment he'd seen that thread of gold begin to wind through the blues of her eyes, he'd not stayed behind to find out. He couldn't. Couldn't hear her choose retribution over them.

111

It wasn't that Owiot didn't understand what had been done to her. The violence perpetrated against her. He hated the fairy for her part in turning his female dark. But war and death were not the answers. It was not the way.

Brother Coyote came padding silently out of the woods, looking up at him with his perpetually mischievous grin.

Owiot shook his head. "Not today, Brother. I am in no mood."

Coyote gave a reedy, throaty chuckle and Owiot had to bite his back teeth.

"I am not running from her. I am giving her space. Giving her time."

Coyote snorted and began to guide Owiot off the path, toward a massive oak tree with leaves burning like flame in the distance. The vexing Spirit animal that knew him far better than almost anyone else loped toward a fallen fire apple, snapping it up in his great big jaws and swallowing it in one greedy gulp.

Owiot sighed, settling against the base of the tree, watching as his brother consumed his weight in fruit. Finally satisfied, Coyote loped over to him and collapsed upon his legs, his big fat belly now overstuffed and full of food.

Sighing, Owiot proceeded to scratch Coyote behind his ears. "You vex me, Brother. But then you always have."

Coyote snorted softly. That perpetual grin still firmly fixed in place. But when he turned to look at Owiot, his eyes were no longer the yellow of his animal familiar, but twin pools of liquid silver mercury.

His Brother wanted to show him something. Owiot frowned, peering into the shifting miasma of colors that had begun to take on shape and form. That of Fable and that of him.

In the left eye stood Fable. Tall, proud, and full of seething hatred.

Bowed low before her was a tide of people all wearing white, but their robes were dipped in blood. Pools of blood that poured like a waterfall down from her throne—a throne built of the skulls and bones of her victims. In her hand, she held a goblet full of green, noxious poison.

Her gorgeous face was twisted into one of perverted and evil delight, and her maniacal laughter echoed to the rafters as one body after another after another dropped dead at her feet.

And all around her, the world burned...

Gasping, Owiot clutched at his chest, heart thundering with fear at the future revealed for her. What had happened to her? Why had she chosen to return to the black arts and surrender her soul in the process?

But the moment he looked into Coyote's right eye, he had his answer.

Fable held Owiot tight to her breast. His eyes were closed and his skin ashen. Standing over them was the monstrous vision of a beast that salivated poison. Owiot's flesh was riddled with it. Blood stained his front and back. And he knew without asking that the beast had dealt him a killing blow.

His darkness screamed, clutching at his chest and begging the fates to alter what had been done, but none would.

And as he opened pain filled eyes, he smiled softly at her and whispered brokenly... "it was always you, my darkness. Always..."

Then he exploded in a shower of starlight, and Fable—with a tear stained face—and mad, glowing eyes stood, turned toward the fairy still flitting around the beast and with a snarl of pure, unadulterated rage, stretched out her arm and smote the little blue fairy dead, howling as the madness of the blackness finally consumed her soul.

Sucking in a sharp breath, Owiot clutched at his chest, shaking his head and trying to tell himself that this couldn't be real. This couldn't be their fate. But Coyote had shown all he was willing to show tonight; he was now snoring on Owiot's thighs and lost to his dreams.

The only way for them to escape this fate would be for Fable to choose love over revenge.

For her to choose to walk away with him now, and not wait.

He could just walk back there, tell her their future, tell her what she would lose if she didn't decide to let go of her need to hate, but then he'd always wonder what choice she'd have really made on her own. And not only that, he'd always wonder if she'd have rather chosen revenge over him, even knowing the outcome.

What if, like Aiyana, she grew to despise the very sight of him down the long road of their existence? What if someday she woke up to the realization that she'd have far rather ended Galeta's life than to be permanently tied down to the man lying beside her on the bed?

Owiot settled his hand deep into Coyote's reddish-gray fur and closed his eyes, trembling because he knew the answer.

He did not care about his own death. Death was a natural part of life. He'd lived long enough if death came now for him he would embrace it like his brother and move on to the next phase of his journey.

No, what mattered most to him was that Fable not turn into the creature of destruction and chaos as he'd witnessed. But the only person who could make her not choose that path was herself alone.

Fable had to choose either life or death.

Bowing his head, he prayed to the Great Spirit, begging not simply as a man in love, but as the son of the Great God himself, to hear his plea to save the life and soul of the woman who meant more to him than even his own.

Coyote snored.

# Chapter 18

Instantly she grew aware that she was no longer alone. Sniffing, she wiped at her eyes with the back of her wrist and stared into the face of one who'd always loved her more than his own life.

Her grandfather, Hades. Dressed in his usual colors of deep black and gray, with his penetrating and soulful blue eyes and ebony colored locks, she had always thought him the handsomest male in the world—until now.

Now her thoughts were consumed by Owiot.

"Little flower," he said in his deep, bassy baritone.

With a cry of anguish and pain, she raced into his outstretched arms, wrapping her arms tight around his neck and sobbing uncontrollably as all the hurt and pain finally exploded from out of her.

And he let her, holding on tight and squeezing almost to the point of pain, but letting her know in no uncertain terms that she was not alone.

Finally, when she got her turbulent emotions under control, she pulled back a little, but stayed within the safe confines of his embrace and shook her head. "Are you even supposed to be here?"

He snorted. "Your aunt and grandmother probably won't like it, but I couldn't stay away, little one."

She snorted, wiping up the mess of tears on her face. "Only you could see me and still think of me in that way. I've done awful things, grandfather. Unforgivable things."

"As have I," he murmured. Then snapping his wrists, he created a bench of ebony colored skulls for them to sit upon.

She'd always loved her grandfather's macabre sense of style. Grinning softly, she joined him on the bench.

"Talk to me, sweetling, tell me what is the matter," he finally asked when he'd gotten them situated.

She shrugged, glancing down at the now wilted flower still gripped in her hand. "I love him."

His smile caused a rainbow to suddenly appear in the sky. Grandfather might deal in death, but ever since his joining with grandmother, he created life too.

Hades had been built for sorrow and sadness, but the power of love had transformed him into so much more. Fable wanted what he had.

"That is good to hear. Then why haven't you told him this already and left? You know he loves you too."

Even though she suspected it, her heart still beat like a drum in her chest at her grandfather's words. She swallowed painfully.

"I suspected that might be the case."

Flexing his powerful shoulders, he stared down at her with keen, intelligent eyes, before finally sighing deeply.

"I sense a but in there somewhere, Fable."

She cringed. Anytime grandfather used her given name she knew she was in trouble.

She shrugged, and he groused under his breath.

Grandfather was a very good grouser. He made the trees themselves shake almost as violently as Button could when he got grumpy. She'd always hated when grandfather got grumpy with her.

"Fable," he drawled. "I already know what it is, so why don't you just spit it out already?"

Frustrated with her stupid emotions, she squared her shoulders and glowered down at the silly flower she still couldn't seem to let go of.

"Galeta, that's what. I wanted out of here, grandfather, I did. I do. I was ready to tell him everything, ready to turn over a new life. But I've been given an opportunity to exact my revenge against the bitch who turned my life upside down and...and..." she trailed off pitifully because saying it aloud made her feel heartily ashamed of herself.

"Fable," Hades said soft, "I'm going to tell you something, granddaughter, something you already know, but that you've probably forgotten."

Looking up at him miserably, she waited for him to continue.

"I know the dark pull of vengeance. The need for revenge. I understand what it is to feel justifiably homicidal."

She couldn't help but chuckle at his turn of phrase. Grandmother had found grandfather strung out like a stuck pig when she'd first encountered him way, way back in the day.

Hades had been accused of murdering Persephone, and all the gods of the pantheon save for Auntie Themis, and Auntie Aphrodite had wanted to see him burn for it.

Only grandmother's quick thinking had gotten him out of the mess.

"How did you let it go? How were you able to just move on with your life? How?" she asked softly.

His lips twisted. "It would be a lie to say it was easy, I chose love, and la-dee-da, we skipped our way into eternal happiness. Your grandmother is many things, and life with her has been an adventure in many ways, but my love for her was not what finally caused me to release my hate."

She frowned, confused by his statement. Because she'd been so sure that love had fixed him. That that was the basis and foundation of true love, an immediate cure-all that would fix all of life's woes and make her forever happy.

Rolling her wrist, she waited silently for him to continue.

He sighed deeply. "I simply came to the realization that it was too exhausting to continue to hang on to it. That no one cared about my hurt or pain as much as I did. No one lost sleep over it. Not a one of them realized the heavy strain I'd been under and suddenly wanted to apologize. For them, life had simply moved on, and that was an end of it. I was little more than a passing fancy in the framework of their thoughts."

"That seems wholly unfair."

"Yes, but that's life, my girl." He gripped her hands. "Since when is it ever fair? Is it fair that humans have such short lives as to be pitied? Is it fair that love can be found and lost all in the same day? Is it fair that a couple that strived for years to have a child should have one only to then lose it a few days later? No. None of that is fair. But it is what it is. It's called life, dear. And life is full of glorious wonders and unimaginable pain, but you live it, and you move on because that's the only thing you can truly control. Even in Kingdom, where death doesn't come as easy as it does to those that are Earthbound, there is very little in this life or the next that you can control, the only thing you can change is your heart. How you choose to live your life. You can let the hurt and pain twist you into a monster, or you can let that same pain make you stronger and mature."

Tears were falling again, but this time, they were tears of relief. Because she knew what she had to do.

"I want to kill her, grandfather. I want to hurt her as she hurt me..."

She admitted the innermost weakness of her heart to him. But the strangest thing happened when she did.

Rather than being overburdened by the pain of the past as she'd always been, instead confessing that truth had made her feel lighter somehow.

Hades smiled softly. "I know you do. And trust me when I say, Galeta the Blue will not have an easy road of it in these games. Did you really think that your grandmother wanted to see that awful fairy gain her own happily ever after?"

She frowned. "I did wonder why that bitch was here to begin with."

He snorted. "Your grandmother and I have matured in many ways in our long lives shared together. We've learned that the best way of letting go of hate is to sometimes take the opposite road. But that doesn't mean that we can't have a little fun while doing it."

Laughing, thinking of all the dastardly ways that grandmother was likely to punish The Blue for all her years of treachery seemed suddenly more than good enough to Fable.

And with one final *click* the last of her need for revenge faded away within her. Just as grandfather said, she didn't suddenly feel love for the fairy or even wish her well...but what she did feel was freedom from carrying around the heavy burden of hate.

Let fate take care of the damned fairy. Fable was ready to begin her life anew with the man she loved with all her heart.

Smiling wide, she threw herself into her grandfather's arms. He expelled a little *oomph* of surprise, but she heard his smile in his words as he said, "Now, little flower, will you please relieve my worries and go find your mate, tell him you love him and get the hell out of this twisted game your grandmother and Aphrodite have wrought?"

Chuckling deeply, feeling as though she could fly, and so impossibly happy that she wondered if it was actually possible to die from it, she popped a quick kiss on his cheek.

"Yes, grandfather, I will. And when you see mother and father next, please tell them that I'll be returning for a visit this winter, with my mate in tow."

He grunted deeply. "I will. And I love you, Fable, my beautiful dark one."

Her smile took up her entire face; she practically burned with it. Her cheeks would ache tonight, no doubt, but she no longer cared.

"I love you too, grandfather." Jumping to her feet, and ready to go find her man, she was stopped by a light touch on her hand. "Oh, and Fable, one last thing. Just so you know, we'll be keeping Mirror in these games just a wee bit longer, if you don't mind."

She cocked her head, wondering why in the world Mirror needed to stay, but trusting that her grandfather had a very good reason for it.

"Oh, okay, I guess."

"Good. Now, I think it's time be reunited with your lover, don't you?"

And so saying, he winked, waved and vanished right along with the bench built of skulls. And standing in its place stood Owiot, looking dazed and confused.

"What is—"

With a cry of utter joy and longing, she flung herself into his beautiful body, tackling him to the ground as she peppered his face with kisses.

He laughed heartily. "Fable...my darkness, what—"

"I choose you, you beautiful, beautiful man," she said in between ardent kisses. "Always you. Forever you. I love you, starlight. I love you."

He paused in his laughter, and his eyes grew intensely serious as he whispered, "And I love you too, Fable of Seren, with all my heart and soul and the very flame of life that burns within my chest."

No sooner had they spoken the words the coiling magick of grandmother's power washed over them, lifting them high into the sky and through a shifting tunnel full of starlight.

She clutched onto his shoulders, nuzzling her nose with his. "So it's probably going to take us a while to get back to the Enchanted Forest."

"*Mmhhm,*" he agreed with a gravelly voice, "and just what did you have in mind, my love?"

Chuckling, she dug her toes into his shins and shoved up just enough so that their mouths aligned. "Well, I was thinking that maybe we could do what we did the other night when you went all the way down on me, except maybe this time, we could both do it to each other at the same time."

He growled, and the wild beast that dwelt in his soul came suddenly roaring to life. Owiot wasn't a passive lover, he took her violently, almost aggressively, and she loved every bloody minute of it.

And that's how they returned home, through a shifting tunnel of stars, and making happy, happy music together.

# Epilogue

*Fable*

Walking back through her castle was the hardest thing Fable had had to do in a long time, coming face to face with all the bodies laying haphazardly in her halls—but especially with Snow's, who Owiot now carried. They'd stopped quickly in the forest to retrieve her body and brought her back to the castle so that Fable would only need to murmur the awakening spell once.

Still dressed in her buckskin clothing and with her dirt-smudged cheeks and face, dirty and split fingernails, and cracked and bruised lips, Snow had definitely looked better.

Now the girl looked dead and gaunt. Sterling's severed horn–which Fable gripped tight in her right hand— was a reminder all over again of everything she had lost to the princess.

There'd been no prince to kiss Snow White awake. That simply wasn't the way Snow's story would end. Not here in the real world anyway. Maybe in fairy tales, but in this world only the queen's desire to awaken the child could do it.

Kneeling, Owiot gently laid Snow White's body down beside the other sleeping bodies, taking care to arrange her limbs thoughtfully and respectfully. He glanced up at her with questions burning in his eyes, but ones Fable had no answer for.

For once she was willing to own up to the fact that she'd done wrong, but that didn't mean that any of this was easy for her. Waking Snow White now would come with its own set of problems. Having to confess to the girl who'd once been more like a daughter to her that she'd been so very, very wrong in her treatment of her. How in Kingdom was she supposed to do that?

Pride could be such a terrible and heavy burden to bear. In no way did Fable want to have this conversation, but if she didn't she'd never truly heal either. Not completely or fully, not the way she needed to. It stuck in Fable's craw to admit it, but she needed to hear Snow White say she forgave her before Fable could truly begin to learn to forgive herself for all her past misdeeds, not just the death's of George and Brunhilda, but everyone else she'd harmed in her tenure as queen.

Sleeping as Snow was, it was easy to remember the innocent, beautiful girl who'd once hugged her with such vigor and whispered repeatedly how much she'd loved her.

Slipping Sterling's horn into a pocket hidden in her gown, Fable took a deep breath full of misery and regret. The lives she'd stolen, the dreams she'd shattered, all the terrible, awful things she'd done since becoming ruler of the Enchanted Forest began to bear down upon her with its crushing weight.

Fable shoved her hand against her rapidly beating chest. So much had happened to her in a few short days. Things that had changed her outlook on life forever. She was no longer the same woman. But who would believe her now, after all she'd done? Who could truly forgive her for the heinous crimes she'd committed?

If Fable were in their shoes, she'd never believe the change could be real. So why should they?

Owiot gripped her fingers tight. "You're not alone, my darkness. I'm right here."

She looked over at him and instantly felt her beating heart begin to still and settle into a more normal rhythm.

"What if she—"

"*Ssh.*" Owiot turned into her and planted a delicate whisper of a kiss against the corner of her lips. "Don't do that to yourself. First, let's look to see if we can find the witch's mark upon her."

Biting down on the corner of her lip, she nodded anxiously. "Okay."

They looked for all the big things first. Pieces of jewelry, articles of clothing that seemed incongruent to a girl living wild and struggling to make ends meet.

"Nothing," Fable whispered brokenly several minutes later after rolling Snow first one way then the other as she'd run her hands over the girl's body.

"That doesn't mean it's not there, Fable. Keep looking," Owiot said, eyeing her sternly.

And she would probably never tell him so, but she loved that he didn't let her walk all over him. Owiot, calm and patient as he was, was all male and very much his own man.

No one would ever take control of his mind and heart. He simply was who he was, and that was probably the best part about him.

That, and he was the sexiest thing alive too. That certainly didn't hurt.

She smirked, and he narrowed his eyes. "What's the matter with you, you suddenly look like you want to ravage me."

She snorted. "And so what if I do, male? You're mine now. Or have you forgotten."

He waggled his brows. "I've not forgotten, female. And I have a surprise for you once we finish here. But come, let's finish first. It feels strange to flirt with my blushing female over what amounts to cooling corpses at the moment."

She rolled her eyes. "Yes, boss."

Owiot only snorted.

Kneeling down beside him, Fable decided to take things more slowly and really look rather than simply rely on touch alone. Starting with Snow's feet, she slipped off the girl's boots and looked not just on the soles or the tops of her feet, but between each toe.

Nothing but smooth skin.

"Owiot, sweetheart, turn your eyes away while I take the girl's pants off."

He snorted again, but did as asked, standing and turning his back to them. Fable smirked, she wanted Owiot to see no woman nude—dead or alive—except for Fable herself.

Yanking Snow's pants down, Fable studied one shapely leg, then the other, moved to the apex between them, only giving it a very cursory glance, she was pretty certain Brunhilda had likely not marked the girl down there, but one had to be thorough.

After determining there was nothing at all, she flicked a little magick over the girl to cover her up with a blanket of shadow and moved up to her chest and back and hips.

And again, nothing.

She studied the front, sides, and backs of her arms, between her fingers, and was starting to get a sick feeling in the pit of her stomach that Snow hadn't been enchanted to hate Fable at all, she simply did.

And the truth of it was, Fable could understand why. Evil or not, George had been the girl's father, she'd only been a little thing when she'd witnessed her evil stepmother brutally slaughter him.

Of course, there was hate.

Fable hated The Blue, and all the fairy had done was trick her. Not stolen the life of someone she'd actually loved.

It was a sobering and disturbing thought and also a disquieting one. At this point, Fable no longer believed that Snow would ever forgive her, that there was no magical curse upon the girl, but rather one of Fable's own making that had caused such division between them.

Once she'd traced her fingers across the length of the girl's neck, front and back, and peeked inside each nostril, she finally had to concede defeat.

"Oh, Owiot, what have I done?" She sniffed and stood, shaking her head miserably as her heart bled with the heavy burden of her sins bearing down on her.

He hugged her tight, kissed her brow, and then asked, "Did you check her hair?"

"No." She sighed. "But there's no point. I know there's nothing there. The child hates me, Owiot, and she has every right to. I never wanted to accept that as fact, but I'm ready to now. I killed her father, justified or no, it doesn't matter to her."

"Would you mind if I checked?"

She waved her fingers. "I don't care. Do whatever pleases you. But I already know the truth."

He knelt beside Snow and Fable hugged herself tightly, allowing herself for once to feel every pain, every hurt she'd ever inflicted upon the child.

True, Snow had hurt her too. But the truth was, Fable had hurt her first by killing the one thing she'd loved most in the world.

How could she possibly blame the girl for that?

"Fable, come here," Owiot said slowly a moment later.

Blinking, she looked at him from the corner of her eye, her pulse beginning to stutter with skipped beats.

"It's not possible. You didn't find—"

"Just come here, love." He waved her over.

Her steps felt like lead as she moved to his side.

"Here," he held his finger over a spot on her scalp, "tell me what you feel."

Frowning, she dropped to her knees, and moved to where his finger was, but no sooner had she gotten close to his finger she felt the very faint, but obvious pulse of black magick.

Gasping, she gently moved aside his finger and where it had been she saw a very tiny, fractured heart shaped mole on the girl's scalp.

"What is this?" she breathed, looking at Owiot.

His look was grim as he said, "It is the very epicenter of hate. The witch did mark her, Fable."

Shaking and jittery, she looked back at the tiny, tiny mole no bigger than a freckle and shook her head.

"That poor girl," she breathed, strangled by the knowledge that unlike Fable herself, Snow White had had no choice but to drown in the darkness of Brunhilda's curse.

"I blamed her for everything, Owiot. All my pain, all she'd done, I didn't know..."

He took her trembling hands in his and held on tight. "But you do now, my beauty. And you can fix this. Free her, Fable. She may never love you again, but you can at least free her of this terrible curse."

Nodding gently, she murmured, "To free her I would need to tap into my own darkness, you understand that."

She glanced at him.

"Yes. But you have light in you now too. Use both, and you will not drown."

"That's what Baba Yaga does, isn't it? It's why she didn't lose herself as I have?" She'd noticed that the day of the battle with the witch.

Baba walked in neither light nor darkness, but in shades of gray. Neither wholly good or bad. It had come as something of an epiphany to Fable, that so long as she kept just enough of the darkness out and let just enough of the light in, she too could walk the gray path unhindered.

He nodded. "It appears so."

Wetting her lips, Fable closed her eyes and slipped deep inside of herself, into that endless well of yawning power.

But this time, when she looked there wasn't merely a void of black, but also a pool of lambent white. She took not just from one, but from both, drawing on the ancient powers of both darkness and light and wove a spell of breaking.

When she opened her eyes, she held not a sphere of black magick, but a ball of radiant gray. She grinned at Owiot, who grinned right back at her.

"What that witch has done, let now it be undone. So say I, so mote it be."

Then she held the sphere of power over the girl's head. Instantly the ball sailed out of her grip, and toward Snow's face. Going down, down, down, until it touched her flesh, and then sank right in.

The transformation was immediate. A bright wash of golden light poured through Snow's pores, making her glow from the inside out, at first bright and intense, but slowly fading with intensity, until finally, she was simply flesh and blood again.

Fable frowned.

"Did it work?" Owiot asked.

She shrugged. "I don't know. I hope so. I'm not familiar with gray magick."

He grabbed her hand and squeezed. "Then I guess the only way to find out in truth, is to wake her up. Wake them all up."

Stomach a twisting nest of nerves again; she prayed to the gods for courage, and without giving her much time to think it through, snapped her fingers and called a cease to the spell.

Sleeping curses took differently for everyone. Some woke up immediately, and others took far longer.

The peoples in the halls were the first to rise. Men, women, children, animals, they all woke, some more lethargic than others. But all of them looking around in a confused stupor.

She stood where she was, not daring to speak a word as they turned to her, all of them looking upon her with recrimination burning brightly in their eyes. They knew what she'd done, but she was the Evil Queen, and none would dare say a word to her face about it.

Owiot stood by her side as promised, clinging tight to her hand, and she was glad he had because otherwise she might have scampered away like a bunny being chased by a wolf.

The only thought hammering through her skull was that her sins were far too deep and ugly to ever be forgiven by anyone.

One by one the people's left, murmuring in their wake, casting curses at her and glancing worriedly at Snow White still lying still at their queen's feet.

An hour had finally passed, and the only ones that remained were Fable, Owiot, and a still sleeping Snow White.

"What's happened," she finally whispered, "why hasn't she stirred, Owiot?"

He shook his head, no doubt as confused as she was.

"Did I do wrong when I lifted the curse from her? Did I—"

He shook his head. "Don't, Fable. Don't do this to yourself. We will figure this out. But in the meantime, she cannot remain this way."

"No," she looked down at the beautiful girl she'd once loved so well, and realized now that she wouldn't stir, she still very much did, "No, we can't."

Waving her hand, she created a box for her. A beautiful glass box with etchings of briar roses along the sides and bottom, and changed Snow out of the ugly clothing into that of a beautiful snow-white gown with designs of blood red flowers along the hem, it was a gown fit for a princess.

Building a pedestal made of gold for that box, she sat the sleeping princess upon it, and each day and each night she returned to that box, peering into it as she pressed her fingers upon it and whispered the same thing over and over, "Please forgive me, little princess. Please forgive me."

From that day forward things changed in the Enchanted Forest. Fable and Owiot themselves went to every hut, every home in the village and she apologized for what she'd done. Making restitution whenever possible and promising to be a good Queen now, an infinitely better one.

And though none believed at first, as the years slipped by, the people began to see the change in their Queen—many, if not most, attributed this change to their new King Owiot. That his love for their Evil Queen had changed her heart.

120

But Owiot knew the truth. He'd never been needed to fix the hurt and pain in Fable's heart, she'd simply chosen to finally be brave enough to right the wrongs herself.

And as the years rolled by, very few remembered Fable the Evil Queen. Instead, she'd become Fable the Kind-Hearted, and he'd become Owiot the Benevolent. The kingdom thrived and the peoples rejoiced, but always there was one point of sadness amongst the realm.

That of the sleeping princess who'd never awoken in the twenty years since their Queen's return.

Until one day, a fairy who'd once been Blue but now was Pink returned to make things right...

*Writing this tale was a difficult one for me. Even now that it is done, I did not want to do it. The truth is, I can remain anonymous no more. You see, though this was a happily ever after, I very nearly destroyed Fable and Owiot's chance at love. Who am I? I am The Blue, or rather I was...and now I suppose I need to tell you what happened to me and why I've been sentenced to right the wrongs. I guess it all started...*

*Once...*

*Upon...*

*A...*

*Time...*

Love my books? Want to know when the next Dark Queen book will be released? Make sure to sign up for my newsletter! And if you really want to get to know more about the queens and all the characters to come, come hang out at The Harem.

# Author's Notes

The next queen is coming soon, though it's a mystery who she'll be. If you want to know, stay tuned to either Jovee Winters's FB page or sign up for her newsletter, which is probably the best way to keep up to date.

The next queens, in no particular order, are as follows:

*The Centaur Queen*

*The Fire Queen (Fiera's Story)*

*The Fairy Queen (Galeta The Blue's story)*

*The Mesmerizing Queen (The Pied Piper's Story)*

*And if you want to start at the beginning, make sure to pick up your copy of The Sea Queen!*

# About Jovee Winters

Jovee Winters is the pen name of a *NY Times* and *USA Today* bestselling author who loves books that make you think or feel something, preferably both. She's also passionate about fairy tales, particularly twisting them up into a story you've never thought could be possible.

She's married to the love of her life, a sexy beast of a caveman who likes to refer to himself as Big Hunk. She has two awesome kids she likes to call Thing 1 and Thing 2, loves cooking, and occasionally has been known to crochet. She also really loves talking about herself in the third person.

## Want more Kingdom?

Did you know I also wrote a slew of Kingdom tales featuring many popular characters such as The Mad Hatter, Robin Hood, and Captain Hook—to name a few. I wrote them as Marie Hall. Below you'll find the complete listing for those stories.

Marie Hall Books

# Kingdom Series (Fairy Tale Romance)

Her Mad Hatter (Free everywhere! Book 1, based on Alice and the Mad Hatter)
Gerard's Beauty (Book 2, based on Beauty and the Beast)
Red and Her Wolf (Book 3, based on Little Red Riding Hood)
The Kingdom Collection (Books 1–3, with bonus deleted scenes)
Jinni's Wish (Book 4, based on Arabian Nights)
Hook's Pan (Book 5, Based on Peter Pan)
Danika's Surprise (Book 5.5, novelette and first introduction to the upcoming Dark Princess Series)
Kingdom Chronicles (Books 4 & 5, and includes Danika's Surprise)
Moon's Flower (Book 6, based on the legend of the Man in the Moon)
Huntsman's Prey (Book 7, spinoff Dark Princess Series)
Rumpel's Prize (Book 8, loosely based on the legend of Rumpelstiltskin and Beauty and the Beast)
Hood's Obsession (Book 9)
Her One Wish (Book 10)

CPSIA information can be obtained
at www.ICGtesting.com
Printed in the USA
LVOW11s2343010617
536671LV00002B/168/P